A JOURNEY TO THE HEART

Gina leaned against the door for a minute, and all the strangeness washed over her. There was no doubt about it—somehow, she had traveled back in time. And, according to Esme, the only way to come back was to complete some task. But what could it be?

What could Gina Charles, who knew nothing of Victorian times, accomplish that would possibly be so important that she would be sent back in time? As she pondered, she stepped away from the door and walked smack into a man hurrying down the hall.

She stumbled, and the man grasped her arms and steadied her. "I beg your pardon. Are you all right?"

She glanced up at him and froze.

Magnetic dark eyes gazed down at her out of a handsome face . . . a face she knew well. Her gaze rose higher. The dramatic white streak in his dark hair confirmed her suspicions. This was Drake Manton in the flesh—very warm and very firm flesh.

He repeated, "Are you all right?"

She nodded stupidly, and he shot her a reassuring smile, then hurried off again.

Suddenly, her task became crystal clear. She had come back in time to save Drake Manton's life.

Dear Romance Reader,

Last year, we launched the Ballad line with four new series, and each month we'll present both new and continuing stories set everywhere from medieval England to the American West—the kind of passionate, romantic stories you love best, written by the most gifted authors. At the back of each book, we'll tell you when you can find subsequent books in the series that have captured your heart.

This month a group of very talented authors introduces a breathtaking new series called *Hope Chest*, beginning with Pam McCutcheon's **Enchantment.** As five people unearth an abandoned hotel's century-old hope chest, each will be transported back to a bygone age—and transformed by the timeless power of true love. Kathryn Fox presents the next installment of *The Mounties*. In **The Second Vow,** a transplanted Irishman who must escort the Sioux across the U.S. border meets a woman whose loyalty to her people is as fierce as the desire that flames between them.

In the third book of the charming *Happily Ever After Co.* series, Kate Donovan offers **Meant To Be.** The free-spirited daughter of a successful matchmaker is determined to avoid matrimony—unless a rugged sharpshooter can persuade her that their union is no accident of fate . . . but a romance for all time. Finally, rising star Tammy Hilz concludes the passionate *Jewels of the Sea* trilogy with **Once an Angel,** as a woman sailing toward an uncertain future—and an arranged marriage—is taken captive by a man who will risk anything to save her from a life without the love only he can offer.

Kate Duffy
Editorial Director

Hope Chest

ENCHANTMENT

Pam McCutcheon

ZEBRA BOOKS
KENSINGTON PUBLISHING CORP.

http://www.zebrabooks.com

*For Trana Mae Simmons, ghost hunter extraordinaire,
whose transparent friend inspired one of the opening
scenes of this novel at a PASIC conference in New York.
Just leave him at home next time, okay?
As always, thanks to the wonderful Wyrd:
Laura, Deb, Karen, Paula, Von, and Mo for enduring
support and friendship. Special thanks also go to
Lorrie Molli and Jeff Johnson for their incredible flexibility
in giving me time to write this book, and hearty
appreciation to Linda Kruger for packaging and selling
the series for us. Thanks!*

Chapter One

Gina Charles gaped at the couple in the back seat of the limo. Bette was flat on her back with her dress hiked above her waist and Jerry was pumping away above her, the tails of his sport coat flapping as if he were going for a world record.

Gina knew she should excuse herself and back away from the open door, but this was *her* limo, with *her* fiancé and *her* maid of honor. She could do nothing but stare in silence as she tried to take it in.

Scruffy, Gina's feisty black cairn terrier, squirmed in her arms and yipped. Bette gasped and Jerry looked up with a start, uttering an expletive. A number of emotions flashed through Gina—embarrassment, shame, and a hot, roiling anger. How could they do this to her?

Someone behind her giggled. The entire wedding party had arrived to be ferried to the rehearsal dinner and now they were all poised behind her, peering into the limo.

Gina couldn't handle it. Slamming the door, she burst into angry tears and pushed through the crowd to run to her own car, parked nearby at the curb.

"Don't worry," Gina heard her mother, Madeline, say, "I'll handle this." As Gina fumbled through her purse, Madeline grabbed her arm. "Don't make a scene," her mother hissed.

"I didn't make it." Gina shook off her mother's restraining arm and wiped away an angry tear. "They did." Where the hell were her keys? She had to get out of here.

"Wait—I'm sure there's some explanation."

"Yeah, right. Like what?" Even through her anger, Gina found room for disbelief. Her mother was skilled at manipulating facts to fit her own version of the truth, but Gina didn't want to hear how she'd spin this one.

Finally, she found her keys and unlocked the door. Tossing Scruffy and her purse in the passenger seat, she dropped behind the wheel and automatically fastened the seat belt. She somehow managed to start the car, but when she tried to close the door, her mother seized it in a death grip.

Madeline scowled. "Stop that this instant, young lady. You can't go anywhere. Your wedding is tomorrow."

Jerry hurried over, stuffing his shirt back into his pants with a harried expression. His blond, tanned good looks were a bit mussed now and she couldn't stand to look at him.

Unfortunately, she could still hear him. "Wait, Gina—sweetheart—this doesn't have to change anything."

Gina stopped tugging on the door to give him an incredulous glare, wondering what she'd ever seen in him. "You've *got* to be kidding."

"No, really. It was nothing—just one last fling."

"Yeah? Well, you flung it in front of our families and friends—and you did it with my best friend."

Make that *former* best friend.

He had the grace to look sheepish. "I swear, it didn't mean anything. *She* doesn't mean anything. I love only you, honey."

Gina wasn't buying it. She'd just changed her whole life to be with him, and he couldn't even keep his brain in his pants on the eve of their wedding. She should have known better than to trust a car salesman, especially a successful one. Gina glared at her mother. "Let go of the door."

Madeline only tightened her grip. "No. Listen to him—you can't throw away your life like this."

"Ha. You mean I can't throw away your dreams of a big wedding and a wealthy son-in-law."

"Don't be silly—you know I only want what's best for you," Madeline protested.

Jerry stuck his head in the opened door. "Gina, *baby,* let's talk this over, okay?"

Scruffy growled at him, echoing Gina's sentiments. "No way. Talk to Bette. Hell, *marry* Bette. Our wedding's off—*permanently.*" With that, Gina drove both hands and her shoulder into her jerk of a fiancé.

The force of her shove knocked Jerry into Madeline, and her mother lost her hold on the door. Thus freed, Gina floored the accelerator and peeled away from the curb.

The door slammed shut and Gina glanced into the rearview mirror. Jerry was trying to run after her, the idiot, but Madeline was heading with grim purpose to her own car.

Gina had to lose them and get out of Richmond—now. She made a series of wild, random turns and found herself heading west on I-64 toward the mountains. She glanced back, but didn't see any pursuers. Good, she'd lost them. Now what?

A sign appeared, pointing the way to Hope Springs. Hmm, the Allegheny Mountains, hot springs, and hope. That's just what she needed.

She glanced down at Scruffy, who appeared a little bewildered by all that had happened. "It's okay," Gina whispered, scratching Scruffy's ears with one hand as hot tears spilled down her cheeks. "We'll just stay in Hope Springs for a little while."

Just long enough to find some way to put the pieces of her life back together again and figure out what to do next.

The afterlife is tedious, Drake Manton thought as he drifted through the thin walls of the motel. If he'd known he'd be doomed to spend the rest of eternity confined to Hope Springs, Virginia, he would have been a lot more careful about how he died. If only he could *remember* the incident. . . .

Drake passed through another room where a couple snuggled together to watch television and paused for a moment to watch the science fiction movie unfold with a sense of wonder. One compensation for being a ghost was that he had been witness to many marvels over the years, but it didn't make up for the lack of human contact.

He spent much of his time as a voyeur, caught up in the day-to-day lives of the people in the town. But the familiar soon lost appeal, so he searched for diversion by watching those who passed through Hope Springs, staying only temporarily.

He glanced at the couple in the bed. They were doing more than cuddling now, and that type of voyeurism didn't appeal to him. As usual, the living couldn't see him, so Drake moved on, searching for Gina Charles, the woman who had checked in earlier that day, shedding copious tears.

He found her in the next room, fast asleep, with her small shaggy dog snoring softly beside her. Gina's tear-ravaged face and the half-empty containers of chips, ice cream, and wine scattered about the room bore mute testimony to her despair.

He surveyed her thoughtfully. What could such a beautiful woman have to be so sad about? Her glossy dark brown locks tumbled in profusion about her head and shoulders, and she slept with one hand curled against her ample bosom, as if protecting her heart.

It was just such misery he'd tried to ease when he was alive. But now that he was dead, there was nothing he could do. Still, the urge to comfort her permeated his incorporeal being. He sat on the bed, staring down at her. Her lovely face and the sight of her full, ripe body in its scanty covering would have stirred him to lust when he was alive, but all physical sensation had fled along with his body.

Now, it stirred him to compassion. He wished he could take her in his arms, wipe away her tears, and provide solace in the time-honored fashion, but that was impossible. Knowing she wouldn't be able to feel him, yet needing to do this for his own sake, Drake curled up behind her and reached out to soothe her. He was fully prepared to find his hand pass through her winsome form, but instead, his hand closed over a mound of womanly softness.

Gina leaped up with a screech and scrambled out of the bed, startling the dog who burst into a fit of high-pitched yips.

Good Lord, had she felt that?

She grabbed the neck of the bedside lamp, and throttled it furiously. It didn't budge.

Bemused, Drake wondered why she was wrestling with a lighting fixture. "The switch is at the base," he said helpfully.

His comment just sent the dog into further paroxysms of barking. With a small shriek, Gina ceased her attack on the hapless lamp and scrabbled about on the bedside table. Grabbing something, she pointed it at him threateningly. "Don't move."

"Or what?" he asked, amused as he glanced at her weapon of choice. "You'll brush my hair?" Actually, he was more than amused—he was overjoyed that someone could finally see him, hear him, feel him.

She threw the hairbrush at him, but missed by a foot. The dog was making little rushes at him now, advancing and retreating, as it continued yapping. Gina kept one hand out to ward Drake off as she inched her way toward the door in her scanty nightshirt. "What do you want?" she asked, her voice quavering.

He smiled reassuringly and pitched his voice to be heard above the dog. "Nothing. Don't worry, I'm not going to hurt you."

She reached the wall and flattened herself against it. "Then why were you in my bed?"

"I didn't think you could see me."

"Yeah, right."

"I assure you, it's the truth. Most people can't—I'm a ghost."

"And I'm Mrs. Muir," she snapped back.

Drake almost chuckled with the delight of her spirited reaction and the novelty of conversing with a living being, but he had to calm her. Unfortunately, Gina continued to edge toward the door as the infernal mutt persisted its hysterical barking.

Someone pounded on the door, yelling, "Shut that damn dog up!"

In a flash, Gina was at the door. She fumbled with the security latches, then wrenched open the door and tumbled out into the night. She accosted the man outside, a burly truck driver who had checked in just before her, and grabbed him by the arm. "Help me—there's a strange man in my room!"

She seemed more irate than frightened, and the man's expression changed from annoyance to resolute determination. He peeled her off his arm, then set her behind him. Flipping on the light switch, he peered around the room, fists clenched. "Where is he?"

"There." Gina pointed at Drake, now standing at the foot of the bed.

The man advanced farther into the room. "Where?"

Drake had hoped the man could see him as well, but his gaze passed right through him. It appeared only Gina could see him—and of course, the dog, who continued to bark.

Gina scooped the dog up in her arms. "Hush, Scruffy." Scruffy quieted, but continued to emit a low growl. "He's right *there*," she said. "At the foot of the bed."

The man relaxed his fists and glared at her. "There ain't no one there."

Apparently emboldened by the truck driver's presence and Drake's lack of reaction, she came back into the room and glanced doubtfully at Drake. "There is, too. Can't you see him?"

Tiring of this farce, Drake said, "No, he can't. No one has been able to see me since I died, except for animals. And you."

Gina shot him a disbelieving glare, then addressed the truck driver. "Are you telling me you can't *hear* him either?"

"Hear what?" The man peered suspiciously around the room and stooped to check under the bed.

When the driver's head passed unimpeded through Drake's torso, Gina collapsed into a nearby chair with a whimper and her eyes grew wide.

Her would-be rescuer rose, then stopped suddenly, his gaze arrested by the half-empty wine bottle on the floor. "Lady, you're seeing things. Maybe you shouldn't drink so much." Giving her a disgusted look, he stomped toward the door. "Sleep it off—and keep that damn mutt quiet."

As the door closed firmly behind him, Gina muttered, "Scruffy is not a mutt. He's a purebred cairn terrier, just like Toto in the *Wizard of Oz.*"

That little hairy nit had a pedigree? "I'm sorry," Drake said. "I didn't mean to frighten you—I didn't know you could see me." *Or feel me.*

She stared blankly at him. "But *he* didn't see you. And he passed right through you."

"Yes, I know," Drake said as gently as he could. "I told you, I'm a ghost."

She froze, her eyes wide, and he could see the pieces of the puzzle visibly click into place. She opened her mouth to scream again, but he swiftly moved to smother it with his hand, feeling a frisson of excitement at the realization he *could* touch someone.

Her eyes grew even wider and she struggled for release, but he held her gently imprisoned in the chair between his arms with his newfound power of touch. "Shh," he said soothingly. "I won't hurt you."

The dog scrambled frantically between them, to no avail. Since Gina seemed to be attempting to speak beneath his hand, he removed it cautiously, prepared to replace it at the mere hint of a screech.

"Wha—what do you . . . want?" she asked, her voice trembling.

"Nothing." At her disbelieving expression, he added, "I just want to talk to you. If I wished to ravish you, I could have done so by now."

Some of the fear left her eyes at this manifest truth. "Why me?"

"Because you're the first person who's been able to see or hear me since I died." He concentrated on projecting soothing thoughts in hope of diminishing her fear.

Apparently, it helped. She relaxed and a perplexed expression replaced the fear. "If you're a ghost, then why can I feel you?"

Relieved that she seemed to regain some of her former spirit, he said, "I don't know—this is new to me, too. Perhaps . . . Are you a spiritualist?"

She snorted. "No, I'm a dog trainer, not a ghost trainer."

He backed away cautiously, prepared to move

swiftly if the need arose. "So you believe I'm a ghost now?"

She shrugged. "I can't believe you're anything else when the evidence is so plainly in front of my face." Though her words were brave, her voice quavered and he suspected she wasn't as blasé as she pretended.

Her voice rose as she ticked off the reasons on her fingers. "Let's see, you got into my room through a bolted door, a man walked right through you, you're transparent, and you're dressed in old-fashioned clothes no modern man would be caught dead in."

He glanced down at his clothing. "Actually, I *was* caught dead in them."

"Very funny." She slumped farther into the chair, cuddling the little terrier to her chest. "I may not be the smartest person in the world, but I figure either you're a ghost, or I'm delusional." Her mouth twisted in a grimace. "Naturally, I prefer to think I'm not crazy."

"You're not. At least, I don't think so." Though there was the one episode. . . . "I assume you have a good explanation for strangling the lamp earlier?"

She blushed. "I intended to use it to brain you, but it's bolted to the furniture."

"Ah, I see." Drake was encouraged by her calm reaction and the fact that she no longer seemed to feel the need to "brain" him. An unfamiliar elation rose within him. Finally, the monotony of his death had been alleviated by the simple fact that at least one person on this Earth could hear him, see him. More than that, this had to be a sign that she was the key to ending his boring existence.

"So why am I the lucky one?" Gina asked.

"I don't know why you can see me—this is a first for me, too."

"No, I mean why were you groping me?"

Mortification swept through him, though he couldn't feel sorry for savoring the softness of a woman's body once again. "Please accept my apologies. I saw you crying earlier, and I was merely offering solace."

"By copping a feel?"

Exposure to modern movies had given him understanding of that peculiarly crude expression. "Again, I apologize. I didn't think I could actually feel you—or you me. I wanted only to comfort you."

"Oh. Well, you can't. Nobody can."

"Why not?"

Her face crumpled. "This was supposed to be my wedding day."

Though Drake found it difficult to suppress his elation at conversing with a living being, he contained it. She couldn't help him until he helped her first. To do that, he needed to determine the cause of her distress. "Did your fiancé jilt you?"

"No." Gina sniffed as a tear tracked down her cheek. "I left him—the creep."

"Then why are you so upset?"

"Because of the *reason* I dumped him."

Drake sat on the edge of the bed and gave her his most encouraging look. "Why don't you tell me about it?"

Gina sniffed again, but appeared relieved to have someone to confide in. "We were supposed to rehearse the wedding ceremony, but my fiancé decided to rehearse the wedding night instead—with my maid of honor." She glowered. "Ha! Maid of *dis*honor is more like it."

"The man is obviously a low-bred cur."

Scruffy growled again and Gina shushed him.

"Worse. At least a dog is faithful. But Jerry couldn't even be discreet about it—the whole wedding party found them making like minks in the limo. And it was going to be the perfect wedding, too," she wailed.

Sniffing and wiping her eyes, Gina continued, describing her wedding plans in intricate detail, all the way down to using Scruffy as the well-trained ring bearer.

One hundred and sixteen years of living in limbo had taught Drake patience, if nothing else, and his work as a mesmerist had shown him the value of a sympathetic ear. So, he listened.

It seemed to help. Gina settled down after relating her tale of woe, ending with, "The worst part is, I sold my dog training business, sublet my apartment, and cut all ties to my former life just so I could devote the rest of my life to Jerry. Now what will I do? My life is gone."

"Perhaps your parents will help you."

"Forget it. My father would have, but he died three years ago. And Mom . . ." She snorted. "Even after we found Jerry and Bette doing the wild thing, Mom still wanted me to go through with the wedding. Typical."

Drake's eyebrows rose. Not exactly a model loving mother. "No wonder you ran away."

"Yeah, but what am I going to do now? I have nothing to go back to."

He considered for a moment. Though he wanted to assist her, he wanted even more to keep her nearby so she could help him. "What do you *want* to do?"

She paused, thinking, and a spark of determination entered her eyes. "I want to start over, somewhere new. Somewhere far away from Jerry, my mother, and my so-called friends."

"Then that's what you should do. Why not stay here in Hope Springs?"

"Here? Why?"

Because he couldn't leave the confines of the area, but he was loathe to tell her that. In fact, it would be better to let her think he could follow her anywhere. "Why not?"

He needed time to think, to plan how to elicit her help. Seeing the dark smudges beneath her big brown eyes, he said, "You don't need to make that decision right this moment. For now, you should sleep."

She yawned. "Good idea. I'm beat." She shut off the light and crawled back into bed, giving him a stern look. "But no more groping, okay?"

"All right." He wouldn't touch her again, but he also wouldn't let her out of his sight. Gina Charles was the key that would allow him to escape this limbo-like existence, and he wasn't going to leave her side until he found it.

Gina woke with stuffy sinuses, swollen eyes, and a sick headache—the inevitable result of a prolonged crying jag. She moved and her stomach churned. Then again, maybe the wine had something to do with this awful feeling.

Scruffy whined and nudged her with his cold, wet nose, wanting out. Reluctantly, she swung her feet to the floor. The memory of yesterday's events penetrated her grogginess, and her eyes flew open, searching the room.

Sure enough, the ghost was still there, sitting in the room's lone chair and watching her with his penetrating dark gaze. Gina closed her eyes and groaned. Great. Bad things always came in threes. First the wedding disaster, then the ghost. She wondered when the other shoe would drop, and what form number three would take. It would have to be a doozy to top numbers one and two.

"Good morning," the ghost said in a deep, vibrant voice.

He made a striking appearance for a dead man, with a dramatic streak of white slashing through long, dark, hair. With his good looks and those sexy eyes and voice, Gina bet he had been quite a lady's man in his day.

But she was through with men—even dead men. It was beyond stupid to be attracted to a ghost, even on the rebound. She glared at him as Scruffy's urgings became more frantic. "Have you been watching me all night?"

"Yes," he admitted. "I wanted to be here when you wakened."

Great, an attentive ghost. That's all she needed.

Ignoring him, Gina crossed to the door and opened it. No one else disturbed the serenity of the early morning sunshine, and there was a small patch of grass nearby, so she let Scruffy run out and do his thing. Somehow, just seeing her faithful companion with his ears perked up and his tail wagging made her feel better. Once he finished, Scruffy hurried back in and growled at the ghost. Suppressing the urge to growl herself, Gina said, "Now that you know I'm still here, you can go away."

"I'd rather stay." His voice was polite, but unmistakably firm. He wasn't going to budge an inch.

Gina sighed. She didn't know how to get rid of him short of hiring an exorcist, and doubted she could find one in the phone book. She was just going to have to put up with him for now. "Look, I have to take a shower, and I don't want to worry about you peeking in on me." He might be a hell of a hunk, but she didn't want to deal with him when she was naked. "Will you promise to stay right where you are?"

He inclined his head in an old-fashioned courtly gesture. "Of course. You have my word on it."

Shaking her head, Gina grabbed the few things she'd picked up at the discount store the night before and stomped into the bathroom. She took Scruffy with her, partly to keep him from getting too noisy in the other room, and partly to act as a lookout while she showered. She put him on guard, knowing he'd alert her if the ghost tried to show his see-through face in here.

Luckily, he was as good as his word and she was able to shower unobserved and dress in the jeans, navy T-shirt, and tennies she'd bought last night. Knowing it was useless to delay the inevitable, she opened the door and walked back into the other room, toweling her hair.

He rose to his feet, and since it didn't look like he was leaving any time soon, she sighed and introduced herself, then said, "If you're going to stick around, at least tell me your name."

He smiled and gave her a sweeping, elegant bow. "Drake Manton, Mesmerist, at your service."

"Mesmerist? You mean like a hypnotist?"

"Something like that. But in my day, mesmerism started out as the study of magnetism in the body, thought to cause problems with the mind. You might say we were the precursors to your modern-day psychiatrists."

An old-fashioned shrink. Just what she didn't need. But if concentrating on him made her forget the shambles of her life, she was willing to ignore it for a while. She sat on the bed. "What's your story? How did you become a ghost?"

He seated himself and steepled his fingers, his mouth curving into a smile. "I died."

She rolled her eyes. "No kidding. I mean, *why* are you a ghost? Are you haunting the scene of your death until you find your murderer or something?"

His mouth twisted wryly. "I don't know. I can't remember how I died. I have always assumed that if I could learn the manner of my death, I would leave this ghostly existence and pass on to somewhere more rewarding." He paused, giving her a penetrating stare. "Perhaps . . . you could help me?"

"No way," Gina said. "I'm not going to go around visiting cemeteries and digging up bones just so you can find out what killed you." Besides, she'd sworn off men forever—dead or alive. On the spur of the moment, she said, "I'm going to become a nun." That ought to do it. Of course, she wasn't Catholic and didn't know if they would allow Scruffy in the convent, but those were minor problems, easily overcome.

Drake raised a sardonic eyebrow. "It won't be necessary to dig up my bones. All I'm asking is for you to visit a morgue of a different sort—old newspaper records. That's one thing I can't do for myself." One corner of his mouth quirked up, giving him a rakish appearance. "Perhaps you could postpone taking your vows until then?"

Nuns had to take vows? Come to think of it, they had to wear ugly clothing, too, and give up a lot more than men. Gina waved a hand airily. "Okay, so I might not become a nun after all." But she didn't want to get bound up in some ghost's problems, either. She had enough of her own. "I'm sorry for bothering you with my troubles." She left unsaid the fact that she really didn't have the energy right now to cope with his, but hoped he got the hint.

He didn't. "It wasn't a bother, and I do need your help."

"I doubt I can help you. I can't even help myself."

"But it's such a small service, and one only you can do for me."

Gina dropped the polite facade. "I'm sorry, but the answer is no."

"Won't you reconsider?" Behind his polite question lurked a thread of steely determination. When Gina shook her head, Drake sighed. "Then I fear I shall have to haunt you for the rest of your life."

Gina bristled and Scruffy, reacting to her unease, growled.

Drake raised his eyebrow again. "I don't think Scruffy approves."

Okay, he had her there—she didn't think she could put up with him for the rest of her life. Maybe this little task wouldn't take long. "What do you want?"

"All I want you to do is look through the old newspaper files, to see if you can find a record of my demise."

She supposed she could do that. "Then you'll leave me alone forever?"

He hesitated, then said, "If all goes as I hope, I should leave this existence as soon as I learn how I died."

"And if you don't?"

"Let's deal with that if the situation arises, shall we?"

Gina sighed. It wasn't a promise, but it was better than nothing. And, to tell the truth, she was rather glad of something to distract her from the mess Jerry had made of her life.

Leaving Scruffy in the motel room, Gina grabbed a quick bite to eat and drove to *The Hope Springs Times* offices with Drake's ghostly presence beside her, giving directions. The helpful newspaper staff showed her how to run the machines to read the old microfiche editions of the paper, then left her alone in the room. Thank goodness—she didn't want to have to explain why she was talking to apparently empty air.

"What am I looking for?" she asked Drake.

"I remember I arrived in Hope Springs in June of 1885. My tombstone says I died that same year, but doesn't say what month or day."

Gina shivered at the casual way he spoke of his grave. As a flesh and blood man, she would have found his dramatic good looks fascinating, but as a ghost, his touch was as cold as ice and he was kind of creepy. The sooner she could help him and be rid of him, the better.

Hours later, they finally found what they were looking for. In the December 22, 1885 edition of *The Hope Springs Times,* she spotted a drawing that was unmistakably Drake. The sketch exaggerated his white streak and compelling eyes, portraying him with his hands raised dramatically and lines of magnetic force radiating from his fingers. It was accompanied by a story with the headline, *Mesmerist Dies in Hotel Fire,* and a drawing of the hotel.

"That's it," Drake declared, peering over her shoulder as they read the article together.

The article stated that Drake Manton, Mesmerist,

had perished in a blaze that destroyed the recently built tower of The Chesterfield, a luxurious Victorian hotel and resort situated two miles above the town. The fire had also claimed the life of a Mrs. Rutledge, and the moral tone of the article implied that Manton had received his just desserts for daring to carry on a scandalous assignation with a married woman.

It figured—in life, Drake had been just like Jerry, her jerk of a fiancé. Gina stood, carefully avoiding Drake's insubstantial form, and stretched. Though she was disappointed in what they'd found, satisfaction filled her with the simple act of helping someone. It felt good.

She glanced at Drake who was avidly scanning the text on the screen. "You're still here," Gina said accusingly. "Why?"

Drake turned slowly, fixing his compelling gaze on her. "I don't know. Perhaps it's because this article doesn't ring true. I'm no philanderer. It's a lie—that must be why I'm still here."

Wishful thinking was more like it. "Or maybe you're doomed to spend eternity as a ghost *because* you're a philanderer."

Drake glared at her. "I can't believe I'm doomed forever. If so, why can you suddenly see and hear me when no one else has been able to?"

"I don't know." Then again, maybe he was right. He seemed so cocksure of it, and reporters of that time weren't exactly known for their accuracy and objectivity.

"You must be the key," he muttered with a frown. "But how?" His face cleared and he turned to her. "I know—we'll visit the site of the fire."

She glanced at the sketch of The Chesterfield, a

magnificent brick edifice trimmed in the white gingerbread so prevalent in those times. "I don't think it's still standing, or I would've heard of it."

"The hotel is no longer in operation, but its ruins are still there." He paused, brooding. "That's it. You must come with me to The Chesterfield. We'll find the answer there."

"How can we possibly find any answers? That was over a hundred years ago."

"I don't know. I only know the answer has to be there. Please, come with me."

"I'm not sure this is such a good idea," she hedged. "It's getting kind of late." And she'd been working on his problems all day when she needed to solve her own.

"There's plenty of daylight left. Today is the summer solstice, the longest day of the year. Please, come."

Gina didn't protest further. Even dead, Drake had a persuasive charm she found hard to resist. Besides, she rather liked being needed, and it wouldn't hurt to see this through to the end. "Okay. But first, I need to check on Scruffy."

She pulled out some change and put it in the machine. After she printed a copy of the article, she stuck it and the remaining change in her back pocket, then went to retrieve the terrier.

She drove as close as she could to the site of the former resort, then parked and got out, peering at the ruins. The Chesterfield was a mere shadow of its former glory, with its mortar crumbling, its brick walls half caved in, and its formerly showy gingerbread hanging slack and rotted.

Scruffy ran off to explore and Drake called out, "I found a way up over here."

Since Drake was a bit more difficult to see in the bright afternoon sunshine, she followed the sound of his voice through the thick foliage surrounding the ruins. Scruffy was already there, bounding up the small path former explorers had made. "Scruffy, come here." She didn't want him wandering around the ruins. They might not be safe.

He obeyed—she wasn't a dog trainer for nothing—and she scooped him up and looked around, squinting with the brightness of the sun. "Drake, where are you?" Had he already disappeared?

"Here, just inside the ruins."

Now she could see him—a faint shimmer against the remains of the hotel. "I don't know about this. . . . It could be dangerous."

Ignoring her complaint, Drake said, "You needn't go any farther. I think I found it."

"Found what?" The steps and porch looked somewhat safe, so she picked her way carefully toward him.

"This." Drake gazed intently at an old wooden chest, half hidden in the shadows.

"Weird. I can't believe this is still here after all these years."

He nodded. "I don't remember seeing it before, either, and I've passed through these ruins many times."

A stir of excitement made her drop to her knees. She blew some dust off the front of the chest to reveal beautifully carved flowers, blackened brass handles, and the initials EMS. "It looks like an old hope chest. I wonder if there's anything inside."

The lid opened with a creak and Scruffy sneezed as Gina batted at the dust rising from the chest. She peered in eagerly as Drake hovered behind her.

"Well?" he asked impatiently.

"Nothing," Gina said in disappointment as the faint scent of cedar rose to tantalize her. "Just a bunch of junk." She stirred the contents—a broken neck chain, a pair of severed handcuffs, a sheriff's badge, and a dented brass nameplate.

Finally, below all the rubbish lay something of interest. Shifting Scruffy to her left arm, Gina reached in and pulled out an old dueling pistol. It, too, was ruined—blackened by fire, with the grip half-melted—but there was something about it that intrigued her.

"That's it," Drake said in triumph.

"How do you know—" Gina broke off, feeling suddenly light-headed. "Drake?" she said uncertainly.

He leaned toward her with a concerned expression and she dropped the pistol to raise shaking fingers to her spinning head. She wobbled, feeling faint, and realized he had suddenly become more substantial. Either that or she was becoming *in*substantial.

Vertigo overwhelmed her, sucking her down into a whirling maelstrom of dizzying speed. *What's happening to me?* But there was no answer as she crumpled to the ground and lost consciousness.

Gina came to, slowly, to find herself lying on a very hard surface while Scruffy frantically licked her face. She pushed him away and opened her eyes to see the concerned face of a woman she'd never seen before.

"How do you feel, dear?" the woman asked in a brisk tone. She sounded British.

"I'm not sure. . . . Where's Drake?"

"He hasn't arrived yet, but he'll be along shortly."

Puzzled, Gina held a hand to her spinning head and stared at the woman. Her dark hair was worn in an old-fashioned mode that made it look like a ballooning pincushion with a knot on top, and her severe dark dress with its crisp white collar and cuffs went all the way down to her ankles. How odd. Had Gina made it to the nunnery after all?

The woman offered her a hand and helped her up in a no-nonsense fashion as Scruffy frisked around them. "How do you do, Miss Charles? I'm Miss Sparrow."

Puzzled, Gina shook the proffered hand. "Hi." She glanced around and found herself on an airy verandah. She and Miss Sparrow were at one end, and a small party had gathered at the other end in wicker chairs, chatting amiably. There was something odd about them, but Gina's confused mind couldn't quite figure out what it was. She swayed woozily, muttering, "Toto, I don't think we're in Kansas anymore."

"That's the girl," Miss Sparrow said in a bracing tone as she steadied her elbow. "Now that you're here, everything is all right and tight."

"Here? Where's here?"

"Why, the past of course," the woman said as if it were obvious. "You've traveled back in time."

Gina grew totally still. Back in time? Was the woman loony? Gina blinked, then focused on a nearby sign. *The Chesterfield.* Slowly, the facts penetrated her fogged brain. This hotel remarkably resembled the ruins she had entered, only now they appeared to be restored to their former glory. And the people at the end were dressed in a fashion peculiar to Victorian times.

Gina blanched. No, it couldn't be. Either this woman

was perpetrating an elaborate hoax, or Gina was stark, staring mad. Either way, one thing was for certain— the other shoe had finally dropped.

Bad Thing Number Three had arrived with a vengeance.

Chapter Two

Gina's common sense returned. No, it couldn't be. Time travel wasn't possible—it existed only in the strange, twisted minds of science fiction writers. Then again, she hadn't believed in ghosts until yesterday, either. . . .

There must be some other explanation. A movie set? That didn't fit—everything had changed too fast. An elaborate hoax? That didn't jibe either—who knew she'd be here? Her fogged brain couldn't come up with any other logical explanation save one—she was dreaming. So, she'd just have to go along with the strangeness until she woke up.

Gina became aware that Miss Sparrow was tugging gently but insistently on her arm. "Come along, dear," the woman said. "Before someone sees you dressed like this."

Gina glanced down at her jeans and T-shirt. "What's wrong with what I'm wearing?"

"Nothing, for *your* time, but in 1885 it just isn't proper."

"Oh," Gina said, feeling as if her head were still stuffed with mush. "Uh, okay. What'll I wear?"

"I'll show you."

Miss Sparrow renewed her pull on Gina's arm. Gina checked to make sure Scruffy was behind her as the woman towed her into a secluded part of the hotel.

Suddenly, Miss Sparrow came to a complete halt and muttered, "Oh, bother."

Gina glanced up. Coming toward them was a middle-aged woman in a severe black outfit that left her looking like a deformed "S." A bustle stuck out behind her, making her small chest curve out in front, and a ridiculous feathery hat perched on her head like a bird about to fly off. She looked like a skinny pouter pigeon. Only, no pigeon ever wore such a sour, pinched expression.

Good grief. What on earth had caused her to dredge up this image from the tortured depths of her imagination? And why was the woman carrying a fur muff in the middle of the summer? It didn't matter—dreams weren't meant to make sense.

Miss Sparrow seemed to be trying to shove Gina behind her, so Gina cooperated. She didn't know why the Wicked Witch of the West had shown up in her dream, but it was probably a good idea to avoid her. She glanced around, wondering if a house was about to fall on the sourpuss.

"Mrs. Biddle," Miss Sparrow said in a calm tone, "how may I help you?"

Mrs. Biddle looked down her nose at Miss Sparrow, no easy feat since she was at least two inches shorter. "I thought this was a respectable hotel," she said in a nasal tone. "What is this young person doing here dressed in such an outlandish costume?"

Jeez, look who's talking. Slowly, it dawned on Gina that the woman was referring to *her*. She opened her mouth to give the old biddy what-for, but Miss Sparrow forestalled her.

"Miss Charles has just arrived from . . . the Far West, where she was brought up in a family of men. I'm afraid she never learned to dress like a lady. She's here to work and learn."

So that was the explanation her mind had dredged up for her appearance in this dream. Okay, it worked.

Mrs. Biddle just sniffed. It was obvious she had far more to say on the subject, but just then, Scruffy, who had been sitting calmly at Gina's feet, looked up and growled at the furry muff.

The muff opened its protruding eyes and growled back.

Startled, Gina realized the muff was really a dog—a plug-ugly Pekingese. Suddenly, her belief that this was a dream wavered. She would never willingly dream about a Pekingese—she found the yappy dogs with their smashed-in faces repulsive.

Maybe this wasn't a dream. Miss Sparrow and her iron grip had certainly felt solid enough . . . What about Mrs. Biddle? Experimentally, Gina reached out and poked the woman in the side. Odd—she was just as solid as the rest of them. More so, for she appeared to be wearing some sort of heavy-duty girdle underneath to hold her assets, meager as they were, rigidly in place.

Mrs. Biddle gasped in affront. "Young woman, what is the meaning of this?"

Maybe this wasn't a dream after all. Then . . . What was it? Could she have really traveled in time? Or had she somehow made it to Oz? She glanced around, looking for a yellow brick road, or a contingent from the Lollipop Guild, but they were nowhere in sight. So, where was she? Her question would have to wait, for Mrs. Biddle was expecting an answer.

"Uh, sorry," Gina said. "You had a bug crawling on you. Don't worry, I got it off."

The witch sniffed in disbelief and glared down at Scruffy. "And *what* is that creature?"

No sense in giving the muff the advantage. Gina picked Scruffy up so the dogs were face to face, and shushed him. Scruffy obeyed, but the Peke continued growling. "He's a cairn terrier."

"Never heard of them," Mrs. Biddle pronounced. "But my Princess here has a royal pedigree from China." She stroked the ugly dog who lolled its tongue in bliss.

"So does Scruffy—his real name is Reginald Scruffington the Third, and *his* line goes back to—" She broke off. Scruffy's line went back to the first cairn terrier admitted to the American Kennel Club . . . in 1913. "Well, they're very well known where I come from," she finished lamely.

Mrs. Biddle gifted her with a condescending smile—the sort she might give a child. "I daresay. But a mere westerner's claims cannot compete with the glory of a Pekingese who has been bred by royalty for generations, hmm?"

The Peke chose this moment to demonstrate its glory by lunging and snapping at Scruffy.

At a single word from Gina, Scruffy magnificently ignored the provocation while the so-called Princess disregarded all its owner's pleas for it to be a "good little doggy."

Smugly, Gina said, "Too bad Princess's behavior doesn't reflect her breeding."

Mrs. Biddle puffed up, obviously prepared to do battle, but Miss Sparrow took the wind out of her sails. "It's been nice chatting with you, but we really should be getting along. The Major is expecting us."

Those magic words effected an immediate change in Mrs. Biddle. Though her dog continued yapping, her stiffness melted away and she smiled, simpering. "Well, now, I wouldn't want to keep the Major waiting. Give him my best, will you?"

"Of course," Miss Sparrow said, then dragged Gina off before the woman could detain them any longer.

Gina whispered, "Good boy," to Scruffy and gave him a quick scratch between the ears. He'd earned it.

As they moved swiftly down the great hall toward their destination, they garnered many odd looks from other women dressed just like Mrs. Biddle, though with more color and more pleasant expressions. Gina received a blurred impression of the ornately decorated hotel, though the only thing that registered was the truly atrocious wallpaper reminiscent of the worst of the Victorian period.

It seemed impossible, but . . . maybe this time travel business *was* true? With a feeling of dread, she realized everything certainly *seemed* real.

But Miss Sparrow didn't give her time to think as she whisked her into a room before anyone else could stop them. "Well, that was unfortunate," she said with a sigh. "Of all people to run into, Birdie Biddle must be the worst."

Birdie? Well, it fit, but what was with the avian names around here?

Miss Sparrow continued. "But I suppose it couldn't

be helped. We'll just have to get you into something more suitable before anyone else sees you."

As Miss Sparrow sorted through a rack of navy skirts the same shade as her own, Gina realized they were in a storeroom of sorts. Miss Sparrow pulled out a skirt and a white blouse and held them up measuringly to Gina. "I think these will fit. Why don't you try them on?"

"Now wait a minute. Before I do anything else, I want an explanation. Where am I and how did I get here?" She set Scruffy down and, like the good dog he was, he went to a corner and lay down to watch the proceedings.

Miss Sparrow smiled. "As I said before, you have come back in time to 1885. You're at The Chesterfield Hotel and Resort."

"And how did I get here?"

The woman's eyes slid away from hers and she plucked unnecessarily at the skirt she held. "You came through a time portal that operates only on the solstices," she said briskly and held the outfit up to Gina again. "Have you ever waited tables?"

"No, and don't change the subject." Gina suspected there was far more to this than Miss Sparrow let on. "Who are you? And why do you seem to be the only one here who understands what's going on?"

"I'm sorry, didn't I introduce myself?" the woman asked with aplomb. "I am Esmeralda Sparrow, the head housekeeper of The Chesterfield. And it's my job to know everything."

That answer wasn't quite complete, but before Gina could ask more, Miss Sparrow added, "But please, call me Esme."

"Okay, Esme, but I want to know—"

"However, I caution you to do so only when we're

alone. It wouldn't do to have others thinking you are acting above your station."

"My station?" What the heck was she talking about?

"Yes. You'll have to work in the resort, of course, which means you'll report to me—all the girls do. The only question is, where best to put you?"

Gina was swept along by the housekeeper's efficiency as she questioned Gina thoroughly about her work history. No, she'd never worked as a waitress, maid, hostess, or in any other capacity a hotel would find useful.

"Well," Esme said, "I'll just have to teach you, then." She offered the outfit again, complete with a contraption that could only be a bustle. "Why don't you try this on?"

Gina balked at the thought of tying a bustle onto her back end. "Why in the world would I *want* to make my butt look bigger?"

"It *is* the fashion," Esme said with a raised eyebrow.

"Good grief, why?"

"Men find it . . . attractive," Esme said. For once, her no-nonsense tone took on a hint of embarrassment.

Gina just shook her head. "Fashions sure have changed since then . . . now . . . whatever," she said, impatient with the confusion of describing the time changes. Worse, she was dismayed by the realization that she had finally accepted the inevitable—she really *had* traveled back in time. But there would be no ruby slippers to take *her* home. It made her want to cry.

"Why do I have to change at all?" *I just want to go home.*

Some of her inner turmoil must have shown, for the housekeeper's expression softened. She led Gina to a chair. "Let me explain. This resort caters primarily to invalids and those seeking a cure for their ills. So, we have a doctor on staff, and Dr. Ziegler is very interested in diseases of the mind. I'm afraid if he sees you in these clothes, speaking as if you're from the future, he'll think you mad . . . and commit you."

Fear shot through Gina. She'd heard horror stories of what mental institutions were like in these times. "Can't I just go home?" she asked plaintively.

"Yes, you'll have that option. But first, there is something you must do here."

"What?" Gina asked desperately. "Tell me—I'll do anything. Just let me go home." Suddenly her messed-up life didn't seem so bad, so long as she could wear sensible clothes and not have to hide from overzealous doctors.

"That is something you'll have to discern for yourself," Esme said, not unkindly. "In the meantime, you'll need some way to occupy yourself. I suppose I could train you to wait tables, but don't you have any talents we could use?"

"I can train dogs—that's my best talent." She also had a talent for picking losers as fiancés, but Gina doubted that was the kind of job qualification Esme was looking for.

"Well, then, we shall just have to make this work." Esme pulled a dark gray dress from the rack. "Here, put this on. It's a maid's uniform but it will have to do for now. The Major will be calling for me shortly."

Well, at least it didn't have a bustle. As Gina put on the awkward heavy dress with the housekeeper's help, she wondered just who this Major was, and even more, how the woman knew the Major would soon be calling for her.

"Who is he?"

"Major Payne is the hotel manager," Esme said as she twitched Gina's dress into place and had her put on some sturdy shoes. "Though all the girls work under me, he has to approve all the hiring." She gazed at her handiwork with satisfaction, saying, "We just need to put up your hair. Come, I'll do it for you."

Gina allowed the woman to manhandle her hair into a style similar to the one Esme wore as Gina tried to make sense of everything. It was too much to take in all at once, so Gina decided to concentrate on the one thing she could do—find out what her task was so she could return to her own time and some semblance of normality.

Just as Esme finished Gina's hair, a tall beanpole in a navy uniform with maroon trim stuck his head in the door. He grinned at the housekeeper, saying, "The Major's looking for you." His speech was directed at Esme, but his gaze was all for Gina, speculative and appreciative.

It wasn't lost on the prim housekeeper. "Thank you, Rupert. I'll be right there." At her obvious dismissal, Rupert withdrew. Seeing Gina's grin, she added, "Rupert is one of our bellboys. He means well, but I suggest if you have any dealings with him, you count all your pennies before you leave—and your fingers and toes. Twice. Rupert is a very . . . enterprising young man."

Gina nodded. Rupert was kind of cocky and cute, but he was too young for her and she had no intention of dating anyone anytime soon anyway—especially not in the past.

Esme swept her out of the room and Gina made sure Scruffy followed so she wouldn't lose him—he was her only link to the life she'd left behind. Forward. Whatever.

Saying, "Let me handle this," Esme knocked lightly on a door labeled "Manager."

"Enter," a man bellowed from inside.

As they did so, Scruffy hid beneath Gina's skirt, evidently wary of entering the room where the parade-ground command had come from.

A man rose from behind a desk and nodded at them, harrumphing. He clasped his hands behind his ramrod-straight back and twitched his handlebar mustache at them. "Miss Sparrow, I wished to speak to you about Mr. O'Riley—" He broke off, staring at Gina. "And who do we have here?"

"A new employee for your approval, Major. This is Miss Charles."

The Major smoothed his mustache and ran his gaze over Gina's form, inspecting her thoroughly. "A new maid, eh?"

"Not exactly," the housekeeper said. "I have finally found a solution to the problem of unruly pets running about in the hotel."

"How so?" he asked, scowling.

Gina watched in wonder as Esme skillfully and subtly convinced him it was his idea to hire a dog trainer, adding that Gina could also take care of pets when their owners were indisposed.

Gina balked at the idea of being a dog sitter, but, realizing it was better than being a waitress, she kept her mouth shut.

The clincher to Esme's argument was her reminder that no other hotel in Virginia could offer this service.

"Quite right." Major Payne looked thoughtful, then said, "How do we know she is qualified?"

Calmly, Esme asked Gina to demonstrate her prowess with Scruffy. Major Payne looked surprised to see the small dog appear from beneath Gina's skirt, but watched intently as she put Scruffy through his paces.

"Very good," he pronounced, but evidently felt the need to deliver a lecture. Frowning at Gina, he admonished her to do her best to keep the guests' animals under control while simultaneously not offending them and their pets.

It was quite clearly a dismissal, but since Esme didn't move, Gina was uncertain what to do.

"Wait outside," the housekeeper said gently. "I believe the Major has something else he needs to discuss with me."

With a sense of relief, Gina left the room with Scruffy in tow, hearing the Major say, "That blasted O'Riley is drunk again," before she shut the door.

She leaned against it for a minute, and all the strangeness washed over her. There was no doubt about it—somehow, she had traveled back in time. And, according to Esme, the only way to get back was to complete some task. But what could it be?

What could Gina Charles, who knew nothing of Victorian times, accomplish that would possibly be so important that she would be sent back in time? As she pondered, she stepped away from the door and walked smack into a man hurrying down the hall.

She stumbled, and the man grasped her arms and steadied her. "I beg your pardon. Are you all right?"

She glanced up at him and froze.

Magnetic dark eyes gazed down at her out of a handsome face . . . a face she knew well. Her gaze rose higher. The dramatic white streak in his dark hair confirmed her suspicions. This was Drake Manton in the flesh—very warm and very firm flesh.

He repeated, "Are you all right?"

She nodded stupidly, and he shot her a reassuring smile, then hurried off again.

Suddenly, her task became crystal clear. She had come back in time to save Drake Manton's life.

Drake admonished himself to be more careful. In his single-minded rush to meet Dr. Ziegler, he'd almost run down a maid.

But surely he could be excused for a bit of abstraction. Finally, he had arrived at the culmination of months of searching for just the right place to put Dr. Mesmer's theories into practice. The Chesterfield seemed ideal. Not only was it a popular convalescent spot for invalids, but the resident physician, Dr. Ziegler, was well known for his interest in the diseases of the mind.

Following the directions the tipsy porter had provided, Drake made his way down the long hallway through the west wing to the bathhouse. He liked what he saw. Though the scent of sulfur was strong in these rooms, the entrance itself was light and airy, with a profusion of potted plants lining the walls and staircases to take advantage of the ample light and humidity.

He climbed the stairs to the second floor and was gratified to find the doctor's office just where the porter said it would be.

Drake knocked on the door and a male voice bade him enter. *This is it. My big chance.* Drake ignored a flurry of movement behind him and, straightening his jacket and tie, he stepped into the room and closed the door.

A small, spare man with graying hair sat at the desk

and blinked at him owlishly through his spectacles. "Yes?"

"How do you do, Dr. Ziegler? I'm Drake Manton."

As Drake shook the man's hand, he could tell his name had sparked no recognition in the older man. "I wrote to you last month, about the possibility of using mesmerism on your patients. You indicated you might not be averse . . . ?"

"Ah, yes. Please, sit down."

Drake sat in the chair indicated. The man had recognized him, but the frown on his face was not encouraging.

Fingers steepled, Dr. Ziegler pursed his lips, then spoke. "I found the notion of using mesmerism to cure patients interesting, particularly the magnetic aspects, but I have initiated more inquiries into this theory. While Dr. Mesmer has gained some followers, others claim he is a charlatan."

Drake sighed in exasperation. This wasn't the first time he'd heard these accusations. He opened his mouth to speak, but paused when he heard some scratching sounds at the door. When Ziegler ignored them, he shrugged and said, "Dr. Mesmer himself may be . . . eccentric, but his ideas are positively revolutionary. His ability to use his own body's natural magnetism to affect the patient's body and cure them of mental illness is amazing. Since you have an interest in that area, I thought you would be eager to try new techniques that might heal your patients' suffering."

Dr. Ziegler scowled. "I don't experiment on those entrusted to my care. I prefer more conventional, tried and true methods to treat my patients."

Drake's hopes sank. It was the same old story, with a new storyteller. Everywhere he went, he met stodginess and a reluctance to try anything new. Of course, he could try to set up his own mesmerism practice in a large city, but building a practice was a slow undertaking at best without the support of a local physician.

He was impatient to begin right away, which was why he had approached Dr. Ziegler. People would be more likely to trust Drake if he was supported by a physician they knew. Then he could finally help people . . . as he had promised himself after his complete failure to help Charlotte.

Unable to let his dream wither and die, Drake said, "Many other prominent men and women have studied mesmerism and found it beneficial."

"Such as . . . ?"

"Charles Dickens for one—"

Ziegler waved his hand in dismissal. "A mere scribbler."

Rather than trot out more names and give the man the opportunity to discredit each of them, Drake changed his tack. "I assure you, this is a major breakthrough in the science of mental illness. If you would approve my lectures here at the resort, I'll be more than happy to explain all the ramifications of mesmerism in theory and in practice."

Drake detested the necessity to ask for permission, but the pompous hotel manager had refused to allow him to even lecture on the subject unless he obtained the resort doctor's approval.

"No, I—" Dr. Ziegler broke off as the noises at the door became more pronounced and turned his scowl from Drake to the door.

Raising an eyebrow, Drake rose and swiftly jerked it open.

A young woman with dark chestnut hair tumbled

inward with a yelp, landing in a flurry of gray material in front of him.

Dr. Ziegler frowned and rose from his desk to peer down at the maid. "What is the meaning of this?"

The girl blushed and scrambled to her feet and Drake thought he saw a flash of something dark and furry beneath her skirts. "I'm sorry, I was just trying to find Mr. Manton. I didn't mean to bother anyone."

How odd—this was the maid he had almost run down in the hall. Why had she followed him? And how did she know his name?

"So you eavesdropped at my door?" Dr. Ziegler demanded.

"I couldn't hear anything," she assured them ingenuously. "I just wanted to talk to him."

"Perhaps another time," Drake suggested, and made to close the door on her. He couldn't fathom why this strange girl would want to talk to him, but now was not the time.

"Wait," the doctor said, halting him with a suspicious glare. "I'd like to hear what she has to say. Explain yourself, young woman. Why do you want to speak to Mr. Manton?"

Anger kindled in Drake's breast. It was obvious the old man suspected he had dallied with this woman and was now trying to discard her. Granted, she was very attractive, but Drake had given up women since Charlotte had died. And though other men found it amusing to trifle with members of the servant class, he wasn't one of them. Stiffly, Drake said, "I assure you—"

"No need," Dr. Ziegler interrupted. "I would like to hear it from the young lady herself. Your name, my dear?"

She glanced uncertainly at both of them. "Gina. Gina Charles."

"And your purpose in seeking out Mr. Manton, Miss Charles?"

She looked flustered. "Oh, nothing important. It'll wait."

The old doctor's visage turned kindly. "Has this young man treated you improperly?"

Drake stiffened, but the obvious horror on Miss Charles's face put the lie to the doctor's suspicions.

"Good Lord, no," she exclaimed, flashing an apologetic glance at Drake. "I just wanted to talk to him about . . . mesmerism."

Dr. Ziegler cast a surprised look at Drake. "You've heard of him and are familiar with mesmerism?"

"Oh, yes," Miss Charles asserted, waving her hand airily. "It's quite well known where I come from."

"And that is . . . ?"

"The fu—" She broke off, coughing. "I mean, uh, the few . . . wise people of Richmond."

Her manner of speech was not convincing. Evidently, Dr. Ziegler felt the same, for his scowl returned as he said, "Perhaps you would be so good as to explain mesmerism to me, then."

She shrugged. "Sure. Those who practice hyp— Uh, mesmerism, put their patients in a trance-like state that allows the mesmerist to determine what's bothering them and help them get over it."

It was a strangely worded yet simplistic explanation that left out a great deal of the scientific theory, but it fit the facts. Oddly enough, Dr. Ziegler seemed intrigued.

"Go on," the doctor said. "What sort of 'bothers' has mesmerism assisted them to 'get over'?"

"Oh, lots of things," Gina said, more confidently

than any servant Drake had ever met. "It has helped people break bad habits, lose fears and phobias, and regain lost memories."

Granted, she knew a great deal about mesmerism, but there was something about her that didn't ring true. She didn't act like a servant, and he suspected she was lying, but he couldn't discern for what purpose.

Dr. Ziegler shot a chiding glance at Drake. "You didn't mention this ability to regain lost memories."

That was because Drake wasn't aware of the possibilities, though now that she had brought it up, he could see the application clearly. "I simply hadn't mentioned it yet," he demurred.

Ziegler turned back to the young woman. "And why have you sought out Mr. Manton? Do you have one of these ills you spoke of?"

The woman bristled, then apparently recalled that she *had* asserted she was looking for Drake. "Nothing very serious," she assured them. "Just a . . . memory loss I thought he could help me with." She paused, then elaborated, "There are a couple years of my life missing, and I thought he could help me get them back."

What a plumper. If she had any memory loss at all, Drake would be very surprised. But he kept his suspicions to himself—Dr. Ziegler seemed to accept her story at face value and was even looking favorably upon mesmerism.

"Do you think you can help her?" Dr. Ziegler asked.

Drake gave the pert baggage a once-over. "I have no doubt of it." He didn't know what she was up to, but he would soon find out.

"Very good. Then take Miss Charles as your patient and keep me informed of your progress."

The maid looked triumphant, and Drake once again wondered what her true game was. "And the lectures?" he prodded. "Will you approve them?"

"Certainly," the doctor said. "After Miss Charles's description, I am anxious to hear how this mesmerism works, and the resort guests may find it entertaining."

Entertaining! Drake's purpose was to illuminate, to elucidate, to educate . . . not *recreate*. But he bit his tongue and thanked the doctor. With the interview at an end, the doctor showed him out the door, the impudent Gina right behind him.

She grinned. "So, I helped you, huh, doc?"

It went against the grain to admit it, but this saucy chit had succeeded where he had failed. Unfortunately, now he had to live up to the outrageous claims she had made for mesmerism.

Chapter Three

Gina smiled at Drake, feeling quite pleased with herself. She had helped him already, so she must be well on her way to saving his life.

"Don't call me 'doc'," Drake said and nodded toward the closed door. "That honorific is reserved for physicians such as Dr. Ziegler."

Jeez, was this stuffy guy the same one who'd groped her only last night?

Then his words penetrated and Gina felt the blood drain from her head. "Doctor . . . Dr. Ziegler?" She glanced at the door. Sure enough, there was his name, big as life. She'd been so intent on following Drake and listening at the door that she hadn't paid attention.

"Yes, Dr. Ziegler, the resort's resident physician. Is something wrong?"

Of course there was something wrong—she had just run into the one man she had vowed to avoid at all costs. Quickly, Gina ran through their conversation. Had she done or said anything to make the man believe she might be a candidate for the loony bin? No, thank heavens, all she'd said was that she'd lost her memory. Surely they didn't lock people up for that.

She turned her attention back to Drake, only to see him turning away. "Wait!" She took a step toward him, and tripped over Scruffy who yipped at the indignity.

Drake turned with an eyebrow raised and gazed down at her feet. "I've heard that yelp before. Either your shoes have an unusual squeak, or ... ?" He trailed off, inviting an explanation.

She looked down. The feathery black tail wagging out from the hem of her skirt was a dead giveaway. "It's my dog," she said unnecessarily. At first, she'd assumed Scruffy had chosen to stay under her skirt to hide, but there was no reason for that now. She suspected he was playing some kind of strange dog game of his own invention. "Scruffy, come out."

Obedient as always, he emerged with a canine grin. But his grin disappeared and his jaws snapped shut when he looked up at Drake. Cocking his head, he stared at the mesmerist with an expression of perplexity on his furry face. Gina grinned. Scruffy was probably trying to associate the ghost he'd barked at with this more physical specimen.

"Well, there's a fine fellow," Drake said as he bent down and scratched the dog's ears. His face softened, making him look more human, not to mention gorgeous. That heart-stopping smile gave Gina butterflies in her stomach.

Luckily, Scruffy chose to like this flesh and blood version of Drake Manton and licked the man's hand enthusiastically. In fact, he practically drooled all over him. Gina couldn't remember Scruffy ever showing such affection for another person besides herself. Any moment now, he'd be humping the man's leg.

Strangely enough, it made the handsome but stuffy Drake even more appealing. It was hard to resist a man who loved dogs. Evidently Gina wasn't the only one who thought so—several women eyed him admiringly as they passed.

Then again, maybe his strong physique and good looks had something to do with it.

Oblivious to their scrutiny, Drake chuckled, then rose and gave Gina a quizzical look. "I didn't realize it was customary for maids to bring their pets to work."

She rolled her eyes. "I'm not a maid, I'm a dog trainer."

"I see. That accounts for the dog and your—" He broke off, as if regretting what he had been about to say.

"My what?" she asked belligerently, hands on her hips.

"Your . . . less than demure attitude."

Gina wasn't about to be held to some nineteenth-century standard of behavior. "My attitude is none of your business, buddy." And she was tired of people telling her what to do.

His face impassive, Drake inclined his head. "As you say. Now, if you'll excuse me?"

Ah, heck. He was leaving again. *Smooth move, Gina. Drive him away, why dontcha?* "No, wait."

He paused again, raising a sardonic eyebrow. "Pardon?" She could tell he was annoyed, but he hid it well. At least men were more polite in these times. "May I ask why?"

"Because . . ." Darn, she had just blindly skipped

on after him with no plans on what to say or how to keep him from getting killed. "Because I have to help you," she finished lamely.

"I appreciate the sentiment, but I don't require assistance." He was still polite, but he was getting impatient as well.

Shoot, she was going about this in the wrong way. Casting about for some way to delay him, she said, "Look, I helped you before, didn't I?"

"If you can call that help. You almost had me accused of trifling with your person."

Well, technically, he *had* trifled with certain portions of her "person" . . . but not until after he was dead. And, speaking of being dead, she had to make sure he didn't get that way.

What could she do? She couldn't tell him she knew when and how he was going to die—he'd make sure Dr. Ziegler committed her. "Hey, I helped you with the doctor, didn't I?"

"Only because Dr. Ziegler believed the truth."

"And now I'm your patient," she added triumphantly.

He paused. "But you weren't exactly telling the truth about two years of lost memory, were you? And you don't really need a mesmerist?"

Gina toyed with the idea of lying and insisting she needed his help, but she had just realized that the best way to ensure he wasn't killed here at The Chesterfield was to make sure he got the hell out of Dodge . . . er, Hope Springs. So, she didn't want to say or do anything to encourage him to stay. The sooner he left, the sooner she'd be able to go home.

"No, I don't really need a mesmerist. I just said that so you'd listen to me." She paused and took a deep breath. "Look, I can't tell you why, but it's imperative you leave this hotel right away."

He raised an eyebrow and said in a low, dangerous tone, "Is that a threat?"

Gina retreated. Oh, my, he was a lot more intimidating in the flesh. "No, no," she said in horror. "I just know you're in terrible danger if you stay."

"I must stay. After all, you convinced Dr. Ziegler to let me lecture on mesmerism."

Had she really done that? Dismayed, she resolved to be more careful in the future.

"Not only that," Drake continued with a steely tone in his voice, "but you have convinced him that I must take you on as my patient."

"Well, heck, I'll just get well real soon, then, so you can leave."

"On the contrary, Miss Charles. I won't be a party to this charade. You must confess your deception to Dr. Ziegler and accept the consequences."

Not if the consequences involved her winding up in the madhouse. "I don't think I—"

"Ah, Gina, there you are," Esme cried as she entered the bathhouse. "You left before I could inform you of your duties."

With an expression of relief, Drake bowed and said, "I'll leave you to it, then. Good day, Miss Charles." Then, with a last scratch on the head for the ecstatic Scruffy, he left.

"Darn," Gina muttered and turned a baleful eye on Esme. "Do you know what you just did?"

"Never mind. Your conversation wasn't going all that well, anyway, was it?" Then, without waiting for an answer, Esme said, "Come along, I'll show you to your room."

She took off walking at a brisk pace and Gina had no option but to follow her. "But you—"

"Not now," Esme said with an admonishing look over her shoulder. "Wait until we're in your room."

Okay, that made sense. Besides, Gina needed all her breath to keep up with the housekeeper and avoid tripping over Scruffy as she hurried down the stairs and out of the bathhouse into the spacious hallway. When they had almost reached the lobby, Esme took a sudden right turn and went up another set of stairs, to a set of rooms above the hallway they had just sprinted down.

Taking a large set of keys from somewhere, Esme opened a door and gestured Gina in. "This is your room. Ordinarily, you would share with another girl, but we are a bit shorthanded this season, and under the circumstances," she glanced down at Scruffy, "I think it best if you have one to yourself."

Thank heavens—Gina had been afraid she'd have to leave Scruffy in the stables or something. She glanced around at the small room. Two beds, two dressers, one washstand, and several other pieces of furniture all crowded into one small space. Okay, it was small, but she didn't need much for the short period of time it would take to convince Drake to leave.

"Guess what?" she said brightly. "I've figured out what my task is."

"I rather thought you might," Esme said with a slight smile.

"You *knew* already?"

"Yes, of course."

"But I thought—"

"I said you had to learn it for yourself," Esme reminded her. "I never said I didn't know."

Semantics. Gina hated semantics. "Whatever—it doesn't matter. The important thing is that I figured out I have to keep Drake Manton from getting killed. So, I need to make him leave the resort so I can go home right away. Got any ideas?"

"That is something you'll have to determine on your own."

Gina gave her a suspicious glare. "You mean you know and you're just not telling me?"

Esme smiled. "No, I really don't know—I only know that you must try." She paused, looking apologetic. "But I'm afraid you're under a misapprehension. It doesn't matter whether you complete your task tomorrow or three months from now."

Uh-oh. Gina had a feeling she wasn't going to like what was coming next. "Why not?"

"Because the time portal is only active on the solstices. You came through on the summer solstice. You can only go back on the *next* solstice."

Gina had never paid much attention to these things. "Uh, just when *is* the next solstice?"

"It's the winter solstice . . . on December 22," Esme said gently.

She had to stay here, back in the past, for *six months?* Gina sank down on one of the narrow beds and hugged Scruffy for comfort. What the heck was she going to do back in the past for so long? Despair enveloped her at the thought of trying to make it on her own in a time she didn't understand, with no money or skills to speak of.

Well, one thing was for sure—she needed room and board, which Esme had already so thoughtfully provided. Since there was nothing Gina could do about it, she might as well accept it . . . for now. Sighing, she said, "Okay, take me to my duties."

* * *

Two weeks later, Drake was only a little closer to
scheduling his lecture series. The Major had finally
approved them, albeit grudgingly, once Dr. Ziegler
had added his support. The only problem was, Drake
had been unable to find a location where he could go
over his notes in peace and practice his first lecture.
It seemed everywhere he went, he was hounded by
females.

If it wasn't Gina Charles trying to buttonhole him,
it was Mrs. Biddle cornering him to puff the virtues
of her daughter, or some other blasted woman making eyes at him. Not even his room was safe—they
all seemed to find some reason to disturb his concentration "just for a moment."

In desperation, Drake decided to seek out the tipsy
porter who had helped him the first day and ask the
man for a suitable place to concentrate. And, from
what he had discerned of Jack O'Riley's habits, the
porter would be either running errands or asleep
behind the palms in the lobby.

As he approached the porter's favorite hiding
place, he heard the man's distinctive Irish brogue,
but a female voice brought him to a halt. From her
crisp British tones, he gathered the woman was Miss
Sparrow, the head housekeeper. He didn't want to
intrude, but he didn't want to miss Jack, either. So, he
hovered nearby where he couldn't help but overhear
their conversation.

"Really, Mr. O'Riley, this won't do. This is the second time this month the Major has threatened to
dismiss you. You must curb your drinking."

" 'Tis a fine day when an Irishman can't have a

bit of a tipple, now," O'Riley complained in a tone designed to cajole the woman into forgiving him.

"That's as may be, but the Major isn't at all happy. If you aren't careful, you may lose your position here altogether. Do try to confine your . . . tippling to your off-duty hours, won't you?"

Drake heard the porter heave a heavy sigh. "I don't know, lass. 'Tis a great deal yer askin'."

If possible, Miss Sparrow's tone turned even crisper. "Then do it for your daughter's sake. Bridget is happy here, and the poor motherless girl needs some stability."

"Aye, that she does," O'Riley replied mournfully.

"Then see to it that she gets it," Miss Sparrow said with finality. "And make yourself presentable for the guests."

Evidently the interview was at an end, for Miss Sparrow suddenly sailed by in her typical brisk fashion, giving Drake a nod. "Good day, Mr. Manton."

She managed to convey disapproval of his eavesdropping with that simple movement of her head, which made Drake feel like a chastised schoolboy. No matter—at least he had found O'Riley. Drake parted the palms and found Jack taking a sip from a flask.

The porter looked up guiltily, but when he saw Drake, his expression cleared and he offered him a drink.

"No, thank you," Drake said with a shake of his head, entering Jack's hiding place. "And should you be drinking after what you promised Miss Sparrow?"

O'Riley grimaced. "Now don't ye be nattering away at me, too, lad."

"I apologize," Drake said sincerely. What the man chose to do with his life was none of his business.

"That's more like it, then." The porter screwed the cap on his flask and tucked it into its hiding place in one of the pots. " 'Twas just a bit of the hair 'o the dog, if ye catch me drift."

"I see."

Jack O'Riley smoothed back the sparse gray hairs on his head and said, "Now then, what can I do for ye? I take ye didn't seek me out to discuss me drinkin'."

"No, of course not." Drake paused, wondering how to broach the subject. "You know this hotel rather well, don't you?"

"Aye, I've worked at The Chesterfield for nigh on ten years."

He had come to the right man, then. "Then you would know the best way to . . . find a place to work undisturbed?"

"That I would. And who is it ye're wantin' to avoid?" O'Riley asked with a twinkle in his eye. "Young Gina, Miss Biddle, or one of t'other young misses bent on havin' a word with ye?"

Drake smiled ruefully. "Ah, you understand, then." The porter had obviously seen right through him. Even better, the man appeared to understand and sympathize with his dilemma.

"Aye, that I do." O'Riley regarded him quizzically. "Didn't ye know resorts are prime breeding grounds for matrimony? 'Tis where the gentry come to meet others o' their ilk and find a mate."

Drake hadn't given it much thought. Though now that Jack mentioned it, it explained why there were so many young, obviously healthy, unmarried people here. He needed to pay more attention. Sometimes he became so engrossed in his studies that he missed what was going on right beneath his nose. "I didn't realize." Though he should have—his wealthy father had met his mother in just such a place.

O'Riley nodded sagely. "Have ye tried the gentleman's bar? The wimmin can't follow ye there."

"Yes, but it's rather noisy. I need quiet to study my notes."

"How about the men's bathhouse?"

"Too wet." Ink tended to run and splotch in the damp air.

O'Riley turned thoughtful. "Hmm, well, I really shouldn't be sayin' this, but the tower is vacant."

It was hard to miss the magnificent edifice at the front of the hotel, though Drake had wondered why he had never seen any guests in that area. "Why is that?"

" 'Tis just being built. The rooms are nothing but bare walls, with the fancy new plumbing bein' put in, so 'tisn't ready for guests yet." O'Riley's eyes twinkled again. "But ye may be able to charm Miss Sparrow out of a set o' keys and mayhap a chair or two. She can be right sympathetic to a man's woes at times."

"Excellent—"

"Yoo-hoo, Mr. Manton," came a voice Drake had learned to dread.

He had thought himself hidden behind the palms, but though they readily hid the shorter porter, Drake realized the top of his head must be visible above the feathery fronds.

The fronds parted with the help of two small hands, and he found himself staring into Mrs. Biddle's beady little eyes. He groaned inwardly, cursing the day he'd made the mistake of petting Princess, her Pekingese. He had no idea it would make the woman regard him as a prospective son-in-law.

But however he might want to flee, manners dictated he remain. Feeling slightly ridiculous for being caught hiding in the shrubbery, he nodded politely. "Mrs. Biddle."

She simpered . . . a horrible sight. "Oh, Mr. Manton," she said, laughing shrilly, "you are such a card. Do come out and say hello."

Drake had no choice but to comply. As he suspected, Letty Biddle was close behind her mother, though Princess was nowhere in sight. The girl must take after her deceased father, for she was quite pretty with her blond hair and blue eyes. And, to her credit, Letty didn't share her mother's matchmaking tendencies. She was a modest young lady, who kept her eyes demurely downcast whenever Drake was around.

He suspected she was embarrassed by her mother's obvious machinations. And, as far as he could tell, Letty had no interest in him whatsoever. It was all Mrs. Biddle's idea.

"Look, Letty dear," the woman cried. "Here is Mr. Manton. Weren't we just saying how we hadn't seen him in ages?"

"Yes, Mama," Letty replied dutifully.

The elder Biddle patted her daughter's hand. "My daughter is too shy to speak her mind, but she does admire you so."

Drake could think of no answer to that, so he merely bowed.

Letty blushed, but her mother continued undaunted. "Of course, she has many admirers herself. Why, at home, she is simply inundated with invitations and suitors."

"How nice for her," Drake said in a discouraging tone, wondering how he could escape.

"But she doesn't get nearly enough exercise here,"

Mrs. Biddle complained. "There are so few young men who like to walk." She glanced expectantly up at Drake.

That look probably meant something, but he couldn't determine what, so he merely returned a noncommittal grunt and cast a despairing glance in O'Riley's direction.

The porter came to the rescue. Appearing from behind the palms with an insouciance that bordered on insolence, he said, "The Chesterfield has a nature walk scheduled every morning at nine."

Mrs. Biddle speared him with an annoyed look. "Pah. A structured walk with a lot of strangers. My shy little Letty has a more delicate constitution. She needs the attentions of a strong young man who can guide her along the proper path."

Delicate? The girl was as healthy as a horse.

Inexorably, the Biddle gaze turned to Drake. "Would you . . . ?"

This time he understood. He might enjoy a walk, but *not* with the exceedingly shy Letty Biddle. "I'm sorry," he said, searching for some excuse that would take him away. "I have . . . an appointment. With Dr. Ziegler." There—that ought to do it.

Mrs. Biddle was disappointed, but not beaten. With a forced smile, she said, "Ah. Well, we can't keep you then. But we were just on the way to the bathhouse ourselves, to partake of the waters. We shall accompany you."

How was he going to get out of this one? He cast a frantic glance at the porter, who smirked but came to his rescue once again. "As I was just tellin' Mr. Manton, the doctor is in the east wing, seein' to a patient." And that was as far away from the bathhouse as they could get in the hotel.

Undaunted, Mrs. Biddle said, "We would be happy to change our plans and accompany you there."

"Ah, no," Drake said, this time determined not to miss his cue. "I couldn't possibly keep you from taking the waters. It would do Letty so much good."

Drake thought he saw Letty cast him a disbelieving glance, but Mrs. Biddle frowned, obviously beaten.

Drake bowed. "Perhaps we shall meet later." *If I don't see you first.*

The old Biddle had to be content with that. Crossly, she tugged at her daughter's arm. "Come, Letty. We mustn't bother Mr. Manton any longer."

They turned to leave, and Drake gratefully slipped a handsome gratuity into the porter's palm. Such sterling service deserved it. "Will you show me the tower now?"

"Aye," Jack said as he slipped the coins in his pocket. "If ye—"

"Wait," Drake said urgently. He had just caught sight of Gina, who was obviously seeking someone. Having a suspicion he was once more the object of her search, he slipped behind the plants again and hunched over to avoid detection.

Unfortunately, her dog, who had decided Drake was the epitome of canine bliss, sniffed him out and made his way through the screening palms with a joyous bark of greeting. Hoping to quiet him, Drake bent to scratch his ears, but it was too late.

Gina peeked through the palm fronds much as Mrs. Biddle had earlier, only with a far more pleasant expression. In fact, she appeared quite amused. "Gotcha," she said. Then, glancing down at O'Riley's flask, she grinned more broadly. "Well, this gives a whole new meaning to the phrase 'potted palms'."

He didn't know what she meant, but, embarrassed

by being caught hiding behind the plants twice in one day, Drake decided there was nothing he could do but brazen it out. He rose and nodded politely, then stepped out into the lobby as if it were an everyday occurrence.

Gina beamed at him as if he had done something exceedingly clever. Drake softened. It was difficult to be annoyed with a young woman who radiated such friendliness. Especially since her sunny, outgoing disposition was in such distinct contrast with Mrs. Biddle's.

"I was just leaving," he informed her, turning to suit action to words.

"I'll come with you."

"Thank you, but that isn't necessary."

"Yes, it is," Gina said with a smile. "You've been avoiding me too long. Now that I've finally caught you, I'm not going to let you go until I've had my say."

The porter grinned behind Gina, and Drake sighed. Though he might admire Gina's forthright attitude, he wished she had learned some of the circumlocutions used in polite society. But he had to admit plain speaking was effective. He couldn't object without telling her flatly to go away . . . and the code of a gentleman didn't allow him to do that.

He cast a pleading glance at O'Riley, but the porter just shrugged and said, "I'll be after gettin' ye those keys. If ye'd like to wait for me at the tower?"

Well, it was better than waiting around here and perhaps having to dive behind the plants again. Resignedly, Drake turned to leave and Gina followed him.

As they walked toward the tower, her dog trotting along beside them, she chatted about various other resorts and their vastly superior amenities—a not so subtle hint that he should take himself off to one of them.

Borrowing a page from her book, he decided to speak plainly. "Why are you trying to get rid of me?"

"I'm not—"

He didn't let her finish her sentence, but pulled her quickly into a secluded alcove, behind another pair of plants. He had spotted two other young women at the end of the hall who had been pursuing him, and he was afraid if the gabby ladies saw him, he'd never win free.

He peered out into the hallway and saw Scruffy staring at him with a perplexed expression. Before the dog could give him away again, Drake quickly scooped him into the alcove with them.

Gina looked confused. "What—"

"Shh," he cautioned with a finger to her lips and whispered, "Wait until the Misses Harrington pass by."

Gina suddenly went still and Drake grew conscious that they were very close in this confined space. He gazed down into her wide brown eyes, wondering why he had decided to drag her in here with him. He could have left her out in the hall since he doubted she would betray him to the young ladies.

His misgivings vanished as he became aware of her rounded body so close to his, her womanly scent enveloping him, and her brown eyes gazing up into his with surprise . . . and a hint of something else.

When he realized her full, soft lips had parted slightly under his silencing finger, he removed the offending digit.

Unfortunately, the Misses Harrington chose this spot to stop and chat. Under cover of their voices, he whispered, "I beg your pardon. I don't know what came over me."

"That's okay," Gina breathed softly.

Their close proximity, combined with the fact that he could feel her warm breath against his neck made the conversation all too intimate. To obtain some appearance of normalcy, he said softly, "I'm sorry, what were you saying before I . . . interrupted you?"

She paused for a moment, thinking. "Oh. I was explaining that I'm not trying to get rid of you, I'm trying to help you."

Ignoring his body's reaction to her closeness, he cleared his throat and said, "By making me leave?"

"Sort of." She shrugged, and the small movement brought her breasts into soft contact with his chest.

He inhaled sharply. A gentleman would ignore the unintended intimacy and pretend he hadn't felt anything, but Drake found himself wishing she would do it again.

Instead, her cheeks turned pink and she backed away from him in the small space to flatten herself against the wall behind her. "I—I can't explain," she said breathlessly, "but it's imperative you leave the resort."

This was the first time he could remember the brazen Gina appearing so discommoded. Could it be because of his nearness? To test his assumption, he moved closer and felt the awareness between them increase. "Why is this so important to you?"

"It just is." He was so close that she had to lean her head back to speak to him, baring the soft expanse of her creamy white throat in unconscious surrender.

Drake was surprised at the surge of feeling that washed through him. The thought of this lush woman surrendering to him made his blood rush. He leaned closer, bracing an arm beside her head. With his other hand, he drew his finger softly down her cheek. "If you can't explain, then I can't go. These upcoming lectures are the culmination of everything I've worked for. I can't just give them up on a whim for a woman, no matter how beautiful." She didn't need to know that he would never give them up—helping others was the only way to make up his failure with Charlotte, at least in some small way.

Gina's indrawn gasp proved she wasn't as indifferent as she would have him believe. "Compliments don't sway me—I've heard too many false ones," she said and squirmed from beneath his arm to peer out of the concealing palms. "They're gone now. We can come out."

Reluctantly, Drake had to admit he had no further reason to stay hidden, though he was loath to give up the closeness they had created.

Her color high, Gina stepped out into the hall and smoothed her apron, unnecessarily calling Scruffy to heel. Giving Drake a challenging glance, she said, "As someone said to me not so long ago, I'm going to hound you until you leave, so be prepared."

Drake watched her depart with a feeling of bemusement. So she was going to hound him, eh? Oddly enough, he found himself looking forward to it.

Chapter Four

The next several weeks went fast for Gina as she fell into a routine. Today was no exception. A bell ringing in the hall woke her at dawn and she rose to dress quickly in her ugly gray uniform dress. Since they weren't allowed to wear makeup—and she wouldn't know where to find any even if they were— her morning toilette went quickly. She splashed water on her face and pinned her hair up, determined not to be late to the Major's morning muster.

Gina already had a penchant for attracting trouble with her twenty-first century ways and attitude, so she tried to make up for it by abiding by the other rules. It kept the powers that be happy . . . and kept *her* at the resort where she could work on saving Drake. Luckily, the doctor hadn't seen anything amiss with her attitude, at least nothing that required hospitalization, so she no longer feared him. But the Major with his rigid rules was another matter.

She made it to the muster just in time and fell in with the rest of the employees, ensuring she lined up straight with the waitress next to her. The Major obsessed over the silliest things, and he really hated a crooked line. Thankfully, she'd learned early on how to pass his inspection—all she had to do was remain neat and tidy and keep her mouth shut. If she didn't give Major Payne any reason to notice her, she didn't get in trouble.

Today, he banished several employees back to their rooms to rectify problems with their uniforms, but when he came to Gina, he merely looked her up and down, harrumphed, and moved on.

Beside him, Esme nodded with approval and Gina repressed a grin. She'd come a long way from the first day when she'd needed help just figuring out how to put her clothes on.

Once the stiff-rumped hotel manager grudgingly dismissed them, Gina headed off to the kitchen to seek out Chef Sasha. The rotund Russian chef was chewing out a subordinate for some unknown grievance, but when he spotted Gina, he paused and struck a dramatic pose, exclaiming, "You! You haf come for more treats for your little pooches, neh? Vell, this time Sasha says no!"

Gina bit back a grin. They had this conversation every morning and it was always the same, but she knew she had to play the game. Staring pleadingly up at the tall chef, she said, "But, Mr. Sashenka, we must keep the guests happy. And they want their dogs to have the best . . . as only you can provide."

"I haf served the Russian court with these hands. Now you wish me to cook for little doggies?"

Sasha continued grumping for awhile, but he had a soft heart under that dramatic exterior, and once

Gina had praised him enough, he relented. Throwing up his hands in a gesture that nearly dislodged the hanging pots, he said, "Enough. You may haf a few scraps."

Gina thanked him profusely but he waved her away to the corner where she knew choice scraps of meat and bone would already be waiting on a tray. As Sasha turned a blind eye, she signaled one of the kitchen helpers to carry it for her. She'd learned it was much easier to collect the half-dozen unmannered dogs she was to tutor if she was accompanied by the meat tray.

Once she had fed and exercised the dogs, then attempted to teach them some manners, she returned them to their owners. Finally, she had the afternoon free until she had to feed them again. But instead of ferreting out Drake Manton as she usually did, Gina went to her room to think.

Lying on the bed and petting Scruffy, she wondered what to do about the mesmerist. She had to save the man's life so she could go home. Though she'd found a way to fit in here in the past, it wasn't her time, and she felt out of place. Besides, she really missed some of the modern conveniences . . . like hot showers, old movies, steamy romance novels, and Häagen-Dazs.

And, truth to tell, she wanted to save Drake's life for his own sake. As a ghost, he'd been a bit melancholy and demanding, but the live man was really very nice. With his dramatic looks and compelling dark eyes, you'd think he'd be more arrogant and condescending. Instead, he was surprisingly kind. Not many men in this era would be so unfailingly polite to the women who pursued him, or treat a hotel employee as an equal. Though she'd vowed to never have anything to do with a man again, Drake's kindness disarmed her and the pain she sensed beneath his polite exterior made her long to comfort him.

Good grief, what was she thinking? He'd be in even more pain if she didn't *do* something. Death by fire wasn't exactly gentle.

The problem was, Drake had proven very elusive and she needed to come up with a new tactic to convince him to leave. Hinting hadn't done it, nor had outright telling him to go. And when she'd tried to spook him by siccing all the single women in the resort on him, her scheme had backfired. She still found it difficult to pass a potted palm without thinking of his warmth, his tenderness, his—

Forget it. This was getting her nowhere. And all her scheme had done was make him go further into hiding. When he did emerge for brief periods, she found it very difficult to get near him. Besides, if all those matchmaking women hadn't scared him away, what would?

Hmm, that was it. Since he wouldn't listen to reason, she had to scare him away. But how? Threats wouldn't work—she didn't have anything to threaten him with, except Mrs. Biddle as a mother-in-law, and he seemed perfectly capable of avoiding that dire fate all by himself.

What *would* scare a man like Drake Manton? A sudden idea came to her and she smiled. Perfect. What better way to keep him from becoming a ghost than to scare him off with one? Besides, it would serve him right, after haunting her.

Plans bumped around in her head, but she realized they all required one thing—an accomplice. Scratching Scruffy's ears, she said, "But I can't tell anyone *why* I want to scare him away, so who can I get to help me, someone who won't ask difficult questions?"

Scruffy had no answers, but a slow smile spread across her face. She had it. The very person—Rupert Smith.

She tracked down the bellboy and waited until he finished taking a load of baggage to a room, then pulled him aside. "Rupert, I need your help."

The lanky bellboy grinned down at her. "Sure, Gina. What do you need?"

"I need you to help me scare away a guest."

Rupert backed away. "Whoa. I'm not about to run some rig that'll get me sacked. I need this job."

"You won't be sacked, I promise you. My plan is foolproof—we won't get caught. And if we do, I'll make sure they know it was all my idea."

"I don't think I can risk it."

"Come on, Rupert," she wheedled. "I'll give you two weeks' pay if you'll help me."

That had him thinking—money was one of the few things sure to get Rupert's attention. But he wasn't really as mercenary as others had made him out to be. Though he'd left Philadelphia and a large family with many brothers and sisters to make his own way in the world, he still sent money home regularly. All those mouths to feed were a powerful incentive, so the surest way to Rupert's help was through his wallet.

"I don't know. . . ." he said, but she could tell he was wavering.

"All right. Four weeks' pay, then." She didn't have much use for it back in this time anyway.

She watched as Rupert wrestled with his conscience, but the money won. "All right, what do I have to do and who do you want to scare?"

"Drake Manton."

"Why does it have to be Mr. Manton?" Rupert complained. "He's a big tipper."

"I have my reasons." And four weeks' pay ought to be reason enough for Rupert. "Do you really want to know?"

He thought for a moment, then shook his head. "No, I don't guess I do."

"Okay, then. Now first, do you know if any of the rooms around his are vacant?" Silly question—Rupert always knew everything that went on in the hotel.

"The one above him is, on the second floor. Why?"

"Because I want you to keep it that way."

"How?"

"You've got an in with the desk clerk—just tell him there's something wrong with the room or something."

"I don't know. . . ."

"Just do it," she said in exasperation. "Look, what I want you to do first is drop a few hints that the hotel has a ghost. Say a . . . a woman hanged herself in his room and she comes back to haunt single men. On second thought, not just in that room—in the whole hotel." She didn't want Drake to think he could just move to another room to escape the ghost.

"Why only single men?"

"I don't know—maybe she killed herself 'cause her lying creep of a fiancé slept with another woman," Gina said sharply.

Rupert raised both eyebrows but wisely didn't ask any more questions.

Gina waved her hands to erase her last outburst. "Never mind. We're going to make him think he's haunted by making ghostly noises above him, okay? With any luck, it'll make him leave the hotel."

"All right," Rupert said with a shrug. "It's your money."

"Good. We need to get started right away. We only have a week."

Drake had his first mesmerism lecture scheduled on Friday. Fearing it might gain him converts who would convince him to stay, Gina wanted to scare him away before that happened. With any luck, he'd be gone by Thursday.

Gina explained the rest of her plan, then put it into action with Rupert's help. They didn't get much sleep over the next week as they worked all day and spent half the night making spooky noises in the room above Drake's.

Rupert proved to be a great accomplice. She overheard him tell blood-chilling stories of the hanged woman's ghost that almost had Gina believing him, and he was extremely inventive when it came to making eerie sounds. His stories were so vivid, they even overshadowed the much talked-about circus coming to town.

Unfortunately, none of it seemed to faze Drake Manton. Finally, after five days of inadequate sleep, Gina put down the pipe she had used to make ghostly sounds at Drake's window. Slumping to the floor, she said, "This isn't working."

Rupert nodded. "So, you want to quit?"

"Are you kidding? Not on your life. We still have tomorrow night. I guess I'll just have to bring out the big guns."

Aghast, Rupert said, "You're going to shoot him?"

"No, of course not." Silly man—she really had to watch her modern expressions. "I mean I just have to go to Plan B."

"Plan B? What's that?"

Well, it had seemed reasonable when she'd dreamed it up a week ago, but now she wasn't so sure. And if she told Rupert what she had in mind, she was sure he wouldn't approve either. "Never mind. Just meet me here tomorrow night at the same time. I'll tell you then."

The next night, Gina slipped into the room above Drake's an hour before Rupert was supposed to meet her and dressed in her jeans and T-shirt, then stepped into the leather harness contraption she'd talked Sean Quinn, the stablemaster, into making for her. As she'd planned, the straps fit her like a bathing suit—at least, one that had really big holes in it.

The bottom straps went around the top of her legs, the top set went over her shoulders and under her arms, and there were two other sets in between, reinforced by strips running vertically up the front and back.

She'd seen something like this on one of those behind the scenes shows on television—it allowed the actors to appear as if they were flying, but the harness distributed the stress evenly across their bodies so they weren't cut in two by the rope.

Pleased with her ingenuity, Gina slipped a white nightgown on over the contraption so it wouldn't show. Good—it made her look properly ghostly. Now for her face. She used the mirror to put on the "makeup" she had devised for this occasion—white flour liberally dusted over her hair and face, soot to create dark circles under her eyes and blacken her lips, and beet juice to draw a red line around her neck.

She stood back to assess her handiwork and grinned. Yep, she looked like a hanged woman. Rupert opened the door then and she turned toward him to give him the full effect.

She had hoped to catch him off-guard and turn

him as white as the ghost she was pretending to be, but instead, he grinned. "You look ghastly."

"Thank you. That was the general idea." But she would have been happier with more fear and less admiration. "Do I look like a ghost?"

"Yes, if I didn't know it was you, you would have convinced me."

Somewhat mollified, Gina said, "Well, I hope it convinces Drake Manton."

"What are you going to do? Pretend to float across his room?"

"No, what if I bump into the furniture? Or into him? He might find out I'm not really a ghost."

"So what are you going to do?"

"I'm going to hang myself outside his window."

"You're going to *what*?"

"Here, I'll show you."

Rupert looked shy at first when she pulled up her nightgown, but when he realized she was fully dressed underneath and saw the harness, he was intrigued. "What's that for?"

"It's to keep me from really hanging myself when you lower me on a rope down to Drake's window."

"Lower you on a rope? Oh, no," Rupert protested. "You'll kill yourself."

"No I won't. Look, I've thought it all out. You just let me down to the first floor window, and I'll get his attention. To him, I'll look like a hanged woman floating in midair. Like this." She cocked her head to the side and let her tongue protrude. "See?"

"Then what?" Rupert asked dubiously.

"Then after he faints or runs away screaming, I'll tug on the rope and you haul me up."

"How? We weigh about the same. I don't think I could raise you back up."

Annoyed with his faultfinding, Gina said, "Okay, how about this? You lower me, then run the rope once or twice around the chest of drawers over there—that'll help hold me in place. Then when I tug on the rope, you can lower me to the ground."

"What if you fall?"

"So what? It's only a few feet down from there—I won't get hurt."

Obviously still trying to find a way to convince her to give up her scheme, Rupert said, "But if I do that, how are you going to get back in without anyone seeing you like this?"

"I borrowed a cloak with a hood. It's over on the bed. All you have to do is drop the cloak on top of me and you can leave. I won't ask you to do any more, okay?

"Do you think this will really work?"

"Of course it will." They did it all the time in the movies. "Come on, Rupert. You promised. And *I* promise—this is the last time I'll ask you to help me."

Rupert heaved a heavy sigh, but she could tell the boy in him was eager to see how it worked. After all, he was only seventeen. "All right, but this is the last time."

No longer reluctant, Rupert tied the rope to the back of her harness and helped her climb out the window backward. As Gina bumped her way down the outside brick wall, she wondered if this was such a good idea after all. She had envisioned floating serenely in space, not hanging plastered against the wall. Oh, well, too late now. At least there was a small brick overhang above Drake's window which helped her achieve a little distance from it.

She gave Rupert the sign to stop and donned her best ghoulish expression. "Wooooooo."

She waited a moment, but there was no sign of life from inside Drake's room. She tapped on the glass. "Gooooo awaaaaaaay!" she wailed.

Finally, there was some sign of movement from inside.

To give him the maximum effect, she pushed off from the brick wall so he could see her feet didn't touch the ground. "Goooo awaaaaay."

She swung back toward the window and pushed away again. Unfortunately, her next "Wooooooo," ended in a "wooooo—oof!" as she sailed in through the now-opened window and slammed into Drake's chest.

"What the devil?" he exclaimed.

As Gina rebounded, she frantically tugged on the rope. The rope went slack, but as she slumped, Drake caught her under the arms and hauled her into his room.

Damn. Now what? Gina struggled to free herself, to no avail. Drake's arm around her middle was like iron—and so was the rest of his body. Jeez, the guy must work out or something. How the heck was she going to get away?

Holding her with one arm, Drake somehow lit a lamp with the other and peered at her face. "Ah, Miss Charles. I wondered when you would put in a physical appearance."

How had he recognized her? Gina decided to brazen it out. Thrusting her hands against his chest, she said, "Let me go."

"Where's your accomplice? And how far do you plan to take this game?"

Ignoring the jibe about Rupert, she said, "It's not

a game. I'm deadly serious. Let me go." But when that tactic failed to make him release her, she forced herself to go limp and let her face crumple, hoping to lull him into a false sense of security.

It worked. As his arm loosened, she pushed him away and bolted for the door. Yanking it open, she came face to face with Chloe Harrington. Though the girl's hand was upraised to knock, she took one look at Gina's face, screeched, and crumpled to the floor in a faint.

Finally, someone who knew how to react to a ghost.

But, unfortunately, it meant Gina couldn't get out that way. Any moment now, curious guests would be opening doors and peering out into the hall. She slammed the door shut. Maybe she could make it out the window.

Too late. Drake had grabbed her rope and hauled her back by it until he held her once more in his secure grip. "What was that?" he asked, frowning.

Hoping to divert the topic onto something else, anything else, Gina said, "That was Chloe Harrington, getting ready to knock on your door. Did you have a tryst planned or something?" she asked in an accusing tone. He wasn't really supposed to have a fling with one of these women she'd flung at him.

"No, of course not," he said in indignation, but his hold didn't loosen one bit.

"Well, she seemed to think so. She looked very fetching in her best nightie, too."

"Don't be absurd. Why would Miss Harrington come to my room in the middle of the night?"

Jeez, for a supposedly smart guy, he was surprisingly clueless when it came to people's motives. "Why do you think?"

If possible, he scowled even harder. "Nonsense.

Miss Harrington is a chaste young woman who wouldn't dream of doing anything so bold.''

Yeah, right. "Oh, I'm sure she planned on getting a wedding ring out of it."

"What are you saying?"

"I'm saying the scuttlebutt around the hotel is that Mrs. Harrington has so many daughters to marry off that she isn't above tricking a man or two into matrimony." She tried to squirm out of his grip, but no dice. "Now do you understand?"

He looked confused. "Are you certain of this?"

"Not absolutely positive, no. But I'll bet Chloe's mama will be along any moment now."

Another feminine screech came from out in the hall, right on cue. "My baby!"

Smugly, Gina said, "See? Don't worry—she'd be foolish to try anything now." Then, to capitalize on this unexpected boon, she ceased struggling and gazed up at him with a woebegone expression that had worked wonders in wrapping her father around her little finger. "I just saved you from a fate worse than Birdie Biddle. Please, won't you let me go?"

"You're not going anywhere. You're going to explain what you're doing here." He grimaced. "But first, you'd best wash your face."

She'd forgotten her ghoulish makeup. No wonder the woebegone look hadn't worked. Sighing, she let him lead her over to the washbasin. She had enough vanity that she didn't want to look like a corpse around such a hunk, and besides, she didn't want anyone else to catch her like this, either. If the Major caught wind of this, she'd really be in for it.

As she wiped the flour from her face and untied the rope from her harness, she wondered what Drake had in mind for her. Whatever it was, she doubted she'd like it. But without proof of her misdeed, it was his word against hers. She had to make a break for it. Now.

Quickly, she dropped her washcloth and dived for the window. Unfortunately, Drake was too swift for her once again. He caught her around the waist. Determined to escape this time, Gina tried to wriggle away. No dice. In their struggle, they ended up on the bed with Drake sprawled on top of her.

"Let go of me," she said, panting. Any other time, this wrestling match might be kind of fun, but she was in danger of losing her job if she got caught.

He seized her wrists and held them pinned above her head to the bed. "Not until you tell me why you are trying so hard to scare me away."

Gina gave up and blew a long strand of hair out of her face. Her mind raced, trying to come up with an explanation he'd buy. As she stilled, she became conscious of his strong body against hers. Though he had been decently clothed in a dark maroon robe, the robe had parted during their tussle, and Gina couldn't help but wonder just what was being exposed down around her thighs. It felt like he had nothing on underneath.

But she couldn't verify her suspicions as Drake held her motionless, pinned by his strong hands and his fascinating dark eyes. Those sexy eyes. . . . As Gina tried to regain her breath, his nearness and her senses slowly besieged her. She became very conscious of his musky scent, the warmth of his skin, and his lower body pressed intimately against hers.

Yum. He was so close she could reach out and taste him.

Oh no, where had that idea come from? This was

worse, much worse than that time when he'd trapped her in the alcove.

"Well?" he asked softly.

It was obvious he wasn't unaffected either. She could feel his reaction—a swelling against her inner thigh. This evidence of his arousal should have turned her off, but it had just the opposite effect. She swallowed hard. "Wha—what?"

He lowered his face so he was only a breath away, the soft lamplight bringing into view the slashing white streak in his hair and the dark, crisp hair curling on his chest between the parted lapels of his robe. Damn. She was a sucker for a furry chest.

Pleasurable, yearning sensations overwhelmed her. She licked her lips and looked up at him with wide eyes, wanting to touch him, needing to kiss him, hoping he would bring his mouth just . . . a . . . little . . . closer.

Drake inhaled sharply, then slowly lowered his mouth to hers. First, he kissed her with a delicate touch that sent her senses reeling. Then, when she couldn't help but respond, he slanted his mouth across hers and she damn near fainted with giddiness.

He released her wrists to clasp her to him more fully, freeing her hands to explore him. She parted his robe even more and burrowed her hands in all that lovely hair on his chest as his kisses turned more urgent.

Sensations overwhelmed her and she was mindless for a while, aware of nothing but the feel of his skin under her hands, the play of his lips on hers, and his warm hands seeking the softness of her breasts through her nightgown and T-shirt.

Damn—she was wearing too many clothes. Gina pushed him away for a moment, determined to remove at least one layer of unnecessary clothing, but he must have mistaken her motives, for he pulled back sharply and got off the bed.

He flashed her for an all too brief moment with his nudity, but swiftly pulled together the edges of his robe and gave her an apologetic glance. "I'm sorry. I—I shouldn't have done that."

"Oh, yes, you should," Gina contradicted him, unwilling to lose the glow his touch had aroused in her. She rose from the bed to take a step toward his warmth. "And you were doing such a good job of it, too."

He smoothed back his hair and averted his gaze, stepping back. "No, I am a gentleman, and gentlemen do not take advantage of young ladies . . . no matter how willing."

"Was that a crack?" she asked suspiciously, remembering how he'd defended Chloe and her so-called virtue.

"I beg your pardon?"

"Never mind." Feeling suddenly ashamed and belatedly remembering her vow to have nothing to do with men, she did the only thing she could think of.

She jumped out the window.

Chapter Five

The next morning, Drake cursed his lack of sleep. This day, of all days, he needed to be fully alert.

He blamed Gina for the bleary eyes staring back at him from the shaving mirror. Not because of her ill-advised appearance as a ghost—he'd deduced early on that she and Rupert were the ones trying to frighten him. So it wasn't her ghostly presence that had disturbed him, but her all too physical one.

He'd lain awake for the rest of the night, reliving those moments when she'd lain beneath him, soft, womanly, inviting. . . . And her unexpected response had merely added fuel to the fire, setting his senses ablaze, making his body crave the satisfaction of being cradled within her warmth.

It was disturbing. He hadn't been this aroused in a very long time. He had denied himself the comforting touch of women, believing he didn't deserve the solace they represented. Not when Charlotte's short life had been so devoid of the blessings of a loving spouse.

And though it had been more than two years, Drake still mourned his little sister, still felt the pain of her passing, still blamed himself for not preventing her death. In expiation, he had dedicated his life to helping other people. It wouldn't bring Charlotte back, but it might assuage his guilt and give him some measure of peace.

Now, Gina threatened to disturb his equilibrium. Worse, he would have to tender her an apology. There was no excuse for his behavior last night. He should have ignored her ripe body beneath his, disregarded her sensuality and unreserved response. Unfortunately, the combination of all three wrapped up in the provocative package that was Gina had been too much for him.

And just when had Miss Charles become Gina in his thoughts? Annoyed, Drake wondered what ailed the woman, no matter what he called her. Instead of lingering on the silky texture of her mouth, he should remember her actions. If she was not mentally imbalanced already, she was definitely heading in that direction.

A tiny voice niggled at him. Wasn't that what he had been trained to do, help people with mental illnesses?

Perhaps, but nothing in his training had prepared him to deal with Gina, especially since she was so intent on making him change *his* behavior.

That was another puzzle. Why the devil did she want him to leave the resort so badly?

He sighed. He couldn't afford to contemplate the enigma of Gina Charles today, nor could he afford to let her distract him from his main purpose. For now, he needed to concentrate on his upcoming lecture. He'd worry about Gina later.

Drake spent the rest of the day going over his notes until the time finally came for his lecture. Knowing he was as prepared as he could possibly be, Drake approached the small theater with confidence. Not surprisingly, it was decorated as lavishly as the rest of the hotel, with heavy velvet curtains lining the small stage. The theater was designed to hold perhaps a hundred people or so, and Drake was gratified to see a good number of people filling the seats.

Surveying those seated below, Drake nodded at the Biddles and Harringtons, who had assured him faithfully they'd be there, though he certainly hadn't pressed for their attendance. He estimated perhaps forty additional people had chosen to attend, which pleased him. That is, until he caught sight of a familiar form entering from the rear—Gina.

She seemed different somehow, and it took him a few moments to realize this was the first time he'd seen her attired in anything but that depressing gray uniform. Well, except for the nightgown last night, and he had best not think of that. And, if the awkward way she moved in the bright blue dress was any indication, she had borrowed the finery from someone else.

Drake frowned. Any other young woman would go out of her way to avoid him after he had compromised her virtue. He should have known Gina would never do the expected.

So, why *had* she come? To cause trouble? He wouldn't put it past her.

She seated herself toward the back, and a man sat beside her who didn't fit in with the rest of the guests. His clothing was a little too bright, his hair too shiny, and he was wearing too much flashy jewelry to appear perfectly respectable. But when the man distracted Gina by engaging her in conversation, Drake was more than happy to accord him all the virtues of a gentleman . . . if he would only continue to hold her attention.

Dr. Ziegler approached Drake and cleared his throat. "Well, young man, are you ready to begin?"

Straightening his jacket, Drake nodded.

As Dr. Ziegler went to the lectern, Drake quickly marshaled his facts and figures in his mind and double-checked to ensure he had his notes handy. He missed most of Dr. Ziegler's introduction, but the smattering of polite applause let him know the moment he had been waiting for had arrived.

This was the first time he had addressed a group, but surprisingly, Drake wasn't nervous. Instead, his confidence was bolstered by the knowledge that the information he had to impart was vitally important.

He smiled down at the audience. "Good evening, ladies and gentlemen. Thank you all for coming. This is the first of a series of lectures I shall present on the topic of mesmerism, and tonight, I will start with a history of the science as it has evolved from Dr. Mesmer's early experiments through later practitioners to the methods in use today."

Eager interest appeared on most of the faces, so Drake went on to explain Mesmer's early belief that it was something he called animal magnetism that had caused the hypnotic effects he had engendered in his patients. As Drake expounded on the progression of mesmerism over the past twelve years, he was careful not to emulate or even mention mesmerism's more colorful and flamboyant practitioners. They had given the science a bad name, lowering it to the status of sensational sideshow entertainment instead of exploring the wonderful potential it held for curing mental illness.

But the more Drake spoke, the more the upturned faces changed from avid interest to polite acceptance. Fearing he would lose them, Drake gave them a preview of the next lecture, reciting an impressive list of the types and kinds of illnesses mesmerism had already helped to alleviate.

It didn't help. Their expressions reflected utter boredom now. Confused as to where he had gone wrong, Drake finished with an open invitation to visit him in Dr. Ziegler's office any afternoon between the hours of two and four.

Scattered, halfhearted applause greeted his closing remarks, leaving Drake even more confused. What had gone wrong? He had been assiduous in presenting his carefully cultivated facts.

Dr. Ziegler came up to shake his hand. "A very illuminating presentation, Mr. Manton, worthy of a true scholar."

Bemused, Drake thanked him, wondering if the doctor had attended a different lecture than the rest of the audience. They couldn't seem to leave fast enough.

All except the Biddles and the Harringtons, that is. Mrs. Biddle dragged Letty up to the stage and declared, "What a marvelous lecture, Mr. Manton. Weren't we just saying so, Letty, dear?"

"Yes, Mama," Letty replied dutifully, though it was obvious she had been as filled with *ennui* as the rest.

The Misses Harrington arrived then, accompanied by their mother, and all the women vied with one another in effusive praise of his resonant speaking voice and his commanding presence at the lectern.

In resignation, Drake realized none of them had mentioned the important message he had tried to convey.

He listened politely but wished himself elsewhere, needing to lick his wounds in private and determine what had gone wrong. He thanked them for their praise, damning as it was, and murmured an excuse to escape their insincere pleasantries.

The momentary relief caused by their departure abruptly ceased when he turned and came face to face with Gina. For a brief moment, he wished he hadn't been so hasty. He would welcome a little insincerity in the face of Gina's blunt honesty.

As if the pain of his humiliation wasn't enough, he had to endure her expression of pity as well. "So," he snapped, "have you come to rub salt in my wounds?"

Well, that's a slap in the face, Gina thought. All she'd planned to do was pat him on the hand and say, "There, there." Now, she felt more like kicking him in the shins. Raising her chin, she glared at him. "No, I just wanted to say I'm sorry it didn't go well for you."

He sighed and dragged a hand through his hair. "I apologize. I shouldn't have barked at you."

Sensing this wasn't the right time to offer condolences or, ever worse, try once more to convince him to leave the resort, Gina turned away.

"Wait," Drake said urgently.

Surprised, she halted. This was a first. Usually he couldn't wait to get rid of her.

Continuing in a low voice, he said, "I believe I owe you an apology."

"It's okay. You already said you're sorry."

"No, I mean an apology of a different sort . . . for my behavior last night. I was somewhat less than gentlemanly."

Gina felt her cheeks heat in embarrassment. Why did he have to remind her of that? She'd been trying to forget it all day. For one thing, she couldn't afford to get involved with any man, especially not here in the past. There was no future in it.

For another, women in this time were so ridiculously virtuous, he probably thought she was wickedly immoral for responding to his kiss. "There's no need to apologize," she said quickly. Besides, it was partially her fault that it had gone as far as it had . . . though it was totally *his* fault that they'd stopped.

When he looked as though he wanted to continue, she narrowed her eyes at him. "Really, don't mention it." She wanted to forget the whole night had happened. When Esme had somehow learned of it, Gina didn't know which the housekeeper found more appalling—the fact that Gina had worn her nightgown to try to scare Drake away, or that she had worn her jeans and T-shirt underneath.

In any case, Esme had removed all her twenty-first century clothing for "safekeeping." The only thing Gina had left to remind her of the future was the article she had secreted under the mattress.

"As you wish," Drake said in a placating tone, then paused for a moment, thinking. "I'll probably regret this, but I wonder if you might help me with another matter."

"What's that?" she asked, grateful for a change of subject.

"Despite your wish to get rid of me, or perhaps because of it, you're the only one who has been honest with me. Could you . . . would you . . . tell me where my lecture went wrong?"

Where didn't it? But Gina kept the flip response to herself. Drake seemed honestly bewildered as to why his talk had bombed. She paused, wondering how to phrase his problem without offending him, but the chatter of female voices interrupted her.

Uh-oh, it looked like Drake's fan club was inching back this way. Nodding in their direction, she said, "Why don't we discuss this somewhere else?"

A faint grimace twisted his mouth. "An excellent idea. Where?"

"It's rather hot in here," especially with all the clothes Esme insisted a proper lady must wear on an evening out, "why don't you give me twenty minutes to change, and I'll meet you in the gardens."

His eyebrows rose, and Gina remembered Rupert had described the gardens as a popular "trysting place" for couples. Darn—she'd put her foot in it again. She added quickly, "It's cooler there by the fountains, and I need to walk Scruffy."

As the women drew nearer, Drake nodded. "Twenty minutes, then," he said and hurried off.

Gina stopped at her room to change into her uniform. It might be ugly, but it was a great deal cooler than the horribly confining dress Esme had lent her. It was kind of fun playing dress-up, but in the sweltering heat of August in Virginia, it wasn't very comfortable . . . and air conditioning wouldn't be invented for many years to come.

Scruffy was eager to go out, so she led him out the side door and hurried to the gardens. As Drake greeted the ecstatic dog, Gina became conscious that they were visible from the hotel so she urged him down one of the paths concealed by the enclosing shrubbery.

They walked in silence for a moment, and Gina sighed in appreciation. In daylight, the formal gardens appeared rigidly controlled in perfectly manicured splendor, but at night, they held an entirely different appearance. Fairy-like fireflies darted about, lending a magical air, and the darkness made her other senses more acute, enhancing the gentle sounds of burbling water in the fountain and the lush, heady fragrance of evening-blooming primroses, honeysuckle, and wild roses. No wonder this was The Chesterfield's version of lover's lane—it was very seductive.

Their wandering brought them to a stone bench in a secluded bower. Silently, Drake gestured toward it, inviting Gina to seat herself.

She did so, grateful for the coolness of the stone and the light breeze that whispered through the surrounding foliage. Scruffy jumped up beside her and Drake sat on the other side of the dog to scratch his ears and stare off into the night, his odd white streak gleaming in the moonlight.

Not wanting to break the enchantment, Gina waited until Drake was ready to speak. Finally, with a sigh, he asked softly, "Where did I go wrong?"

In the darkness, Gina searched for a kind way to tell him his talk had been incredibly dull. "I don't think the audience found your lecture interesting."

He slanted her a glance full of self-mockery. "You mean they found me boring. I know that, but what I don't understand is *why.*"

He seemed genuinely confused, so Gina decided to enlighten him. "It was the wrong slant for that audience. You spoke to them as if they were all scholars, as if they were interested in learning for its own sake."

He frowned. "Isn't everyone?"

She almost laughed at his naiveté. "No—most people want to be entertained. They came looking for amusement and got a history lesson instead. No wonder they were bored."

"Not everyone," Drake protested, sounding defensive.

"No, but the doctor is a scholar himself, and . . ." She paused. There was no way to put this delicately. "And, uh, I believe some of your female admirers have an ulterior motive in saying they enjoyed your lecture."

Though the shadows of the shrubbery obscured most of Drake's face, she saw his lips twist in a rueful smile. "Perhaps you're right. At least *your* motives are clear—you've made no secret of the fact that you want me gone."

Gina shrugged. She couldn't deny it, especially now that the man who had sat next to her at the lecture had given her another option to get Drake to leave. Lester Suggs was a booking agent for the lecture circuit. If she could just help Drake find a way to wow his audience, Mr. Suggs might schedule him for a long tour around the country. Anything to get Drake out of The Chesterfield and away from the doom that awaited him.

Unfortunately, Drake wouldn't take any suggestions from her unless she could understand why he cared so much about mesmerism. How could she get him to confide in her? Hmm, she'd always been a good listener. Maybe if she encouraged him to talk . . .

Deliberately changing the subject, she asked, "Why are these lectures so important to you?"

"Why do you ask?"

"I can help you improve them, but only if I know your objective—what you want to accomplish."

Incredulity colored his voice as he asked, "You think *you* can help *me*?"

Stung, Gina said, "Well, you weren't doing so well on your own, were you?"

"Very true."

"Then maybe I *can* help."

"Perhaps," Drake admitted, though doubt still tinged his voice. "But I hope it doesn't involve dressing up like a ghost to terrorize innocent guests."

I guess I deserve that. "Of course not. I promise— no stunts. But I have experience in entertaining an audience and I can help you . . . if you'll tell me what you're trying to accomplish."

Drake was silent for a moment, but the darkness or her soft, matter-of-fact tone must have lulled him into confiding in her. In a low voice, he said, "I—I want to help people."

Surprised, Gina asked, "Why?"

Again, silence filled the night until Drake said, "There was someone . . . two years ago. I was unable to help her, and she died."

A stab of jealousy pierced Gina, but she quickly suppressed it. She had no business being jealous. In fact, her *only* business was to get him to leave the resort so she could go home.

Though she wanted to know more about this woman who had died and meant so much to Drake, this wasn't the moment to probe. At least, not for *that* information. "So tell me, what kind of help do you want to provide? What do you want in an ideal patient?"

He didn't need to pause this time. "The ideal subject would be someone whose illness is mental in origin, perhaps someone who has tried physical or other traditional means of treatment and failed."

So this mesmerism really was the precursor to modern psychiatrists and psychotherapy. Well, Gina had spent some time in therapy, trying to come to terms with her father's death and her mother's coldness. She knew all the buzz words and was familiar with pop psychology, which was far more than anyone in this time knew. Heck, that made her an expert.

The only question was, what type of person did he want to appeal to? "Will anyone do? Or would you prefer to have someone influential as your first . . . subject?"

He frowned, considering. "Mesmerism isn't just for the rich and powerful—it should be available to every person, depending on need."

When he hesitated, she added, "But . . . ?"

"But in order to spread the word about the benefits of this treatment, I need to start with people like the guests here at the resort. That's why I came here."

Okay, that made sense. "Then the first thing you need to understand is that these people are bored. To get their attention, you need to put on a dog and pony show."

He glanced down at Scruffy. "A . . . pony show? I don't understand."

"I mean that to intrigue them, you have to catch their interest. And the best way to do that is to be entertaining."

He shook his head. "I'm sorry, but that goes against everything I believe in. Sensationalists such as Dane Carl Hansen have given mesmerism a bad name, reducing it to silly parlor tricks."

Ah, so he was familiar with the concept. Good, that would make her job easier. "But did he then use this ability to help people?"

"No," he admitted.

"Well, there's the difference between you," she

said in triumph. "You can borrow his methods, but turn them to your gain. To *other* people's gain."

"It doesn't seem right, somehow."

"Nonsense—you aren't going to make people interested in mesmerism by lecturing them with dull history. You need to jazz it up a bit."

He eyed her skeptically. "And you are good at this . . . jazz?"

"I'm very good, if I do say so myself." Learning to be a handler and putting on a good performance for the dog show judges had taught her that. "I know how to impress a crowd."

When he didn't say anything, she added, "Isn't it worth a little sensationalism to achieve your objective, to find the kind of people you want to help?"

"I don't know . . . what do you have in mind?"

"I'm not sure yet, but I'll figure something out. Do we have a deal?"

"Perhaps. You do seem to have a flair for the dramatic, but . . . why are you willing to help me with this?"

Honesty seemed best in this situation, and he was already aware of her primary objective. "Frankly, I hope this will help you leave The Chesterfield earlier." If she could make his next lecture interesting enough, she was sure she could convince that nice Mr. Suggs to book Drake in a series of lectures across the country . . . far from The Chesterfield and the fiery fate that awaited him here.

He pondered for a moment longer. "Very well, I agree. On one condition."

"What's that?"

"You must tell me why you are so determined to have me leave."

Playing for time to come up with a suitable story,

she said, "Okay, but not until *after* your next lecture."
That would give her a month to come up with something he'd believe.

"All right." He grasped her chin and gazed at her
with those dark, sexy eyes of his, saying softly, "But
none of your tricks, now. If I am to change everything
I believe in, you must promise you will do me the
courtesy of telling the truth."

Gina gulped. He was difficult to resist when he
turned the full force of his personality on her. And
it was even harder to lie when he so obviously believed
in her honesty.

"All right," she said, and meant it. "But I warn
you, you're not gonna believe it. . . ."

Chapter Six

Drake had two hopes on the day following his first lecture. First, that he would have several clients waiting for him in Dr. Ziegler's office despite the failure of his presentation. And second, that Gina would forget he had ever promised to listen to her wild ideas.

His first hope was doomed to failure. The only "clients" who had come to visit him were the Biddles and the Harringtons. It was apparent they had paid close attention the night before, for they claimed several nervous conditions from the list he had cited. But, as he suspected, their so-called symptoms didn't match the ailments they claimed.

"I'm sorry, Miss Harrington," he told the disappointed Chloe and her mother, "but I don't think I can help you."

He escorted them to the door, ignoring their downcast expressions. If he thought Chloe was really in need of his help, he would be more than happy to treat her. But he didn't want to waste his time or theirs on fruitless therapy.

Though he had dismissed the Biddles and their spurious claims earlier, Mrs. Biddle still hovered around the office. Waiting, no doubt, to ensure Chloe didn't steal a march on Letty.

Thin Mrs. Biddle and short, plump Mrs. Harrington eyed each other like two prime fighting cocks, ruffling their feathers and circling each other, looking for an opening.

But Drake had never been fond of cockfights and this was one bout he didn't plan to attend. Saying, "Good day, ladies," Drake attempted to shut the door.

Birdie Biddle was too fast for him. Interposing herself in the doorway, she said, "Are you quite sure you can't help my Letty?"

"Quite," he said firmly in a discouraging tone. "Letty and Chloe are both healthy young women who have no need of a mesmerist."

Thus assured that her rival had gotten no further than she had, Mrs. Biddle couldn't resist sending Mrs. Harrington a satisfied glance.

Unfortunately, she didn't move from the door. Drake wondered if he would have to remove her bodily until salvation in the form of Gina appeared. Seizing on her appearance as an excuse, Drake checked his pocket watch and said, "Ah, Miss Charles, excellent. I still have some time left. Won't you come in?"

Gina grinned at him and played along. Sweeping past one matchmaking mother, she paused at Mrs. Biddle's form in the doorway, saying, "Excuse me."

Mrs. Biddle looked her up and down with suspicion

in her eyes, and Drake realized Gina was once more attired in the bright blue dress.

"I thought your services were intended for the hotel *guests,*" Mrs. Biddle said to Drake with a disapproving glare at Gina.

Drake despised snobbery of any kind—he had seen far too much of it in his so-called peers growing up, and it belittled none but the snob. Reprovingly, he said, "My services are available to anyone in need, regardless of social level."

Mrs. Harrington seized the moment to gush. "Why, of course they are. And sweet little Gina is quite the odd one, isn't she? I'm sure you can help the dear girl." She cast a triumphant glance at her rival, though she didn't realize the danger came from an entirely different direction.

Game as any cock he'd ever seen, Gina thrust her chin out pugnaciously and clenched her fists, apparently ready to enter the bout as an unscheduled contestant. Drake intervened quickly. "I would be happy to help you, Miss Charles. If you would please wait for me inside?"

Gina shrugged and Mrs. Biddle had no choice but to move aside. Drake followed Gina into Dr. Ziegler's office, shutting the door behind him.

"So I'm your patient again, huh?" Gina asked.

Drake smiled ruefully. "I'm sorry for that. You see . . ." He paused, wondering how to phrase his difficulty.

Gina grinned. "Never mind—I can see your dilemma. In fact, I'm the one who warned you about them to begin with, remember?"

He sighed in relief. "So you did." But he feared his relief was short-lived. Apparently, she had come to dash the second of his hopes—that she would have forgotten their agreement. "How may I help you?"

Her smile widened. "You've got it backward. I'm the one who's going to help you. And I have your first lesson all ready."

Ah, just as he'd feared. . . . "What lesson?"

She brandished a pair of colorful tickets. "Mr. Suggs was kind enough to give me a couple of free passes. We're going to the circus!"

As if being in her presence isn't circus enough for anyone. He frowned. "Is that really necessary?"

"Absolutely. You've been stuck in Dullsville for so long, you don't know how to have fun."

Dullsville? "I'm from Boston."

"Ugh. Even worse." She planted her hands on her hips. "Come on, now, you promised to let me help."

"How will going to the circus help?"

"It's best to see for yourself. Come on, now. It'll be fun—it's opening night for the Barnum & London Circus down in Hope Springs." She arched an eyebrow at him. "Or would you rather spend the rest of the evening hiding out from Letty and Chloe?"

If those were his only two options, he would definitely choose the circus. "All right, then." Picking up his hat, he turned toward the main door, then thought better of it. It was quite possible the cockfight was still in progress on the other side. "There's another exit. Shall we?"

"Sure," Gina said, grinning. "Let's sneak out."

Drake suppressed an answering smile. He suspected Gina enjoyed baiting him, that she took perverse delight in exposing polite discourse for the fraud it was. Truth be told, he found her amusing as well, but he didn't dare encourage her.

Not for the first time, he found himself wondering

about her upbringing. Though she worked as a hotel employee, essentially a servant, she didn't act like any servant he'd ever known. He couldn't imagine his mother's parlor maid or housekeeper teasing him, walking with him in the moonlight, or inviting him to the circus. And it had never even occurred to Gina that it might not be considered proper for him to escort one of the resort employees to an entertainment.

It had occurred to *him*, of course, but after his indignation over Mrs. Biddle's snobbishness, he could hardly turn Gina down for that reason. Besides, it might be diverting. "I've never been to a circus," he admitted as they left the bathhouse.

"My father took me when I was little," Gina said, and her wistful expression made him wonder what had happened to her father. "But I haven't been back since. And we're both gonna love it," Gina promised. "P.T. Barnum is supposed to be one of the greatest showmen ever."

Three large tents had been set up not far from the town below the resort, and The Chesterfield had thoughtfully provided transportation to the event. As Gina and Drake climbed into one of the waiting carriages, he thought he caught a glimpse of more than one disapproving look turned their way, but he ignored them. Gina didn't seem to notice as she chattered away about the circus.

Soon, they arrived and it was like entering an entirely different world. The energetic sounds of the calliope, the smell of popcorn mixed with the odor of sawdust, and the bright stripes of the tent and colorful outfits of the circus folk lent a festive air.

Gina scorned the side shows, heading straight for the "big top." She charmed their way into good seats near the center of the ring and pulled Drake down onto the wooden bench. "Isn't this great?" she asked.

Drake couldn't help but return her smile. Unlike most women of his acquaintance, Gina was unaffected, enthusiastic. She, apparently, had never been taught that overt enthusiasm was unladylike and vulgar. And frankly, Drake could see nothing wrong with her zeal. He found it surprisingly refreshing and far more healthy than most modern young women who were taught to suppress their feelings. He regarded her wistfully, wishing Charlotte had been as free. Perhaps then she wouldn't have taken her own life.

"Look," Gina exclaimed. "There's the ringmaster. They're going to start."

She squirmed with excitement and Drake relaxed, resolving to enjoy the show. But he derived far more entertainment from watching Gina. Her every emotion played across her face as she clearly delighted in the tumbling feats of the acrobats, the skill of the jugglers, and the antics of the clowns.

But it was the equestrian exhibition that held her undivided attention as skilled riders performed seemingly impossible feats on horseback. She greeted the lion tamer with detachment, whispering, "The big cats are hard to train. I can do ten times more with Scruffy."

And, surprisingly, she was totally unimpressed by Jumbo, introduced by the ringmaster as "The Towering Monarch of His Mighty Race, Whose Like the World Will Never See Again." Though the rest of the audience oohed and aahed over the elephant's dimensions, Gina watched indifferently as the huge pachyderm paraded around the ring.

Once it was over and the other spectators filed out, Drake remained seated, hoping to avoid the crush. "Did you enjoy the spectacle?"

"Yes. For the limitations of these times, it was great."

"These times?" What did she mean by that?

"Never mind—the question is, did *you* enjoy it?"

Surprisingly, he had. "Yes," he admitted, though his enjoyment came more from Gina's reactions to the circus acts.

"Good." She smiled. "And what did you learn from it?"

Was he supposed to have learned something? "Not to put your head in a lion's mouth?" he ventured.

She stared at him, mouth agape. "You made a joke," she said in awe.

"It has been done before." And surely it was a very small jest, hardly worth her reaction.

"Well, sure, but not by you. I was beginning to wonder if you had a sense of humor."

"Of course I do," he said indignantly. In fact, he had once been considered quite the wit, but since Charlotte's death, he had found little amusing. Changing the subject, he asked, "What lesson was I supposed to learn?"

"The value of a sweeping gesture, the suspense of a dramatic pause, the atmosphere of wonder created by grandiose language."

He frowned. "Didn't you find it a trifle overdone?"

"Well, maybe a little. But did you see any bored faces in *this* audience?"

No, he had to admit everyone's attention was riveted on the performers in the ring, exactly where the ringmaster had directed them. "I see what you mean, but—"

"By using the same techniques, you can get the audiences at your lectures just as interested."

"You flatter me," he said, knowing he couldn't possibly emulate a circus performer.

"No, I don't. Trust me, you'll be great once I'm done with you. You have terrific stage presence."

On the contrary, he would look the fool. "I'm sorry, Miss Charles," he said with real regret, "but I'm afraid I will be unable to keep my part of our agreement."

Her face fell. "But—"

"No," he said firmly. He regretted that he must be the one to wipe away all her enthusiasm and joy, but he must be adamant. "It would undermine everything I believe in. I cannot and will not emulate a circus performer."

A week later, Gina had still not convinced Drake to change his mind. Unfortunately, the man was very stubborn, but if he thought he could out-stubborn her, he'd better think again. She was going to bug the hell out of him until he capitulated.

She approached Dr. Ziegler's office promptly at 3:30. Drake had very kindly set aside this time every day since the circus for her to present her arguments to try to change his mind. He pretended it was out of a sense of fair play and to have some time free from the matchmaking mamas, but she suspected he enjoyed their battle of wits as much as she did.

Speak of the devils . . . There they were, *sans* chicks. Gina nodded at the two women and tried to breeze past them, but for once, they worked as one and blocked her way.

"Why if it isn't little Gina," Mrs. Harrington said nastily, though Gina towered over her.

The woman pretended to be a sweet southern belle, but Gina saw right through her. In fact, both of these women had tried to make her life miserable this past week once word had got around that Drake had escorted her to the circus. But since they were guests, she had to be polite. "Excuse me, please," Gina said. "I have an appointment with Mr. Manton."

She stepped around the plump woman, but Mrs. Biddle blocked her way. Glaring down her thin nose at Gina, Mrs. Biddle said, "Really, Miss Charles, I don't think it's quite the thing for you to thrust yourself upon Mr. Manton's notice like this. You are earning a reputation for yourself."

Gina bristled. "Me?" Mrs. Biddle made her sound like she slept around. Well, since they'd removed their gloves, so to speak, Gina had no compunction in returning the favor. "Would you care to hear what sort of reputation *you* two are earning in this hotel?"

Mrs. Biddle scowled. "*Our* conduct is above reproach—"

"Yeah, right. If you call throwing your daughters at a poor, unsuspecting bachelor above reproach."

Mrs. Harrington's eyes flashed with malice. "I believe you have mistaken the matter, dear," she said in her sugary tones. "Which is understandable, given your background. A *lady* would understand."

Gina snorted derisively. "Oh, I understand how the game is played, all right. The first one to nab a husband, wins, right? Well, for your information, I'm not in the market for a husband."

The two exchanged puzzled glances. "Then why are you pursuing him?" Mrs. Biddle asked.

Pursuing him? "Did it ever occur to you that I might actually be seeking his help?"

"No," they said in unison.

Well, true, she wasn't, but they didn't know that. Thoroughly ticked off now, Gina popped off with the first thing that came into her mind. "Well, you're right. I don't want to marry him—I just want to seduce him."

They gasped in unison.

Pleased by their shocked reactions, Gina added, "Then once I'm done with him, I'll just throw him away." She added a contemptuous tossing gesture for good measure.

Mrs. Harrington sputtered. "Really, this is too—"

"Ridiculous," supplied a deep voice from the door. Drake stood there, regarding them all with a grave expression, though Gina thought she saw a bit of a twitch at the corner of his mouth.

The two women quickly wiped the condescending expressions from their faces and turned fake smiles on him. But before they could say anything else, Drake said, "Miss Charles is merely having a bit of fun with you."

The women cast doubtful glances at Gina, but she just rolled her eyes, refusing to confirm or deny his statement. And, to tell the truth, she felt a little embarrassed that he'd caught her at it. Thank heavens he seemed to understand she was kidding.

Drake continued. "In fact, that's why I'm seeing Miss Charles—for a disturbing tendency toward levity in inappropriate circumstances."

Gina challenged him with her eyes, but he wouldn't look at her.

"I see," Mrs. Harrington said, but her glance at Gina showed she wasn't quite sure whether to believe it.

Drake opened the door invitingly. "I believe it's time for our appointment?"

Gina swept past the two women and couldn't help but cast them a smug glance as the door closed in their faces.

"So," Drake said with a small smile, "have you come to ravish me?"

Gina felt her face heat, but she wasn't willing to give him the upper hand by going on the defensive. "You never know," she said flippantly, and was rewarded with his surprised expression. "Maybe later. But first, I want to talk to you."

They seated themselves, and Drake leaned back in his chair to regard her quizzically. "I'm afraid your arguments today won't sway me any more than your earlier ones."

"Why not?"

"I explained this before—what you're asking me to do is simply not within my character. I cannot pose as a circus performer."

"You haven't even tried," she accused him.

"I don't need to try to know it is beyond me."

Well, this was getting her nowhere. Exasperated, Gina exclaimed, "I don't know why you want to help people, anyway. You're not suited for it at all."

"What do you mean?"

Since nothing else seemed to work, she decided to be blunt. "To help people, you have to understand them. You don't."

He frowned. "While it's true my understanding is not yet complete, I have been studying—"

"That's not enough. You have to get inside their heads, figure out what makes them tick."

"I know that, but how will acting the clown help me gain a better understanding of people?"

She sighed. "You make it sound like I want you to

treat your patients by wearing a red rubber nose and squirting water down your pants.''

"Don't you?''

"No, not at all. But in order to get patients into your office in the first place, you have to get their attention. You aren't going to do that with boring lectures. That's why I want you to borrow a few tricks from the circus—but from the ringmaster, not the clowns.'' Besides the added fact that if Drake put on a good enough show, Mr. Suggs would book him on the lecture circuit far from the fate that awaited him here.

"I've told you before, I'm not suited for those sort of theatrics.'' He stroked his chin, deep in thought. "But I think you might be able to help me in my understanding of people.''

Still stubborn. Well, maybe if she eased her foot in the door now, she could wedge it open wider later. "How?''

"You have an excellent understanding of people, one that I lack. You understood what Miss Harrington was doing at my bedroom door before I did, and you are able to get people to do things they never thought they would do.''

"Me?'' Gina said in disbelief.

"Yes, you convinced me to accompany you to the circus, and you seem to have Rupert and Chef Sasha wrapped around your little finger.''

She waved a hand in negation. "Oh, that. That's nothing—anyone could figure them out.''

"I couldn't,'' Drake stated flatly.

Oddly enough, he really believed that. "Sure you could. All you need to do is pay attention and figure out each person's hook.''

"Hook?''

"Yeah, you know—the one thing that motivates them the most. Once you know what makes them tick, you can get them to do what you want."

"That sounds so . . . manipulative."

"Yes, it does, doesn't it? But people do it all the time, whether it's conscious or not. Children are especially good at it. They learn very quickly what behaviors will get them what they want from their parents."

He paused for a moment, lost in thought, then said, "I see. So what are Rupert and Chef Sasha's 'hooks'?"

She shrugged. "That's easy—a few minutes of conversation with either of them will show you that Rupert will do almost anything for money and Sasha adores flattery."

"And the Major?"

She snorted. "If you're under the impression I have *him* wrapped around my little finger, you're out of your mind."

He smiled slightly. "Perhaps I am not so unobservant as you believe. He may pretend to be gruff, but I notice you aren't in his black book as much as the others."

"True, but I've learned the way to deal with him is to follow all his silly little rules and stay out of his way."

"So that is his hook."

"Yeah, I guess you're right," Gina said in surprise. "Then what is mine?"

"I wish I knew." If she knew that, she would have had a whole heck of a lot more success in convincing him to leave the resort.

"Ah, so your hook theory isn't infallible?"

She'd never claimed it was, but for some reason, his certainty irritated her. "Oh, I don't know," she drawled, eyeing him speculatively. There was one hook she suspected would work with Drake, but she hadn't wanted to use it for fear it would backfire. "I have an idea about you, too."

"You think you have found a way to manipulate *me?*" he asked with a raised eyebrow.

Then again, maybe this *was* the right time to use it. "Maybe," she said cryptically and rose from her chair. When Drake would have automatically risen as well, she pushed him gently back into his seat. "No, sit. I want to look at you, see if I can figure you out."

Pretending to consider him, she circled him slowly, tapping one finger on her lips while she let the fingers of her other hand trail along his shoulders. Yes, that was the ticket. A sudden stiffness in his shoulders and the arrested awareness in his eyes let her know she'd gotten his attention.

A thrill shot through her at this evidence of her power, making her even bolder. Stopping in front of him, she leaned closer and stared into his eyes, pretending to seek knowledge there, but really letting him get a whiff of her perfume, and making sure he was very aware of her.

Her heart beat a rapid tattoo as she played her little game. She didn't know exactly what effect this was having on Drake, but it was shredding *her* nerves to pieces.

He appeared cool, but when she glanced down, she noticed his knuckles were white on the arms of the chair. So, he wasn't as indifferent as he might have her believe. Wanting to rip his facade asunder, she ran her hands lingeringly up his chest, and clasped them behind his neck.

Being this close to him made her breathless. She

knew she was tormenting herself as much as she was him, but couldn't help herself.

Time for the payoff. She leaned closer, tilted her head until they were only a kiss away, and whispered, "How's this for a hook?"

Before he could answer, the door flew open. Startled, Gina could only stare as three people appeared in the doorway: Mrs. Biddle, Mrs. Harrington, and the Major.

"You see?" Mrs. Harrington said, her eyes glinting maliciously. "It isn't enough that the brazen hussy coerced Mr. Manton into taking her to the circus, but she's bent on seducing him as well. She said so herself."

Startled, Gina let go of Drake. "No, it isn't what you think."

As Drake shot from the chair, Mrs. Biddle huffed with disgust. "This isn't the sort of thing that goes on in a decent hotel."

The Major stood ramrod straight and glared at Gina with disgust and disappointment. "Quite right. Miss Charles, your behavior is unconscionable."

Damn. It looked really bad this time and for the life of her, she couldn't think of any way to explain it.

Drake tried to interrupt the Major, but the hotel manager quelled him with a glance. "I beg your pardon, Mr. Manton, but this is an internal hotel matter. You'll have your say later." Then, turning to Gina, he said, "There is no excuse for your behavior. I want you out of The Chesterfield in two hours."

"But—"

"No excuses. Two hours." Unfortunately, his expression was as implacable as the women's were triumphant.

I guess that's what I get for acting so smug myself.

Reality suddenly hit with a one-two punch. She was fired. Gina's heart sank. How was she going to support herself until the next solstice? Worse, how on earth was she going to save Drake's life if she couldn't even get near him?

Chapter Seven

Gina couldn't help it—she whimpered. Their expressions were just too much to handle. The smugness of the matchmaking mamas', the implacability of the Major's, and the worry on Drake's face drove her to push past them and run away. She couldn't face them, not until she figured out what to do.

She headed straight for her room and pulled Scruffy into her arms. He must have sensed her agitation, for he licked her nose in the only way he knew to comfort her. She buried her face in his soft coat. "What am I going to do now?"

She had only two hours to get out of The Chesterfield, two short hours until she was cast out into the unknown hazards of 1885. She didn't know what would happen if she took longer than that, but she suspected it would cause a scene, and she didn't really want that.

She glanced around at the room. Well, it certainly

wouldn't take long to pack. She had very little here except for a few items of clothing. The two hours that had seemed so short now seemed like forever. Once she packed, then what? She had no idea how to survive alone in these times. Where could she go? What could she do? She didn't have a clue.

A knock came at the door but Gina ignored it, hoping whoever it was would assume she was gone and leave her alone. She didn't really want to face anyone right now. She needed to think.

But Scruffy let out a short, sharp bark, betraying their presence. The knock came again. "Who is it?" Gina asked wearily, prepared to tell whoever it was to go away.

"Esme Sparrow."

On second thought, Esme was just the person Gina needed. She rushed to open the door and, judging by Esme's concerned expression, the housekeeper already knew of her predicament.

Esme gently closed the door behind her and drew Gina into a hug. "What am I going to do with you?" the housekeeper asked softly.

"It wasn't my fault," Gina choked out past her tears. Until now, she hadn't been able to cry. Nastiness of the Biddle kind just made her mad, but kindness was her undoing.

"Come, sit." Esme pulled her down to sit beside her on the bed, as Gina wiped away her tears. Scruffy snuggled between them, looking up at Gina with a worried expression.

"Perhaps not all of it was your fault," the housekeeper said gently. "But you could have been a little more circumspect. These times aren't like yours."

"They aren't as different as you think." Mrs. Biddle and Mrs. Harrington seemed like early incarnations of her own mother. Gina had never been able to please her, either.

But what did it matter? The past was past, and she couldn't change it. But maybe Esme could. She looked at the housekeeper in sudden hope. "Can you talk the Major into letting me stay?"

"I might, given time," Esme admitted. "But not with Mrs. Biddle and Mrs. Harrington so adamant against you. While they're here, I'm afraid keeping you will be out of the question."

"When do they leave?"

"I don't know—they've registered an indefinite stay."

"Maybe I can find a way to *make* them leave," Gina suggested darkly.

Esme gave her a stern look. "You haven't had much luck doing that with Mr. Manton. Do you really think you'll be more successful with the ladies?"

"I guess not." While their prey—Drake—was still here, they probably wouldn't leave until they'd snared him, hog-tied him, and dragged him to the altar. "Then what shall I do?"

Esme pondered for a moment, then said cryptically, "I can't interfere too much—I've done too much as it is. But I might be able to convince the Major to let you stay if I could promise him you would avoid the Biddles and Harringtons."

Hope surged through Gina, then just as quickly vanished. "No, I can't. My task is to save Drake's life, and they're always hanging around him." She turned a hopeful glance on Esme. "Any other ideas?"

"Not at the moment, but I'm sure something will come up," she said with calm certainty. "It always does."

Esme sounded like a perky Pollyanna, but Gina didn't

share her confidence. "Well, until it does, where shall
I stay?"

"I don't suppose you've made any friends in the
area?"

"How could I? I've spent all my time here, either
working for you or working on Drake. My only friends
are hotel employees—and they can't exactly hide me
in their rooms without the Major finding out." She
paused, searching through her options. "Except
maybe for Sean Quinn." The kindly old stablemaster
lived in rooms next to the horses, and she'd rarely
seen the Major out there. "Do you think he'd put
me up?"

"Perhaps," Esme conceded. "Yes, that might do
until we can find a better solution."

Scruffy licked her hand and Gina squeezed him
gratefully. Things didn't look so bad now, not if she
had the possibility of someplace to stay. But another
thought struck her, bringing her down again. "What
if I can't get near Drake to save his life? Does that
mean I'm stuck back here in the past?"

"Not necessarily," Esme said, looking evasive.

No? "But you said . . ." Gina paused, thinking. Had
Esme ever actually said she had to save Drake's life
to leave? She couldn't remember, though the woman
had certainly implied it. It was probably those darned
semantics again. She fixed Esme with a glare. "What
do you mean? *Can* I go back home? Even if I don't
save Drake?"

"Well, yes," Esme admitted, though she managed
to pack quite a bit of disapproval into those two small
words.

"How?"

Reluctantly, Esme explained, "The same events

that brought you to the past can take you back to the future."

Back to the future? A vision of Michael J. Fox riding to the rescue in a time-traveling DeLorean flashed through Gina's mind, but she shook her head. That was only a movie. "I know you said I can go back on the solstice, but how?" Remembering how Esme had parceled out her information in little bits and pieces, Gina figured she'd better be more specific. "What exactly do I have to do?"

"That depends. What triggered your time travel in the first place?"

"I don't know. One minute I was kneeling in the ruins next to a ghost, and the next, you were there in his place."

"There must have been something," Esme insisted. "What were you doing at the time? What were you touching?"

Gina thought back. They had approached the ruins and she'd found something. . . . "A chest," she said aloud. "I was rummaging in an old hope chest." That's right, how could she forget that lovely chest? "It was beautifully carved . . . and it had some initials. Let's see, they were—" She broke off and turned to Esme in surprise. "They were *your* initials, weren't they?"

When Esme regarded her with a serene expression, Gina reacted with disgust. "That was *your* hope chest. That's what did it—*you* did it."

"It wasn't the hope chest," Esme said calmly, but Gina noticed she didn't answer her accusation, either. "There was something inside the chest that drew you back—something that had significance only to you. What was it?"

"Don't you know?"

Esme merely regarded her with that infuriatingly serene expression that revealed nothing. "The question is, do you?"

Gina sighed, knowing she'd get nothing more out of her. "Just a bunch of junk." Nothing that held any significance. Wait . . . she remembered sorting through it, then finding something interesting. That was it. "The pistol. I found a melted dueling pistol." Funny, she hadn't remembered that until this moment.

"And what happened when you touched it?"

That was when she'd turned dizzy. "That's it—the pistol sent me back in time." She turned to Esme in excitement. "You mean all I have to do is find the pistol in this time and it will send me back home?"

"Yes," the housekeeper said with obvious reluctance, "but only if you have it in your hands on the next solstice."

Darn—she still had to wait a few more months. And she had to find the pistol first. "Okay, where is it? In your hope chest?"

"Not yet."

Not yet? What the heck did that mean? "Then where is it?"

"I don't know."

Gina regarded her in disbelief.

"I really don't," Esme said with a small smile. "I know it will eventually end up in my hope chest, but I don't know where it is at this point in time. That's something you'll have to learn on your own."

Gina had remembered something else as well. "Drake—his ghost, I mean—had an attraction to that pistol, too. Do you think it's his?"

"Perhaps," Esme said with the vagueness Gina had

come to expect of her. "Or perhaps there's another reason his ghost recognized it."

Too impatient to decipher cryptic messages right now, Gina decided to clarify what she did know. "So if I hold the pistol on the solstice, I'll go back to my own time . . . whether I've saved Drake or not?"

"Yes, but is that really your intention? To let him die?"

"Of course not, not if I can prevent it." She couldn't abandon him to that—she'd come to care for him too much. "But what can I do now that the Major has kicked me out of the hotel?" Even more important, how was she going to find that blasted pistol?

Before Esme could answer, another knock came at the door. Bridget O'Riley stuck her head in the door and said cheerily, "The Major wants you, Gina."

Gina frowned. He probably just wanted to make sure she was gone. But if he was kicking her out, she certainly didn't need to stick around for a dressing-down. "Forget it—I'm not going."

But Esme stood and smoothed her dress, saying, "Come. This may be the opportunity we need."

Gina wasn't holding out any hopes, but the house-keeper had an air of calm certainty about her and Gina couldn't deny that some strange things had happened around Esme. Maybe something *could* be done. And if Gina were able to stay here, it was certainly better than sleeping in the stables.

"What about Scruffy?" She didn't want to risk the Major's continued wrath by taking the dog to his office, but she didn't want to leave Scruffy here, either. Her two hours were about up, and for all she knew they'd lock the door on her.

"I'll watch him for you," Bridget offered.

Scruffy liked Bridget, so Gina agreed. Leaving the dog with her friend, Gina reluctantly followed Esme to the hotel manager's office.

At their entrance, the Major stood, holding himself stiffly. He harrumphed, then said awkwardly, "Miss Charles, it seems I owe you an apology."

That was the last thing she'd expected to hear. "You do?"

"Yes, Mr. Manton explained the entire situation."

"He did?" Gina felt silly at being able to do nothing but ask stupid questions, but she didn't know what else to say. She thought about demanding more information, but a small shake of Esme's head reminded her this probably wasn't the best time.

"Yes," the Major confirmed. "Mr. Manton explained how you've been helping him to improve his lectures, and on your own time at that."

She hadn't quite helped him *yet*, but she wasn't going to argue with the Major.

"He has apologized for taking advantage of your extra time, and is quite willing to recompense The Chesterfield for the future use of your services." He harrumphed again and smoothed his mustache with one finger. "Quite generously, I might add."

Gina wondered how Drake had explained away the compromising position they'd been found in, but decided mentioning it now would be a really dumb move.

"What are you trying to say?" Esme asked delicately.

Yeah—Gina sure wished he'd get to the point.

The Major clasped his hands behind his back and bounced on the balls of his feet. "Under the circumstances, I am reinstating Miss Charles, but not in her former position."

Okay, that didn't sound too bad. "So what do I

have to do?" Gina asked. "Rat on the rat catcher? Muck out the stables? Kiss Sasha's feet?"

The Major scowled. "That won't be necessary. You will be assigned to Mr. Manton, as his personal secretary and general factotum, to assist him with his lectures."

Gina inhaled sharply. She couldn't believe it—she was to be given the one job she really wanted and needed above all others. She exchanged a half incredulous, half triumphant glance with Esme then turned back to the Major. "*Thank* you."

"However, there is one stipulation."

"What?" Gina asked, figuring she could agree to just about anything.

"The hotel will not tolerate any suggestion of impropriety in its employees. Therefore, you must be chaperoned at all times when you are with Mr. Manton."

"Chaperoned?" Her elation dissipated a little. "By who?" *Not the old biddies, please.*

"Miss Biddle and Miss Harrington will be with you at all times. Their mothers have been consulted and have already agreed to this arrangement."

So it was only the *young* biddies—she could handle them. Beaming, Gina said, "Okay."

"Remember," the Major admonished her. "You are to behave in a circumspect manner at all times. Any suggestion of impropriety and you will be out the door—for good this time."

Gina grinned. "No problem—I can handle that. I'll be good, I promise." Well, except maybe for one more teensy-weensy infraction. . . .

* * *

About midnight, Drake gave up any further attempt at sleep and got out of bed. The events of the day had been going round and round in his mind. Remembering Gina's playful seduction, the Major's abrupt dismissal, and his own championing of her reinstatement was enough to make anyone restless.

Pulling on his dressing gown and lighting a lamp, he figured he might as well read for a bit in hope that would make him drowsy enough to go to sleep.

But he had barely opened his book when a sharp tapping noise interrupted him. Strange . . . it sounded like it was coming from the window. Surely Gina and Rupert weren't up to their ghostly antics again? He thrust aside the curtains to see Gina's face staring at him, this time devoid of ghoulish gore.

He opened the window and let her see his annoyance. "What the devil are you doing here?" She was about to undo everything he had worked so hard to make right today.

"Shh," she said with a finger to her lips. "Let me in and I'll explain."

When he hesitated, she added, "Hurry—I don't want anyone to see me."

"It would be worse if they found you in my room."

"But only if they catch me—they're far less likely to see me in there than out here, now aren't they?"

Conceding the point, Drake stood aside while Gina clambered into his room. He forbore offering her assistance, fearing that touching her could only lead to more trouble.

Once inside, she said, "Whew, it's hot in here," and took off her dark cloak to reveal only her nightgown beneath.

He regarded her incredulously. "Are you trying to get us both booted out of here?"

"No, of course not. Why would I?"

"Then why are you in my rooms dressed only in your night wear?" If it had been Chloe Harrington, he might suspect her of devious intent, but this was Gina, and a more open woman he had yet to meet.

She glanced down at the voluminous article of clothing in question. "Well, I had to wait until everyone had gone to sleep to come see you and it was faster than changing clothes," she said, as if it were the most practical thing in the world. "Besides, this loose thing is a lot less revealing than my uniform—and it *is* hot in here. What's wrong with that?"

She made it all sound so reasonable, but it didn't mitigate the fact that seeing her in her night wear conjured up images of Gina in bed, her face soft and flushed with desire. Nor did it help that the thin fabric revealed more than it concealed, especially outlined in the window against the moonlight. The curve of her hip, the shapeliness of her legs, and the fullness of her breasts showed clearly . . . not to mention the faint hint of her nipples straining against the material.

As the first stir of arousal made itself known, Drake averted his gaze and realized that arguing with Gina would be futile. Instead, it would be better to hear what she had to say and let her leave. But first, he had to get her out of the silhouetting moonlight.

"If you don't want anyone to see you, you might want to move away from that window. Come, sit down."

"Oh—you're right." But, eschewing the room's one chair, she sat down on the bed where the soft radiance of the moon fell on her, washing her face and form with a silvery glow.

Drake almost groaned. It wasn't an improvement, as his body let him know. Unhampered and free beneath the silk of his dressing gown, his semi-erection flexed into full force. Turning his back, he blew out the lamp and adjusted his clothing, hoping to hide the signs of arousal from her sharp eyes, and pretending he'd snuffed the light to hide her presence from the outside. "So what was so important that you felt it necessary to come calling in the middle of the night?"

"I, uh, wanted to borrow your pistol?" she asked more than answered.

He glanced at her in surprise—that was the last thing he'd expected to hear. "I don't own a pistol," he said in puzzlement.

She sighed. "I was afraid of that."

"Why do you need one?"

"I don't really. It's just . . . never mind. It's not important. What I really wanted was to thank you," she said softly.

Her soft, gentle tone didn't belong to the Gina he knew. Surprised, he stared at her more fully.

"Thank me? For what?"

"For convincing the Major to let me stay. He told me what you did."

Drake shifted uncomfortably. "It was the least I could do, after causing your dismissal in the first place."

She smiled and cocked her head. "But however did you explain our . . . compromising position?"

Did she have to remind him of that? He shrugged as if it were nothing, but the truth was, he had had to do some fast talking to convince the Major their actions were aboveboard. "I merely explained that we were experimenting with a mesmerism technique."

"One that had the patient practically in your lap?" she asked with a grin. "How'd you do that?"

He smiled back and assumed a haughty expression. "With a lofty air and a rather wordy and lengthy scientific dissertation on the efficacy of proximity to manipulate the patient's mesmeric fields." He just hoped the Major didn't try to look up any of the words he'd created for the occasion.

She laughed. "See, I knew you had it in you— you're a born carny."

"I beg your pardon?" What was a carny? And did he really want to know?

"Never mind. The point is, I just wanted to thank you, and since we're going to be chaperoned from now on, I knew this would be my only chance to do so."

"You're welcome. But perhaps you should go now before someone hears our voices and sends the Major to investigate." And before the lust she stirred in him threatened to burst free and embarrass them both.

She rose from the bed. "I will, but I have one more question. Why did you do it . . . really?"

"I told you, I felt responsible for your dismissal."

She cocked her head speculatively. "So you lied to the Major, arranged to have me help you with your lectures though you hate the idea, and agreed to have two husband-hungry chaperones at your side at all times . . . just to help me?"

"Well, yes," he admitted, "but it really wasn't quite as noble as—"

Before he could finish, Gina was in his arms, hugging him fiercely and kissing his cheek with a fervent smack. "Thank you," she said. "No one has *ever* done such a wonderful thing for me. *Ever,*" she repeated, her eyes shining with tears and gratitude.

"You're welcome," he said faintly. He ought to push her away, but the feel of her soft curves against his chest and the adoration in her expression were too much to resist. He found himself pulling her close, wanting to hold her, comfort her . . . love her. "Has no one ever treated you kindly before?" he asked, hoping she wouldn't notice his turgid erection straining against her thigh.

Laying her head on his shoulder with a sigh, Gina said, "Not lately."

That simple confession tore at his heart. Gina was so vibrant, so alive, so warmhearted that he was surprised she wasn't married with six children by now. "Haven't you anyone to care for you? Parents? A fiancé?"

She brushed moisture from her eyes and looked up at him, lower lip quivering. "No, my father died a few years ago, and my mother . . . well, let's just say we don't get along."

"And the fiancé?" Drake repeated, having to know. "I can't believe there isn't a man out there waiting for you, that you aren't married."

Her lips twisted in a grimace. "That's a good one. Oh, I was engaged for awhile, but I found Jerry, my fiancé, in bed with my . . . my best friend."

No wonder she felt deserted, as if no one had ever done her a kindness. Drawing her close once more for comfort, Drake said, "What did you do?"

"Nothing I *could* do," she said into his shoulder. "I just ran away."

As she had when he had discovered her posing as a ghost. And, he realized, when the Major had dismissed her. "You seem to make a habit of that," he murmured, and though one corner of his mind screamed that he shouldn't, he couldn't help stroking down the clean line of her back. Somehow, he managed to stop at her waist, just above the enticing curve of her buttocks.

Gina pulled away slightly and stared him straight in the eyes as she slipped her arms around his neck. "Well, I'm not running away now." Suiting action to words, she deliberately moved her hips against the throbbing column between his legs until it came to rest in her cleft.

He pressed against her, groaning with the sweet agony of it. Dear Lord, he wanted her. More, he wanted to comfort her, show her how very desirable she was, erase the memory of her careless fiancé from her mind. But ... He pulled away. "We can't do this."

"Why?" she demanded, grasping him about the hips and pulling him tight against her once more. "Because I'm not your kind? Because I'm not a 'good' girl like all those silly females who pant after you?"

His robe had parted with her movement, and now there was only the thin material of her gown separating her tender flesh from his bare, aching need. How could he think with her jammed so intimately against him? "No, because you *are* a 'good' girl. How—How can I live with myself if I take your—" He broke off, unable to voice the words, despite Gina's frankness.

"Well, if that's all that's bothering you, don't worry about it. Jerry took care of that. Now, if there are no more objections ..."

She slipped her hand between them to grasp him with mind-numbing firmness, turning his mind to mush, his legs to quivering traitors, and his penis to pure steel. He staggered backward away from her grasp, coming to rest against the wall with his robe gaping open, his full hard length out-thrust and fully visible to Gina's frankly admiring gaze.

But not for long. She moved to clasp him again, cupping him with one hand and stroking his rigid length with the other, sending waves of blissful sensation through him.

"You still want me to leave?" she asked softly.

The shock of her determined assault had left him powerless beneath the onslaught of his senses, but the light of triumph in her eyes brought him up short. "No," he whispered. But if she stayed, things were going to be different—*he* was going to take the upper hand.

He shrugged out of his robe and reached for her nightgown. Bunching the material in both hands, he lifted it over her head and tossed it aside, revealing her naked body limned in moonlight.

Bold Gina became suddenly shy and attempted to cover her nudity. But he drew her hands aside to drink in the heady sight of her plump breasts, womanly curves, and the dark, mysterious place between her thighs. "Don't hide yourself from me."

She winced. "I'm too fat."

"Ridiculous. Who told you that? Jerry?"

At her nod, he added, "That man has a lot to answer for. You're not fat, you're . . ." He paused, searching for just the right words. "You're soft, ripe, lush . . . all a woman should be." And the flush of desire on her face made her breathtakingly beautiful.

It must have been the right thing to say, for Gina's expression softened and she reached for him once more. Avoiding her seeking hand, he said, "No, it's my turn."

Gently, he palmed her full breasts, the source of many a restless dream, and kneaded, rubbing his thumbs over the protruding tips. She moaned and his heart soared with the knowledge that he had the power to please her. He released one breast only long enough to bring his mouth down to taste it. He circled her nipple with his tongue, then drew it into his mouth, sucking gently as he continued to knead the other.

Her clutching hands, quaking thighs, and soft moans let him know she was enjoying this as much as he. Reveling in her responsiveness, he drew her to his bed and laid her down upon it, then proceeded to lavish attention on her mouth, neck, and breasts until she was quivering with need. Only then did he gently part her thighs and, greedily inhaling the musky scent of her arousal, slip his fingers past the dark curls into the moistness awaiting him.

Gina whimpered and spread her legs wider, reaching for him. But he avoided her grasp once more and sought the small nub that would give her pleasure. It took only a stroke or two of his slick finger to bring a cry to her lips and send her body into spasms of pleasure.

Almost over the edge himself after experiencing her fulfillment, Drake could wait no longer. He poised himself above her, and as she opened to him in complete surrender, he plunged inside.

She was tight, warm, welcoming, and very, very wet. *Dear Lord, this must be heaven.* He spared a brief moment to gauge her reaction but saw nothing but willing acceptance. Saying a short prayer of thanksgiving, he began to move within her.

To his surprise, Gina moved with him, raising her hips to help him go deeper, more fully into her. Then pure sensation took over, driving him past thinking to a mindless frenzy. Ever stronger waves of overpowering pleasure washed through him, taking him higher and higher until he reached the pinnacle. He heard Gina's cry of release at the same time as he spilled over the top, arching with a few shuddering, thrusting bursts of sheer joy.

Drained, he collapsed next to her, feeling nothing but peace, repletion, and tenderness for the woman next to him. As he gazed at her face, an impulsive question left his lips. "Will you marry me?"

Gina went rigid. "Are you nuts?" She hopped out of bed and grabbed her nightgown, yanking it on over her head.

Bewildered and surprised, Drake slid out of bed to face her. This was the first time he'd asked for a woman's hand in marriage, and he'd certainly expected a different reaction. Politeness, at least. Trust Gina to do the unexpected. "What's wrong?"

"I just barely escaped marriage with one guy. What makes you think I'd hop into it with another so soon?"

Perhaps because he was ten times the man this Jerry seemed to be? Resorting to the familiar, Drake said, "It is customary after what we just did." He nodded toward the bed.

She snorted. "Not where I come from. And if that's your only reason, it's not good enough."

Just where did she come from that lacked so basic a custom? "And if a babe should result from our union?"

"Don't worry, it won't," she said as she dragged on her concealing cloak. "My Depo Provera injection should still cover it."

Feeling distinctly as if they were speaking two entirely different languages, Drake said, "It wasn't my intention to *insult* you." Just the opposite, in fact. "Am I that hideous?"

"No, of course not." Her gaze swept his still-nude body. "Come on, you know you're gorgeous. It's just that . . . oh, I can't explain."

"Does it have something to do with the fact that you're trying to force me to leave the resort?"

She swung a leg over his windowsill. "Yeah, kind of."

"How?"

"I told you I'd explain after your next lecture."

"Why not now?"

"Because." And as if that were reason enough, she swung her other leg over and dropped out the window.

Drake stuck his head out the window to try and glean more information from her, but it was too late. She was already hurrying off, waving a breezy hand in farewell.

Bemused, Drake shut the window. He ought to be annoyed that she had so cavalierly dismissed his offer of marriage, but, strangely, he wasn't. Grinning, all he could remember was one thing. *She thinks I'm gorgeous.*

Chapter Eight

Gina didn't want to wake the next morning, but Scruffy insisted he needed out. She pulled a cloak over her nightgown and let him out a side door, with a mental apology to the gardeners for what Scruffy planned to deposit on their pristine lawn.

As she waited for her dog to do his thing, her thoughts turned inexorably to the events of the night before. She hadn't gone to Drake's room with the intention of making love. She had only wanted to thank him for standing up for her to the Major. But one thing had led to another . . . and another . . . until she had experienced one of the most memorable evenings of her life.

For once, she had felt desirable, attractive . . . cherished. Far different from Jerry—Mr. Wham, Bam, Take it on the Lam.

She winced. Instead, she was the one who had taken it on the lam this time. But she couldn't help it. She had been so overcome with conflicting emotions that she just couldn't stick around.

She was shocked that he had asked her to marry him, but soon figured out he had done so only because they had made love, and that's what men did in these times after they had sex with a woman. But that wasn't a good enough basis for a marriage. Besides, she wasn't going to be around much longer. All she planned to do in this time was save Drake's life, find the pistol, then go home come December 22.

To what? a little voice asked.

Gina ignored it. There might not be much to go home to, but it *was* home . . . and that's where she belonged. She certainly didn't belong over a hundred years back in the past.

Scruffy finished his business, and she hurried him back to their room, hoping to get a bit more sleep before she had to get dressed. But it was not to be. No sooner had she crawled back in bed than the insistent little bell-ringer in the hall reminded her she had a muster to make.

She got up reluctantly and eyed her uniform with a baleful expression. Since she had been "promoted," the Major had decreed that she must now wear the white blouse and navy blue skirt that comprised the waitress uniform instead of her usual gray maid's uniform. He had intended it to be some kind of weird honor, but she didn't see it that way. The blue uniform was heavier, hotter, and it had one of those dratted bustles.

Somehow, she struggled into the outfit and made the muster on time. There, Esme told her to meet Drake in Dr. Ziegler's office. After feeding Scruffy, she decided to take him with her for moral support.

When she caught sight of Drake outside Dr. Ziegler's office, she faltered. He looked really good, all broad-shouldered and darkly handsome like that. It reminded her of the things they had done together the previous night.

So, what the heck did you say to a starched-up gentleman who had just done the nasty with you the night before?

"Good—good morning," she stammered.

Okay, so it wasn't brilliant but it *was* civil.

One corner of his mouth turned up as he returned her greeting. A warning growl from the other side of the room caught her attention and she turned to see both matchmaking mamas, their daughters, and the Major standing there, confronting her with varying degrees of disapproval in their expressions. Good grief, how had she missed seeing them?

She wouldn't have been surprised to find the growl had emanated from Mrs. Biddle, but the lazy Peke in her arms had directed the commentary at Scruffy. Scruffy returned the favor, but quickly hushed on Gina's command. Thank heavens. She was in enough trouble already without adding a dogfight to the rest.

Mrs. Biddle sniffed and spoke to a point above Gina's head. "I must say I do not approve of this arrangement. However, since Major Payne feels it is fair, I must acquiesce." She turned a simpering look on the man in question.

"I disagree," Mrs. Harrington put in. "I believe I shall stay. I don't want to leave my sweet Chloe prey to such wicked influence."

Gina bristled. *Wicked influence? I'll show her wicked.* She immediately resolved to corrupt the two girls. But before she could come up with something suitably shocking, Drake cleared his throat and gave the Major a penetrating glare.

The Major must have interpreted this look correctly, for he said, "No, that wasn't the plan. The agreement was that the young ladies will chaperone each other. Too many cooks spoil the broth, you know," he said with uneasy heartiness.

Birdie Biddle sniffed again, patting the still-growling Princess. "Then perhaps only *one* young lady should chaperone Mr. Manton and that . . . that . . . young woman," she said derisively. She pushed her daughter forward. "My dear little Letty is perfect for the job. She's pretty, bright, decorous . . . and she just adores listening to Mr. Manton lecture. Don't you, dear?"

As Letty turned bright red, Mrs. Harrington turned purple, spluttering incoherently.

Gina watched the varying facial colors with interest, but Drake apparently decided to rescue them both before it turned ugly. "I'm quite certain Miss Biddle is an exemplary young woman." Then, before Mrs. Harrington could explode, he added, "As is Miss Harrington. However, I believe the original arrangement is best. And now, if you ladies would leave us to it?" He gestured toward the exit in unmistakable dismissal.

The Major made his escape at a brisk march, and the two older women had no choice but to follow him. However, Mrs. Biddle wasn't content to leave it at that. Before she left, she muttered fiercely into her daughter's ear, casting fulminating glances at Gina as she did so.

Once the mothers were gone, the rest heaved a collective sigh of relief.

"I—I'm sorry," Letty stammered, her face still

bright pink as her gaze skittered toward Drake and away again. "Mama means well, but she thinks that I should—But I don't—And I really don't mean to—"

Since Letty seemed incapable of finishing a sentence, Gina decided to interpret for her. Turning to Drake, she said with frank honesty, "What Letty is trying to say is that her mama is trying to push you two together, but Letty isn't interested in marrying you."

Drake gave her a chiding glance but Gina shrugged. She was all for plain speaking. How people in this time communicated with all their hedging about the truth, she didn't know. "Isn't that right, Letty?"

Letty nodded. "I have a—That is, there's a boy—"

"Ah, so you are in love with someone else?"

Letty nodded, blushing even deeper. Gina suspected there was a mystery here, and that Mama probably didn't approve of Letty's choice—if she even knew of it—but she didn't feel like second-guessing any more of Letty's half sentences. Besides, the girl had been embarrassed enough for one day.

But Chloe hadn't. "How about you, Chloe? Do you want to marry Mr. Manton?"

Chloe giggled. "No, that's Mama's idea. I don't want to marry anyone—I plan to be a famous writer and hold elegant soirées that will be the envy of the literary set."

Ignoring the last part of Chloe's burst of confidence, Gina said, "Good. That makes three of us. Now that we know *none* of us want to marry Mr. Manton, we can relax and get on with helping him with his lectures."

Chloe and Letty giggled nervously, but Drake

merely looked amused. Raising one eyebrow, he said, "You didn't ask me if *I* want to marry one of *you.*"

And I'm not going to, either. She cast him a warning glance, trying to remind him silently that they were chaperoned and this wasn't the time or place to broach the subject again.

Chloe giggled. "Do you?"

Gina held her breath. He couldn't. He wouldn't. Would he?

Drake allowed himself a small smile at the expression on Gina's face. She was terrified he was about to say something inappropriate, but that was her bailiwick, not his. "Of course I would," he said, and enjoyed Gina's expression of panic. "I'm sure any one of you young ladies would make a wonderful wife."

All three relaxed, and Chloe giggled. "Don't let Mama hear you say that."

Gina shot him an exasperated glance, but he was unrepentant. He might have been disgruntled when she turned down his offer of marriage, but he had no intention of hounding her. He wasn't in the habit of forcing himself on any woman.

However, he *was* a bit annoyed. In Boston, he was considered quite the matrimonial prize. To have this slip of a girl turn him down without so much as a by-your-leave or thank-you-kindly-sir was a bit lowering.

And though she was quite right in that he had done so primarily because he'd compromised her virtue, he felt oddly disappointed in her refusal. Life would never be dull around Gina, and a man could spend a lifetime plumbing her mysteries without getting bored.

But the fact that she was so vehement in refusing him gave him an idea. He smiled to himself. There was very little that seemed to discommode the saucy chit as much as a simple proposal had. He'd just have to find a way to use it to his advantage.

"Well," Gina said. "Let's get started, shall we?" She glanced around. "But it's a bit crowded in here."

Drake smiled inwardly. Most women he knew would simper or hang on him after a night of passion. Instead, the ever-surprising Gina wanted to put him to work.

He removed a key from his pocket. "I took the liberty of acquiring the key to the small theater from the Major since no one uses it this time of day. Shall we?"

"Good idea," Gina said enthusiastically.

They all trooped toward the theater, Scruffy in tow, and Drake began to wonder what he had gotten himself into. He'd only wanted to help Gina retain her position, and now he was stuck with a parade of women and a small dog . . . all intent on "helping" him with his lectures. Unfortunately, he couldn't back out now without making the Major wonder about his motives and jeopardizing Gina's position.

When they reached the theater, Gina positioned them as efficiently as a general deploying troops. She had Drake gather chairs to place on the stage and directed the girls to sit there instead of taking their place in the audience as they preferred. Uneasily, the girls obeyed Gina's orders.

Placing one chair at center stage, she beckoned to Drake and said, "I've been thinking about your lecture. The primary problem is that you do too much telling. The audience won't be convinced unless you *show* them that mesmerism works. So, the first thing I need to know is how you go about mesmerizing someone. And who better than a pretty young girl?"

Drake grinned. "I would be more than happy to demonstrate my methods on you."

"Nice try," Gina said with an answering grin. "But I wasn't talking about myself. We have two potential subjects right here."

She turned toward Letty and Chloe, who averted their gazes. Chloe giggled nervously, and Letty turned bright red, muttering, "I don't think—That is, Mama would *never*—"

"It's all right," Gina said bracingly. "Wouldn't your mothers want you to help Mr. Manton with his lectures?"

The girls exchanged doubtful looks as Drake watched in amusement. They didn't know it yet, but they were doomed. Once Gina had the bit in her teeth, there was no stopping her.

"I'm not sure . . ." Chloe said.

Gina turned to her, obviously sensing a weakening. "Think how thrilled your mother will be when you tell her that *you* helped him with the demonstration." She let that sink in a moment as Chloe wrestled with the idea. "And Mr. Manton might even be able to help you. Let's see, you said you want to be a famous hostess some day, is that right?"

"Yes," Chloe said eagerly, and Drake knew she was hooked. "Just like Mrs. Drummond back home. She has the most wonderful literary salons. Everyone is just *dying* for an invitation to them. I want to be just like her."

"And what does your mother say about that?" Gina asked gently.

Chloe's enthusiasm faded. "She thinks I'm too silly," she said in a small voice. "I—I giggle when I'm nervous."

"Well," Gina said, shooting a triumphant glance

at Drake. "I think Mr. Manton can help you with that. Can't you?"

"Yes, I believe I can." How odd. The resourceful Gina had not only managed to unerringly pinpoint Chloe's most pressing need, but it was an area he could help with as well.

Gina assisted Chloe to the chair at center stage, and Drake reassured the nervous young lady with a smile. "Don't worry, this won't hurt a bit." And he might even be able to help her develop a bit of confidence as well.

Unaccustomed to having an audience when he worked, Drake was unsure how to proceed. Finally, he decided he would just have to ignore the others on the stage. Facing the seated Chloe, he said, "Now, this is a very simple—"

"Wait," Gina said. "You've got your back to the audience. They need to see both of you." She rushed forward and adjusted their positions until she was satisfied, then nodded and moved away again.

His concentration broken, Drake tried once again to ignore them and focused on Chloe. "As I was saying, this is a very simple procedure." He explained that he was going to put her into a somnambulant state and make suggestions that would help her be more like Mrs. Drummond. Now eager to cooperate, Chloe nodded impatiently.

Holding up his forefinger, Drake asked Chloe to concentrate on it.

"Wait," Gina cried, shattering the mood again.

He glared at her. "What is it now?"

"Don't you have anything more dramatic to do this with, like a crystal or a spinning mirror?"

Loath to break the rapport he had achieved with Chloe, he excused himself and drew Gina aside.

Speaking in a low voice, he said, "I cannot work like this. Continuous interruptions do nothing but disturb the harmony I achieve with the patient."

"But I need to coach you on how to do it better."

"But you don't need to do it while the session is in progress. Why don't you just watch, then discuss my technique afterward?"

Gina seemed annoyed at losing the upper hand, but said, "All right. But try to remember you have an audience to convince and act accordingly, okay?"

He nodded, knowing she really was trying to help. He went back to Chloe and reestablished his rapport. He didn't have any of the gewgaws Gina set such store by, but keeping her strictures in mind, he used a technique he had found useful before, waving his hands in a hypnotic pattern while keeping his gaze fixed intently on the subject.

Gina murmured her approval and he spared one admonitory glance for her before finishing his instructions to Chloe. Chloe proved to be an excellent subject, quickly sinking into the desired state. He informed her that she had nothing to be nervous about, and had no desire to giggle, then paused. How could he imbue confidence in her while putting on the sort of show Gina wanted?

Ah, he had it. Calling Gina and Letty over, he told Chloe that she was a poised and confident hostess, every bit as accomplished as Mrs. Drummond. To prove it, she would now host a literary soirée and treat everyone on the stage as her invited guests until he uttered the word "desist."

The change in Chloe was remarkable. She shed her nervous giggle and uncertainty, and immediately became confident and poised. Offering Gina her hand, she said, "How do you do, my dear? So glad you could come."

Turning to Letty, she said, "And you, Miss Biddle. So nice to see you."

Letty stammered and blushed, and Chloe patted her arm reassuringly, apparently emulating the dowager she admired. "Now, now, dear. No need for shyness. We're all friends here, aren't we? Do come in and meet the others."

Then, turning to Drake himself, she said, "And of course, Mr. Manton. Our honored guest." She linked her arm through his and drew him in to the "soirée" with an arch look. "My, you will be popular with the ladies. Come, let me introduce you."

Bemused by the success of his suggestion, Drake allowed her to draw him in and introduce him to Gina and Letty. Then, spying Scruffy next to Gina, Chloe said, "And who is this gentleman?"

Letty stifled a giggle, but Gina, game as always, hesitated for only a moment before saying with a grin, "This is my . . . cousin, Sir Reginald Scruffington the Third. He's . . . visiting."

"How charming," Chloe exclaimed when Scruffy shook hands with her. "And how are you enjoying our fair city?"

Apparently realizing she was addressing him, Scruffy barked a sharp retort.

Chloe appeared somewhat taken aback, but retained the aplomb of a premier hostess. "I see," she murmured.

Letty broke into giggles, and feeling the demonstration had gone on long enough, Drake halted it by saying, "Desist." Before he brought Chloe entirely out of the mesmeric state, he said, "When I snap my fingers, you will come out of the trance and remember everything that has happened while you were under. Ready?"

He snapped his fingers and Chloe blinked, then raised trembling fingers to her lips. "Oh, my. Was that me?"

"It was indeed," Drake confirmed with a smile. It was always gratifying when he could help his patients.

"Does that mean I can do that from now on?" Chloe asked.

"Not yet," Drake admitted. "But the more sessions you have, and the more you believe you can do it, the better you will get."

Her beaming smile was his reward. It did his soul good to be able to help a young woman who reminded him so much of the happy child Charlotte had once been.

Chloe's expression turned puzzled. "But who was the small dark gentleman with the horrible cough?"

Letty giggled and pointed to Scruffy. "Him. Sir Reginald Scruffington."

"That's Sir Reginald Scruffington *the Third,*" Drake reminded her, and the girls went into peals of laughter.

"Oh, my," Chloe exclaimed with admiration in her tone. "You did tell me to regard everyone on the stage as a guest. But if I could see a little dog as a man, you are a true mesmerist."

Buoyed by his success, Drake glanced at Gina who had been strangely silent during all of this.

"Chloe's right," she said. "See, all you have to do is give the audience a little demonstration, make it fun and maybe jazz it up a bit more, and you'll have them convinced."

So she was still on that road, was she? "I don't know. One small success—"

"Oh, yes," Letty exclaimed. "My turn, now?"

Giving him an I-told-you-so look, Gina smirked and said, "Yes, I think it is."

Drake frowned. "Miss Harrington was easy, since we knew what she wanted. But Miss Biddle . . ."

"Oh, but what Letty wants is obvious, too."

"What's that?" Drake asked, and Letty appeared to be wondering the same thing.

"Letty wants to be able to stand up to her mother and to finish a sentence without blushing. Isn't that right, Letty?"

The girl naturally colored at that, but said, "Oh, yes. If you could—"

Yes, he rather thought he could. Unable to turn down the opportunity to help another young woman and fulfill his promise to Charlotte, Drake agreed and Letty beamed.

She succumbed as easily as Chloe, and he led her through a confrontation with her mother, Gina acting as a totally convincing Mrs. Biddle. Under mesmeric control, Letty managed to assert herself without being rude or disrespectful and acquitted herself admirably. Even Gina seemed struck by her success.

When he brought Letty out of the trance and enjoined her to remember the experience, she immediately blushed, bringing both hands to her flaming cheeks. "Oh, did I do that?" she breathed.

"Yes, you did," Gina confirmed. "And good for you!"

Letty turned back to Drake. "And if I have more sessions—Then I can—Mama—"

"Indeed you can," Drake said with a smile.

"So," Gina said briskly, "we have two excellent candidates for the demonstration in your lectures. Which one shall we use?"

Letty and Chloe exchanged glances. Both obviously wanted the chance, but their upbringing wouldn't allow them to say so.

He knew he was going to hate himself for saying this, but, flush with his success, Drake blurted it out anyway. "Why not both? It would be more convincing with two subjects."

The girls beamed and exchanged joyous glances. Even Gina said, "Good idea."

"If their mothers approve, of course," he added.

Their faces fell.

"I don't know. . . ." Chloe said.

Letty concurred. "Mama won't—"

"Sure they will," Gina said bracingly. "All you have to do, Letty, is tell your mama that if you don't, then Chloe will, and she'll get all Mr. Manton's time and attention."

A ray of hope appeared in the clouds on Letty's face.

"And you do the same, Chloe," Gina admonished. "That ought to do the trick."

Chloe giggled. "Yes, it should. Come on, Letty. Let's go ask."

Excited by the idea, they hurried off, leaving Gina and Drake alone together.

"Well," Gina said. "I'm impressed. You really were able to help them."

"Thank you. So is it your turn now?" Perhaps once he had her under his control, he could finally discern why she was so eager to get him to leave the resort.

She grinned. "Not a chance. Besides, in their excitement, I guess they forgot they were supposed to chaperone us."

He glanced at the dog, resting patiently with his

head on his front feet. "Well, there's always Sir Reginald."

He won a smile from her, but it was short-lived. "I don't think the Major would consider him sufficient chaperonage."

"Perhaps not." Taking a leaf from Gina's book, he moved closer until the magnetic fields of their bodies intersected, eliciting a vibrating tension so intense he could feel it.

Ah, heady stuff. As Gina swayed toward him, he stroked her cheek and said softly, "You know, we wouldn't need chaperones if you would just agree to marry me."

She turned bright red and averted her gaze, just as he'd expected. "You know I can't," she said, pulling away. "And we're not supposed to be alone like this. I'd better go."

"All right, but one more thing," he said softly.

"What's that?" she asked with an apprehensive glance.

"You were right—about the demonstration I mean. Before, I don't think either girl believed in the benefits of mesmerism at all. Now they both do."

She smiled. "Now maybe you can admit that I might be right about the rest?"

"I wouldn't go that far," he drawled.

She laughed, evidently relieved at the change of subject. "Well, I have to admit I was surprised as well. You did an excellent job of helping those two through their fears."

"Thank you. But you give me too much credit. The only reason I was so successful is because you helped me see what they needed in the first place."

Gina fairly glowed with his praise. Calling Scruffy

to her, she turned to leave, saying, "I'd better go now."

He nodded, but couldn't resist calling after her, "All right, but this just proves it."

She turned back for a moment. "Proves what?"

"That we make a great team."

Gina just shook her head at that sally and was off and running once again. Drake grinned. He was going to have to help her with that habit. Someday, she'd never feel the need to run from him again.

Chapter Nine

Drake peered through the curtain from backstage, assessing the crowd that had come to hear his second lecture. If they had attended the first one, they were in for quite a surprise. Over the past month, he had found himself incorporating many of Gina's suggestions. He'd made only one little change at a time, but once she was through with him, the new lecture no longer resembled his original one in any way.

It was now far more showy than he had ever anticipated, but after seeing Chloe and Letty's reactions, he had decided it was necessary to have a little "jazz" as Gina called it. He had felt a little self-conscious and silly at first, but the more he tried her suggestions, the more they seemed to work.

And from somewhere within himself, he found he even enjoyed the theatricality. Besides, he couldn't deny the benefits. Already, Chloe and Letty's mothers seemed a little disconcerted by their daughters' new-found confidence.

The girls themselves, on the other hand, were his best advertisement. Word of mouth, Gina called it. They had spread news of his talents far and wide throughout the resort and the results were plainly visible—every seat in the small theater was filled.

"Isn't it great?" Gina asked from behind him. "Standing room only."

Drake nodded. Granted, his lecture was far more interesting now, but was it effective? Would he be able to draw the sort of patients who could use his help?

"Are you nervous?" she asked.

"No." Not in the way she meant. He knew it all backward and forward—he just wasn't sure it would do any good.

"I'll just warm them up, then, okay?"

"All right." This was one of the parts he wasn't so sure about. Gina had explained the necessity of "warming up" an audience, and though he had bowed to her greater knowledge, he wasn't certain it was quite . . . proper.

Oh, there was nothing *im*proper about her act, but somehow it didn't seem dignified to follow a performing dog. At least he had convinced Gina she must wear the bright blue dress instead of the spangled circus costume she had wanted to wear.

As Gina entered the stage, Scruffy at her heels, the audience quieted. Smiling, Gina said, "Ladies and gentlemen, it's my distinct pleasure—"

She broke off as Scruffy, on cue, tugged at her hem with his teeth. She glanced down at him and pretended to shoo him away. "As I was saying—" But Scruffy interrupted her again, tugging even harder.

There were a few titters of laughter and Gina glared down at Scruffy in mock exasperation. "What's the matter?"

Scruffy answered with a sharp bark which generated more laughter.

"I see," Gina said, glancing toward the wings. "He's not quite ready yet. Is that what you were trying to tell me?"

Scruffy's head bobbed up and down.

"Well, then," Gina said. "I guess we'll just have to keep them entertained for a few moments. Would you like to show them a few tricks?"

When Scruffy signaled his agreement, the audience applauded and Gina put him through his paces. To the uneducated eye, it appeared Gina was showing off Scruffy's wide range of talents, but Drake knew the real demonstration was Gina's skill as a trainer. She made it look effortless, but he knew how much time she had spent making her hand signals unobtrusive yet still visible to the smart little dog, and how much time she had spent practicing to get it just right.

About fifteen minutes later, Scruffy stopped what he was doing and looked toward Drake, uttering a sharp bark.

"Oh, is he finally ready?" she asked, making a show of looking relieved.

Again, Scruffy nodded and the audience laughed. "Well, that concludes our little entertainment then."

The crowd gave her a big round of applause and once they quieted, Gina gave a sweeping arm gesture and cried, "Ladies and gentlemen, it is my distinct pleasure to introduce Drake Manton, Mesmerist Extraordinaire!"

She grinned at him as she left the stage and enthusiastic applause greeted his arrival. Well, it seemed she was right once more. Now he knew what she meant by "warming up" the audience. Scruffy's tricks had certainly made them receptive.

Eschewing the lectern, he gave a brief explanation of what he was about to do, then called Chloe from the wings. Using slow, hypnotic passes of his hands, he put her under, then demonstrated how very suggestible she was in this state. She was unable to "see" someone standing right in front of her, greeted Scruffy as her long-lost brother, and drank vinegar with every evidence of pleasure, believing it to be lemonade.

He did the same sort of thing with Letty, and was gratified to see no sign of boredom in this audience. Instead, they appeared to be hanging on his every word. Quite different from his first lecture.

But once he had brought Letty out of her trance and excused the girls and the dog, a man yelled from the audience, "Ah, it's all hooey. You trained them girls to do that, just like the lady trained that dog."

From his rough dress, the man who accused him appeared to be one of the townspeople who had come to attend the lecture. Surrounded by his friends, he obviously felt brave enough to challenge Drake.

Drake had anticipated this accusation, and so had Gina. Maintaining his aplomb and ignoring the doubtful expressions of the audience, Drake said, "Though these two young ladies have certainly been cooperative, I assure you everything they did was under the influence of a mesmeric trance. I did not *train* them to do anything."

"Prove it," the man called out.

"I'd be happy to. If I successfully mesmerized you, would you be convinced?" At least, he hoped he could mesmerize the man—some people were simply not susceptible.

The man's friends laughed and jostled him, prodding him to accept Drake's challenge. "Do it, Callahan," one called out. "Show him what's what," another said.

When the heckler still hesitated, Drake addressed the audience. "Wouldn't you like to see Mr. Callahan mesmerized?"

They applauded their approval, so, grumbling, Callahan said, "Awright. Let's see you try it." The short, belligerent man strutted up onstage like a bantam rooster to the accompaniment of rude noises and encouragement from his friends.

Unfortunately, no one could be mesmerized in this sort of environment. Regaining control of the audience, Drake called for complete silence as he seated Callahan. Knowing this stubborn man would need something more compelling to put him under than mere passes of his hands, Drake pulled out the spinning disk Gina had insisted Rupert procure for him. Drake didn't know where Rupert could have found such a thing and was afraid to ask. In any case, he hoped it would work on Callahan.

As the audience watched in expectant silence, Drake bade his subject stare at the spinning disk and was relieved when the cocky little man soon went into a complete trance. But now that he had him there, Drake wasn't sure what to do with him. He didn't want to repeat anything he had done with the girls, but hadn't thought to plan anything in advance.

As he stalled for time and inspiration, Drake asked Callahan to stand and face the audience. Seeing Gina off to the side gave him an idea. Beckoning her to come on stage, Drake said, "So, Mr. Callahan. How's your mother?"

"Don't know. Haven't seen her in years."

"Would you like to?"

The man shrugged. "Only if she don't scold me like she usta."

"Well, you're in luck. Your mother is here with us tonight. See, there she is, just coming onstage."

He pointed Callahan toward Gina and the man did a double take. "Ma! How'd you get here?"

The audience laughed, and Gina played on it. Shaking her finger at Callahan, she said, "I heard you've been a bad boy, sonny."

"No, Ma, it weren't me. The police chief got it all wrong. I didn't set them fires, honest."

Uh-oh, it looked like something entirely different was coming out of this than Drake expected. He hadn't intended to let the man incriminate himself on stage, guilty or not.

Gina looked startled as well, but quickly recovered. "That's my boy," she said. "You be good now, you hear me?"

"I hear ya, Ma," Callahan said contritely.

As the audience roared, especially Callahan's friends, Drake turned him to face the front and sought a way to distract the audience from what had just happened, something that would prove to the cocky little man that he had been well and truly mesmerized. Aha, he had it. Calling for silence from the audience, Drake said, "Mr. Callahan, you're quite the cock of the walk, aren't you?"

Callahan thought for a moment then nodded. "Yep, I guess I am."

"In fact, I believe you're the biggest rooster in the hen yard. See all the hens spread out before you?"

he asked, giving a sweeping gesture at the audience. "Why don't you show them how you can strut?"

Obediently, Callahan tucked his hands into his armpits, scratched at the ground with one foot, and puffed out his cheeks, emitting squawking sounds. He strutted around for a minute, indeed looking like the cock of the walk.

When a lull came in the laughter, Drake pointed off to the side, saying, "Look, the sun is rising."

Callahan gazed off toward the "rising sun" and stretched to his full height, emitted a piercing "cock-a-doodle-doooooo."

The audience howled, but Drake quieted the laughter once more and said, "What do you think? Is Mr. Callahan mesmerized?"

Their applause was louder than ever, so Drake took pity on the man and brought him out of his trance, telling him he would remember everything that had happened.

"So, Mr. Callahan, are you now convinced?"

The short man looked pugnacious and more than a little embarrassed. "Naw, I just did them things to play along."

His friends hooted with derision. "I didn't know Shorty was a mama's boy," one of them called out.

"Yeah," another said. "But he ain't Shorty no more. Now he's Cock-a-doodle Callahan!"

The aptly named Shorty turned beet-red and gave Drake a fulminating glare. "I'm gonna get you for this," he muttered. But he didn't follow through, evidently more intent on reaching his friends who were still crowing like roosters.

When they finally quieted under Shorty's threats, Drake judged that he had established his point. Facing the audience alone, he said, "Ladies and gentle-

men, I have used a number of parlor tricks this
evening to show you what mesmerism can do. But
it's not about parlor tricks, it's about helping people.
By putting people in a mesmeric trance, I can assist
them to eliminate their fears, change their bad habits,
and calm nervous dispositions. If you have one of
these ailments, I would be more than happy to give
you a free consultation on the first visit. Just stop
by Dr. Ziegler's office in the west wing any weekday
between two and four. Thank you."

He left the stage to thunderous applause—quite
different from the reception his first lecture had
enjoyed. But the proof was yet to come. Would they
see it just as entertainment, or had he finally reached
people in need?

"You were perfect," Gina exclaimed as he joined
her backstage. "And so were the girls."

They had already left to join their friends in the
audience and enjoy their moment in the limelight.
"Thanks to you," Drake said, basking in the pleasure
of her approval. "You were right—the lecture did
go over much better this way. I just hope it proves
effective."

"It will," Gina said. "Come on, there's someone I
want you to meet."

She tucked Scruffy under one arm and dragged
Drake off the stage with the other, but they were soon
waylaid by a young couple. "So," the beefy young
man said, greeting Drake with a hearty slap on the
back. "You can change bad habits, can you?"

"Yes," Drake said simply, hoping the man wanted
to change his coarse attitude. He'd be happy to help
him with that.

"Good. The wife here could use your help," he
said with a jerk of his thumb in her direction.

The wife in question was a lovely young woman with honey-blond hair, porcelain skin, and fine features, who appeared embarrassed by her husband's crudity.

Drake smiled down at her, hoping to put her at ease. "How do you do, Mrs. . . ?"

"Mrs. Rutledge," the man boomed. "Annabelle Rutledge. And I'm her husband, Clyde Rutledge."

Gina stuck her head in, saying, "Nice to meet you, but we have to be going now."

She tried to tug Drake away, but he resisted. Something in Mrs. Rutledge's eyes reminded him of Charlotte. Speaking directly to the woman, he said, "I would be most happy to help you in any way I can. If you would like to come to Dr. Ziegler's office at two o'clock tomorrow . . . ?"

Her eyes lit with hope but she turned to her husband for guidance, and the hearty man said, "Good idea. We'll be there."

Drake nodded and allowed Gina to drag him away. Thankfully, Callahan and his friends had already left so he didn't have to run that gauntlet, but they were stopped several more times by people who wanted appointments.

"See?" Gina whispered fiercely. "I told you it would work."

"So you did." He was quite willing to give credit where credit was due, and he was becoming quite encouraged by the reaction.

Finally, she found the man she was looking for and Drake was surprised to see it was the seedy little man who had sat next to her at the last lecture.

Grinning, Gina said, "This is Lester Suggs. He's a booking agent for the lecture circuit. So, what did you think, Mr. Suggs?"

The man nodded sagely. "Very impressive. Very impressive indeed. Quite an improvement from the first lecture."

"So you'll do it?" Gina inquired eagerly. "You'll offer him a contract?"

"Oh, I think I can see my way clear to a tour of the West," Mr. Suggs said with a smile that implied he was offering Drake quite a concession.

"Isn't that great?" Gina enthused.

What was she talking about? "I'm sorry, I don't understand."

"A tour," Gina explained patiently. "He's offering you the opportunity to take your lectures on a tour of the West."

"Yes," Suggs said with an expansive grin. "I've had a vacancy come open and you can start in two weeks. Whaddaya say?"

"I appreciate the opportunity, but I'm afraid I shall have to say no."

Gina appeared quite taken aback. "Why?"

"Didn't you hear the people who stopped me? The lecture was a success—I have quite a list of patients who want to see me."

"But—"

"I can't just leave when I've promised to see them, now can I?"

"What's the matter?" Suggs growled. "You turnin' down my offer?"

"No, no," Gina said. "He's just a little confused, that's all. Let me talk to him and we'll get back to you."

"All right," Suggs said, appearing rather disgruntled. "But the offer ain't open long. You got two days or I'm giving it to someone else."

"Thank you," Gina said fervently, shaking his hand. "We'll get back to you in two days."

As Suggs wandered off, Gina turned to Drake with a determined look in her eyes.

To forestall whatever it was she had to say, Drake spoke first, firmly. "I don't want to hear your rationale or your reasoning. I have patients now who need me—"

"You wouldn't have them without my help."

"Granted, but that doesn't change the fact that they need me. I won't desert them to traipse all over the country in some kind of traveling circus. The answer is no—and that's final."

Gina looked stunned. "I went to all this trouble to give you this great opportunity . . . and you turn it down?"

"I didn't ask for this—all I wanted was a few patients."

"I can't believe it," she muttered fiercely as the crowd eddied around them, congratulating them for a wonderful performance. "We need to talk. In private."

"I'm not so sure that's such a good idea," he muttered back. "Remember the last time you approached me privately?"

Gina blushed. "I didn't mean we should meet *there*. Somewhere else."

Drake sighed. Why did she insist on spoiling his moment of triumph? "I'm in no mood to listen to a harangue. And it will do no good. My mind is made up."

"But—" He could almost see the thoughts revolving in her mind like pinwheels as she sought for a way to keep him there. "But I need to fulfill my promise to you."

He looked surprised. "Promise?"

"Yes. Remember, you made me promise that I would tell you why I want you to leave."

That's right. In the excitement, he'd forgotten. And he *would* like to know. "Are you willing to tell me now?"

"Yes, but not here." She glanced around. "I don't see any of our chaperones about. I have to get something from my room first, so what do you say you meet me in Dr. Ziegler's office in fifteen minutes?"

He nodded. He did want to hear this. At least one mystery would be solved.

They met in the doctor's office, and Drake felt a little awkward. Every other time they'd been alone, she'd somehow ended up in his arms. This time he'd just have to keep his distance if he wanted to finally learn the truth.

"So," Drake said, sensing that she felt as awkward as he. "You are finally going to tell me why you've been trying to get me to leave?"

"Yes."

"The truth? Not one of your evasions, now—you promised."

"Yes, the truth. Though you're not going to believe it."

"Tell me anyway."

Gina sank into a chair and Drake did the same, careful to ensure he sat on the opposite side of the desk.

Taking a deep breath, she stroked Scruffy's coat as if for moral support and said, "All right. The reason I've been trying to get you to leave is because if you stay here, you'll die."

Whatever he had expected her to say, this wasn't

it. He raised an eyebrow. "So, you've added soothsaying to your many talents?"

"No, it's not a prediction, it's a fact. I know because . . ." She made an exasperated sound. "Hell, there's no way to say it but flat out. I know because I'm from the future."

"The future," he repeated. And she expected him to believe this? "I see. And how did you manage this feat? Is Rupert going to show up with some contraption you claim to have sent you back in time?"

"No, actually it was a pistol in a hope chest that sent me back."

A pistol? "What kind of fool do you take me for?"

"I don't take you for one at all. I *said* you wouldn't believe it."

"And I don't. You promised you'd give me the truth."

"This *is* the truth. Look, I know it sounds crazy, but I really did come back in time." Her voice rose. "And it's all your fault—you sent me."

"I?"

"Yes—you. Well, your ghost really."

Time travel and ghosts? "Preposterous."

"Ha—that's what I thought, until your ghost crawled into bed with me."

Wasn't a ghost incorporeal? He didn't understand how one could crawl into bed with her . . . though he *could* understand the temptation. "Nonsense. I don't believe in ghosts."

"It doesn't matter. If you go on the way you've been going, you're going to *become* one real soon, whether you believe or not."

This was turning from the ridiculous to the absurd. "Really, Miss Charles, if that's all you can say—"

"No, it's not." She chopped downward with one

hand and her voice turned cold. "Drop your condescending attitude for one minute and just listen, okay? I was right about the lecture, wasn't I?"

"Yes, but—" He broke off, realizing she was right. He should do her the courtesy of hearing her out. "All right, I'll listen. But you have to come up with something more convincing than wild tales of time travel and ghosts."

She took another deep breath, and spoke in calm tones. "I know it's hard to believe, but I really am from the future. The year 2001 to be exact. Haven't you noticed odd things about me? The way I speak, the words I use, the way I don't understand how you do things in this time?"

"Well, yes, but I assumed that's because you were from the far West." That's what he'd heard, anyway.

"No, I'm from the far *future*. When I ran away from Jerry and my wedding, I ended up in Hope Springs and your ghost crawled into bed with me. Since I was the only person who could see or hear you after you died—"

"Why is that?"

"I don't know," she said, sounding miffed. "You thought it was because I could help you find out how you died. So you could 'move on' or whatever and stop haunting Hope Springs."

Ah, he found a fallacy in her reasoning. "Then if you *don't* know how I died, why are you so adamant about making me leave the resort?"

"I didn't know then, but I do now. You pestered me until we went to the newspaper office and found your obituary."

The thought made him shudder, as if a goose had walked across his grave. He still didn't believe a word of this, but he had promised to hear her story to its end. "And what did it say?"

"It said you died in a fire—along with a woman you were meeting secretly."

Ah, he had finally found the root of her concern. "And you were the woman?"

"No," she said with a clipped tone. "The woman you were meeting was Mrs. Rutledge."

So much for that theory. "But that's ridiculous— I just met her for the first time tonight. I don't even know her."

"Maybe not now, but according to the newspaper article, you're gonna get to know her *real* well before you die. Not only that, but you're going to die in a fire, one that was deliberately set at this hotel. Now, who does that remind you of?"

"Shorty Callahan," he murmured. The man had been totally unconvincing in protesting his innocence in the matter of arson. And the man *had* threatened him . . .

Drake shook his head. Lord, she almost had him believing her nonsense. "I'm sorry, but this story is just too farfetched. How can I believe a word of it?"

"You might ask Miss Sparrow."

"Would she corroborate your story?" he asked incredulously. The housekeeper seemed so down to earth, so . . . sane.

For the first time during her recitation, Gina looked doubtful. "I'm not sure. Oh, she knows it's true, but she's awfully evasive. . . ."

"Then you can't prove it."

"Oh, I can prove it all right. I was saving this as a last resort, because I don't think I'm really supposed to show it to anyone." She pulled a piece of paper out of her pocket. "Here. Read this."

He took the proffered paper and scanned it quickly. It purported to be a page from *The Hope Springs Times*. Right next to an article about a spiritualist whose machinations had been exposed, there was a sketch of him and an article about his death, just as she'd said.

No, it couldn't be true. "Did you and Rupert concoct this 'evidence' between you?"

"No, Rupert has nothing to do with it," she said in exasperation. "Look at the paper. Have you seen anything like that in these times?"

"No . . ." It was very high quality, bright white, with perfectly straight edges. But . . . "This isn't newsprint."

"That's because it's a photocopy."

"A what?"

"Never mind," Gina said urgently. "That's not important. Look at the date."

December 22, 1885. "Are you trying to tell me that this is the date of my demise?"

"Yes," she said firmly. "If you don't leave the resort soon, you're going to be a dead man on December 22."

A cold feeling washed over him. Suddenly, he had the unshakable conviction that everything she said was absolutely true.

Scanning his face anxiously, Gina said, "Do you believe me now?"

Just as quickly, he doubted himself. It was just too preposterous. "Perhaps," he hedged. "But it doesn't change my plans."

"What do you mean?" She snatched the paper from his hands so swiftly that a small piece of the corner tore off.

It was just as well—he didn't want its morbid contents in his hands any longer anyway. "Well, even if this is the time and method of my death, then all I need do is avoid the hotel on that day."

Gina paused. "Well, it sounds logical," she conceded, "but I don't think it'll be that easy. To be safe, you'd better leave right away."

She certainly seemed overeager to get rid of him. Curious, he said, "What's your interest in this? Why are you so worried if I live or die?"

"Can't I just be concerned about you?"

He thought about that for a minute, but it didn't ring true. "No, you were trying to get rid of me before you even knew me."

She sighed again. "Okay, I'll tell you why. Apparently, the reason I came back in time was to save your life. I can go back to the future again on December 22, but if you die after everything I've done to prevent it . . ."

"Then you might be stuck back here forever, is that it?"

"Maybe. Even if I do go home, you—your ghost, I mean—promised to haunt me for the rest of my life unless I keep you from doing something stupid."

So, she didn't really care about him at all. He was just the means for her to get back home—or so it seemed in her odd little fantasy. That decided him. She might not care what happened to other people, but he did. "I'm sorry, but I can't leave."

"Why not?"

"I made a promise, and I won't break it."

"You're kidding. What kind of promise could possibly be more important than your own life?"

"One I made to Charlotte," he said bleakly. "My sister—after she died."

"Your sister?" Gina asked softly and reached out to lay a hand on his. "I'm so sorry. What happened?"

It was about time she understood. "Charlotte was two years younger than I, and was always a happy child ... until she married our father's choice of husband." The pain hit him anew, and he had to pause for a moment. "The man was a cad. He ... he railed at her night and day, telling her she was stupid and childish, that she was worth nothing. Finally, she believed it ... and took her own life."

Gina gasped. "I'm sorry. I didn't realize ..."

"That's not the worst of it," Drake said. "She came to me and tried to tell me of her problems, but I was so absorbed in my studies, I didn't see ... I didn't understand ..."

"It wasn't your fault," Gina said as she hugged him.

He gathered her to him, needing the comfort of her embrace. "Yes, it was. I was studying mesmerism at the time. I should have seen what she was going through. I should have known."

"Nobody's perfect," Gina said in a consoling tone.

He held her tight, marveling at how much solace he felt in her arms. "Least of all me ... and Charlotte is dead because of my lack."

"It wasn't you—it was her husband who was to blame," Gina insisted.

"Yes, he bears part of it," Drake conceded, drawing away, "but so do I."

"So that's why you're so intent on helping people?"

"Yes. I know it won't bring Charlotte back, but it will help me atone, in some small way, for not heeding her when she needed me." He gazed down at her, pleading silently for her to understand. "It's a matter of honor, don't you see? Now that people have indicated they need my help—young women just like Charlotte—I can't go back on my promise.''

"Not even to save your own life?" she asked incredulously.

"No," he said firmly. "Especially then."

Chapter Ten

The next day, Gina felt rather at loose ends. They didn't have to practice now that the lecture was over, so she had nothing to do.

Nothing but find Drake and try to beat some sense into him. The lecture had gone very well, just as she'd planned, but the aftermath was another story. After all she'd done to help Drake, found a way to improve his lectures, got him some patients, and saved his life, she couldn't believe he had so casually thrown it all away.

The biggest problem was that he didn't believe her story. She could understand that—she'd found it hard to believe herself. But she had to find a way to *make* him believe it—his life depended on it.

She finally tracked him down in his room. When he opened the door, he raised an eyebrow. "Have you come with more preposterous tales to entertain me this afternoon?"

Well, that didn't bode well for changing his mind. But maybe she had something else that would. She slapped the morning edition of the newspaper into his hand. "Have you seen this?"

He glanced at the headline: *Manton Mesmerizes Hope Springs.* "Yes, it's very flattering."

"Not the article." She pointed to the sketch accompanying it, one portraying Drake with his hands raised, his white streak dramatically highlighted, and lines of force radiating from his eyes. "That."

He glanced at the sketch. "What of it?"

"Look familiar? It's the same one I showed you last night." She stabbed it with her finger for emphasis. "They're going to run it again for your obituary. Do you believe me now?"

"No, but I believe that you know the artist and somehow managed to fake the article."

"Give me a break. When have I had time to go into town to meet these guys? I've been with *you* most of the time." Not to mention Chloe and Letty.

"Why would you need to? You have your lackey, Rupert, to do it for you."

"That's not true." But this was getting her nowhere. "What can I do to convince you I'm telling the truth about where I'm from?"

"Perhaps you could arrange for my own ghost to visit *me* in bed some night? I imagine that would be quite convincing."

"Sarcasm doesn't become you." What she had to say next she didn't want overheard, so she tried to push past him, but he held firm.

"Our chaperones are nowhere about, and it isn't proper for you to be in my room."

"All right, then." She glanced around and didn't see anyone in the hallway, but figuring she couldn't be too careful, she lowered her voice. "Your ghost is in the *future*, remember? *After* you're dead?"

"Oh, that's right. How inconvenient."

"Come on, there must be some way to convince you. And I'm not going to leave until you tell me what it is."

He glared down at her, then thought a moment. "Perhaps there is. If you let me mesmerize you, and your story is the same—"

"Forget it."

His eyebrows rose. "I see. The story *wouldn't* be the same."

"Yes, it would, but I'm not going to let you hypnotize me."

"Why not?"

"Because I don't want you messing around in my memories, asking me questions that are none of your business."

"I see. You don't trust me."

He even sounded a bit hurt. Annoyed, Gina snapped back, "Look who's talking. According to you, I'm in cahoots with the entire hotel! Think of something else."

"No, I believe that's the only thing that would convince me."

"It ain't gonna happen," she repeated.

"It seems we are at an impasse, then."

"For now." But she was going to find a way to convince him, no matter what it took.

He glanced at his pocket watch. "It's almost time to meet my first patient of the day." He stepped out into the hallway and closed the door.

That's right, she'd forgotten he was supposed to meet Mrs. Rutledge at two o'clock . . . the beautiful woman whose name was linked with his in his obituary. "You know," Gina said casually, "the Major thinks I still work for you, so I'd better go along, too." Gina fell into step beside him.

Drake shook his head. "I won't have need of your talents today. You may have the day off."

"Thank you," Gina said insincerely, "but I'll pass. You need me whether you realize it or not."

"For what?"

"Well, to avoid the impression of impropriety, shouldn't you have someone present while you consult with your female patients?" Especially one Annabelle Rutledge.

"No, I'm a professional, much like a doctor, and people must feel free to tell me their secrets. They won't be willing to do that with you in the room."

"But—"

"Absolutely not."

That implacable tone in his voice told Gina she wasn't going to budge him on this. But if she couldn't stop him from seeing Mrs. Rutledge, she could at least make sure there wasn't any hanky-panky going on. No matter what Drake thought now, Gina knew he'd soon be seeing Mrs. Rutledge romantically— she had seen it in black and white. "Okay, then, I'll be your receptionist."

He cast her a doubtful glance. "Receptionist?"

"You know, someone to screen patients, take appointments, and make sure you aren't disturbed while you're with someone else." Surely he couldn't object to that.

"I don't think that will be necessary," he said, then stopped abruptly. They had reached the waiting room, which was packed with people. When the potential patients saw him, they looked up expectantly and all began to speak at once.

Over the confusion, Gina said, "Still think you don't need me?"

He gave her a wry smile. "Well, perhaps you're right this time. I told Mrs. Rutledge I would see her at two. Could you sort out the others?"

"Sure," Gina said in triumph. "Just let me know how long you'll want for each appointment."

"Fifteen minutes for the initial consultation, I think. Then if I think I can help them, we'll schedule hour-long appointments later."

Seeing her chaperones in the waiting room, Gina carefully left the door open as she followed Drake into his office. Rummaging around in the doctor's desk, she found some blank paper and a pen and ink.

Going back to the door, she said, "Mrs. Rutledge, Mr. Manton will see you now."

The blonde rose and her husband followed her to the door.

Drake frowned. "I'm sorry, but I shall need to see Mrs. Rutledge alone."

"Why?" the beefy man boomed in a voice filled with suspicion as his wife looked at him with trepidation.

That's what Gina wanted to know, too, and Mrs. Rutledge looked very uncertain as if she didn't quite know what to do unless someone told her.

"Because the application of the mesmeric technique is most effective when the patient isn't distracted by others."

"But you did it in front of a whole crowd last night," the man exclaimed.

"That was merely for show, and the people being mesmerized were not trying to change their habits, they were just performing the actions I suggested to them."

"But I gotta tell you about her bad habits," the man whispered in a carrying tone.

Mrs. Rutledge cringed, as if she was afraid her husband was about to enumerate them in public. Drake cast her a sympathetic glance and said, "I'm sure Mrs. Rutledge is more than capable of explaining them to me herself."

"I dunno . . ."

Gina could see Drake's point. With this man overpowering his wife, Drake would never be able to get anything out of her. And Mrs. Rutledge needed a little backbone, if nothing else.

"I'm sorry," Drake said firmly, "but that's the way I work. And this first time is most important. I need to judge your wife's temperament and symptoms, to see if I can even help her."

The man looked as though he was ready for war, so Gina stepped in and grasped his arm. "That's right," she said confidingly and turned her most charming smile on him. "It's the only way Mr. Manton can help your wife change those bad habits of hers. Now, why don't you just sit over here and wait a bit, and talk to the nice gentlemen in the waiting room."

As she steered Rutledge out of the doorway with one hand, Gina pushed his wife in through the doorway with the other. Gina cast a quick glance over her shoulder and was glad to see Drake had picked up on her maneuver and was steering Annabelle into the office. Annabelle cast her an odd glance compounded of gratitude and trepidation. Well, she'd soon find out there was nothing to fear from Drake. Mr. Rutledge allowed himself to be persuaded over to one of the waiting chairs, though he didn't look at all happy about it.

Though Gina was dying to know what was going

on inside that office herself, she busied herself by speaking to the others in the waiting room, and scheduling initial consultations. For those who really indicated a need, that is. To the sensation-seekers, she just gave the date and time of Drake's next lecture.

She had gotten most of the way through the waiting room when Drake's door opened, and Annabelle came out with a timid glance at her husband.

Rutledge stood. Without sparing his wife a glance, he glared at Drake who stood behind her. "Well?" he demanded.

"Yes, I think I can help her."

"Good," Rutledge exclaimed, and Annabelle appeared to be relieved.

No matter what adulterous things Annabelle might do in the future, she didn't deserve this kind of treatment. Taking charge before Rutledge could discuss any of his wife's supposed bad habits in public, Gina said, "I'll just schedule another appointment for Mrs. Rutledge, then." She glanced up. "Mr. Wilson, you're next."

The small man went into the office and she scheduled Annabelle for the following week. There were only a few more people left, and Gina took care of them with dispatch.

Now, she had nothing left to do but show people in and out—and sit and think about her situation. Unfortunately, nothing she could think of would sway Drake, and she doubted she would ever convince him of the truth. At least, not without subjecting herself to hypnosis.

But the thought of surrendering herself to someone else's control was abhorrent. What if he had her do something crazy? What if he dug around in her thoughts and feelings while he was in there? What if he found out how she felt about him?

And how do *you feel about him?* a small voice asked inside her head.

Well, to tell the truth, Gina wasn't quite sure. Half the time she was with him, she felt as if she were under a spell of enchantment, mesmerized by his intensity, his gallantry, his magnetic eyes. . . .

The other half, she was irritated by his pigheadedness. But it didn't matter—she didn't want him to know about either half. He was right, she didn't trust him. And, according to the newspaper article of his assignation with a married woman—Annabelle—she had darned good reason not to.

But if he didn't listen to her, he was a dead man. The thought was agonizing, but what could she do?

Unfortunately, if he was still here on December 22, despite her warnings, there was nothing she *could* do. Maybe she should just worry about herself—at least she had some control over that. Since Esme had said she didn't *have* to save his life to go back home, maybe Gina should concentrate on finding the pistol that could send her home.

Where could it be? She tried to picture it, but all she could remember was that it had a long barrel and the grip was half-melted. Melted . . . Hmm, that must mean it was in the fire that claimed Drake's life. No wonder it had sent her back.

So, if it was in the fire, and the only two who had died in the fire were Drake and Annabelle, then one of them must have had it with them. Gina couldn't imagine Annabelle carrying around a weapon like that—she just didn't have it in her. So where did it come from? Drake had said he didn't own any weapons.

Gina paused. Yes, so he had *said*. But could she take his word for it? Would he admit to being armed with a dueling pistol? In this century, men didn't tell ladies things they thought might upset them. And if she asked again, he'd deny it even if he had it—he wouldn't want to admit to having a pistol she might claim as the instrument that had sent her back in time.

Well, then, she wouldn't ask. She'd just go check for herself. She sent the next patient in, then called Letty over. "I have to take Scruffy for a walk, so could you fill in for a little while until I get back?"

"Of course," Letty said, and Gina smiled. A month ago, the girl would have stammered and blushed, but now she was confident enough to take on some small responsibility. For a mesmerist, Drake made a darned good psychologist.

Leaving Letty in charge, Gina went in search of Rupert. She waited until he was through helping a guest, then pulled him aside. "Rupert, I need you to let me into a guest room."

His expression turned wary. "You know I can't do that, Gina."

"Oh, yes you can." She lowered her voice. "I have reason to believe he's hiding a dangerous weapon."

"So? Most men carry a gun."

"So what if he uses it on another guest?"

"What if *who* uses it?" Rupert asked suspiciously.

"Mr. Manton."

Rupert pulled his arm away. "Uh-uh. I ain't getting involved with pulling anything on Mr. Manton again. He was nice enough about it the first time, but—"

"He won't know," Gina insisted. "He's in the middle of his consultations now."

"No—"

"Come on, Rupert. Just let me in to his room. I have a really good reason, but I can't tell you what it is. Trust me, you don't want to know."

"You're probably right, there."

Sarcasm, from Rupert? "Please? I promise no one will know."

"I don't—"

"And if I do get caught, I'll tell them . . ." She paused, searching for a suitable cover story. "I know, I'll tell them Jack O'Riley dropped his keys and I borrowed them. What do you say, Rupert? I just want to make sure he doesn't have a gun, that's all."

"What are you going to do if you find one?"

She hadn't thought about that. "Uh, nothing. I just want to know where it is. And if I think it represents a danger to the hotel or the guests, I'll report it to the Major." She added quickly, "I'll just tell him that I think Mr. Manton has a gun—I won't tell him I saw it in his room." She tugged on his arm once more. "Whaddaya say, Rupert? It isn't much to ask, is it?" When he still looked doubtful, she said, "I'll just pester you until you do it."

That did it. "All right," Rupert said, "But this is the last time I help you."

He walked with her to Drake's room and glanced furtively about. Once the hallway was empty, he used his passkey to let her in to the room, whispering fiercely, "Be careful now. And don't tell anyone I let you in."

"I won't," she promised, and Rupert shut the door behind her.

Now that she was inside, Gina wasn't sure where to look first. Drake had left his trunks inside the room instead of lining the hall as many of the guests had. Probably because they were still half-full. Whatever the reason, it was easy to rummage through them. She didn't find much—mostly books and old papers. His desk yielded much of the same, and she didn't find anything inside any of his pockets.

Well, since it wasn't in his trunks, desk, or wardrobe, where else could it be? She glanced at the bed. Would he hide it there? She checked thoroughly under the bed and the mattress, but found nothing. Darn—it looked like he didn't have it after all.

A small frame on the bedside table caught her eye and she picked it up. It was a miniature portrait of a young girl with dark hair and dark eyes much like Drake's. It must be Charlotte, the sister who had meant so much to him.

A key suddenly turned in the lock, startling her. Oh, no, she couldn't be discovered here—by anyone. Hastily putting the portrait back on the nightstand, she realized she couldn't make it out the window in time, so she dived into the wardrobe, pulling the door shut behind her.

Squeezing in behind his clothes, she held her breath, hoping whoever had entered would leave soon. Drake should still be in the middle of his consultations, so maybe it was a maid. Unfortunately, hidden as she was behind the dark clothing, she couldn't see a thing.

She heard someone moving around, then the door to the wardrobe opened. She held her breath, hoping she had concealed herself well enough. When the door closed, she let out a sigh of relief.

She heard another door open, and the tones of a man and woman having a short conversation, frustratingly muffled by the wardrobe. The door closed again, and Gina listened carefully. Had the intruder gone? Was the coast clear now?

Suddenly, the wardrobe door swung open again and she heard Drake's deep voice. "So, have you taken to wearing my clothes now?"

Gina sighed. Damn, she was caught. Now what? "No," she said in a small voice. She felt a little silly being caught hiding like a child, but she wasn't sure she wanted to face him either.

"Come on out," Drake said, then watched in amusement as Gina struggled her way past the confining clothes. She looked a little shamefaced, as well she should. He ought to be angry at her, but this latest escapade was so very Gina, he just couldn't. It was rather like training a puppy—it did no good to get angry with them. They were just too cute when they were caught doing something wrong.

"Come out quietly," he added. "Mrs. Biddle informed me you were in my room, but I don't think she believed me when I told her you weren't here. No doubt she's lying in wait in the hall to catch you coming out."

Gina grimaced. "How'd she know I was here?"

"Apparently she spotted you coming down this hallway, so she immediately came to me."

"But shouldn't you be interviewing potential patients right now?"

"Yes, I should be, but Mrs. Biddle threatened to go to Major Payne unless I checked . . . so I canceled them and came straight here."

Gina glanced longingly toward the window.

"Oh, no you don't," he said with a grin. "You run away every time things don't go your way, but not this time. This time you'll have to stay and face the consequences. Besides, it's daylight outside. Someone would see you."

She twisted her mouth into a grimace. "I guess you're right."

"I know I am. So, why don't you have a seat?" He gestured toward the wing chair and Gina seated herself as he sat on the bed.

She looked a little uneasy, which was just as well. She was too impulsive—she needed to think about the consequences of her actions. "Since we're trapped here for awhile, why don't we talk?"

"You're not trapped here," Gina pointed out. "Just me."

He smiled ruefully. "Actually, I am. You see, I told Mrs. Biddle I would stay here to do some research in my notes. And I asked Jack O'Riley to let me know when she stops hovering around this hallway. So, until the porter arrives, why don't we talk?"

"What about?" she asked warily.

"We could start with why you were in my room . . . and hiding in my wardrobe."

"I was hiding because I didn't want anyone to find me here," she said, stating the obvious.

It wouldn't get her off the hook. "And why were you in my room?" Seeing the mulish expression on her face, he added, "And no fairy tales, please."

"I was looking for the dueling pistol."

"Here? But I told you I don't carry any weapons."

"I know, but you might have forgotten. . . ."

Her tone was unconvincing. "I see. You didn't believe me." He was surprised to find the realization hurt.

"Not really," she assured him. "I thought perhaps you were just trying to save my feminine sensibilities or something. You know—you're such a nice guy, you might have thought it would frighten me or something if I knew you had a gun in your room."

No, he rather thought nothing would daunt the intrepid Miss Charles. But he was flattered by her description. "Thank you for that, anyway."

She shrugged. "It's true."

"Why are you so intent on finding this pistol?"

She scowled. "You told me I couldn't talk about that."

He sighed, afraid that would be the case. "Tell me anyway." Then, "Wait, I think I know. This would be the pistol you claim will take you back to the future."

"Yes, that's it."

"And how is it supposed to do this? The recoil shoots you into the future? Wait, I know—it's a magic bullet that does it. Or maybe you shrink to the size of a pea and shoot yourself out of the gun?"

"Very funny," Gina said with a disapproving frown. "No, all I have to do is hold it—on the winter solstice."

"Well, that's a relief. I was afraid you might have to use it on me."

She threw him an annoyed glance. "I might yet, if you don't stop with the sarcasm."

"But you're such an easy target. . . ." When she said nothing, he asked, "Why did you think I had it?"

"Because when I found it, it was half-melted, as if it had been in a fire. Since you and Annabelle are the only ones who die in the fire, I figured one of you must have brought it with you."

It made a strange kind of sense . . . if you believed in the ridiculous story to begin with. Trying to see it from her point of view, Drake said, "Well, I don't have it, and I highly doubt Mrs. Rutledge would carry a weapon—especially one as large as a dueling pistol."

"That's what I figured, too," Gina said. "But if neither of you have it, I don't know how it gets to the fire and into my hands."

Strictly through your vivid imagination. But Drake kept the thought to himself. "Perhaps she borrows the pistol from her husband. Maybe Mr. Rutledge has it."

Surprise dawned on Gina's face. "You know, you might be right. We'll have to look there."

"We?"

"Well, yes, you wouldn't want me to get caught there, would you?" she asked with a grin.

"Well, no." But he quickly changed the subject, hoping she would drop the whole idea. "So tell me, when are you going to marry me?" he asked lightly.

She rolled her eyes. "That again. You know I can't, so stop asking me."

"But I can't," he protested with a smile. "Your reaction is always so . . . interesting."

"Interesting? Is that why you ask me? Because I have *interesting* reactions? What am I, a science experiment?"

He regarded her with pursed lips, amused by her outrage. "No, I rather think you are a delightfully vibrant woman who is endlessly fascinating."

Gina flushed. "Oh." Then apparently casting about for something to say, she came up with, "How about Annabelle? How do you feel about her? Did you declare your undying love for each other?"

Annoyed by her repeated assumption that he and Mrs. Rutledge would have an affair, he said, "Of course not. I just questioned her about her symptoms, to see if mesmerism could help her."

"Since you gave her another appointment, I guess

it can. So, what *are* her symptoms?" Gina asked, her eyes bright with curiosity.

"I'm afraid that's confidential." He was surprised she asked.

She pouted. "After all I did to help you get your patients, you're going to keep this from me? I deserve to know."

"I do appreciate everything you've done, but that doesn't mean I can breach client confidentiality."

A gleam appeared in Gina's eye. "You would if I were another professional you were consulting on her case. Wouldn't you?"

"Yes, if I felt the need for assistance, I would contact another professional. Why?" he asked warily.

"Well, you did say I was very good at reading people and you're not . . . so how do you know you're reading her correctly?"

The truth was, he didn't. "That's what I hope to determine in the course of her treatment."

Gina grinned. "Well, why not save yourself *and* your patient some time and grief, and consult with a professional people-reader? Me."

"Perhaps you're right." Her instincts had been invaluable in pinpointing the areas where Chloe and Letty needed assistance. Perhaps she could help with his other patients as well.

"I am right."

"Then . . . all right. Your insights would be useful."

"Good," she said, squirming in delight. "Does that mean I can sit in on the sessions? I think I'll need to, so I can catch what you miss."

He thought for a moment. "Only if the patients don't object, and it doesn't impair their treatment."

"Great. Okay, tell me about the session with Annabelle. What are her bad habits?"

Drake remembered how woebegone poor Mrs. Rutledge had seemed when she related her troubles. "One bad habit is that she prefers to read romance novels rather than attend to her domestic duties."

"That doesn't sound so bad—who wouldn't?"

"Her husband doesn't agree. And she has a problem pleasing him. . . ." He paused, wondering how to phrase this.

"In bed, you mean?"

Why had he worried about Gina's sensibilities? "Yes, there . . . and elsewhere. She has a problem anticipating his needs."

Gina snorted. "Well, I hate to tell you this, but it seems the only bad habit Mrs. Rutledge has is being married to Mr. Rutledge."

He nodded. "That's the conclusion I came to. But I was unsure if I was reading her correctly, or if I was seeing things in her marriage that aren't there." His gaze slid toward his sister's miniature. The same things Charlotte had found wrong in her marriage.

Gina's gaze softened. "Well, if it's any consolation, I think you read her right."

"Thank you. I just hope I can help her. . . ."

"You can," she said bracingly. "You've already helped Chloe and Letty so much—you'll be able to help Annabelle, too. So, what about the other patients?"

Before he could answer her, someone knocked on the door. Gina darted over to hide beside the wardrobe, and Drake cautiously eased open the door, glad to see it was O'Riley. "Is Mrs. Biddle gone?" he asked the porter.

"No," Jack whispered fiercely. "That ol' biddy is settlin' in for the winter. But I have an idea to get rid o' her." Raising his voice, he said clearly and distinctly, "Ye know that woman ye wished to see?"

Playing along, Drake said, "Yes?"

"Well, she wants to see ye now." He lowered his voice to a loud whisper that would be clearly audible to any listeners. "In the bathhouse."

"Thank you," Drake said loudly and placed a token of his appreciation in O'Riley's fist. Closing the door, he beckoned Gina over and said, "O'Riley is a genius. I'll just go meet this nonexistent woman in the bathhouse. Mrs. Biddle is sure to think it's you and will follow me."

"Good idea," Gina said, her eyes twinkling.

"I'll make sure to lead her on a merry chase. Then, once we're out of range, Jack will let you know when the hallway is empty."

She smiled. "Thank you for being so concerned about my reputation. You're too good to me."

Once again, Gina had surprised him, this time with her sensitivity and heartfelt thanks. Giving in to an impulse, Drake stooped and gave her a swift kiss. Grinning at her stunned expression, he said, "I know."

Chapter Eleven

Gina changed from her uniform into a pretty emerald green dress to get ready for dinner with Drake. She didn't have many clothes here and was sick of wearing the same old thing all the time, so she'd spent some of her wages on a dress down in Hope Springs.

She usually didn't change for dinner, but felt she needed to acknowledge this day in some way. As of today, she had exactly two months remaining until the winter solstice. Only two months left in which to convince Drake he was going to die.

Not that it would do her much good. Drake's third lecture last week had gone just as well as his second, so it had generated even more clients for him—more clients who convinced him he needed to stay at the resort. And Lester Suggs was long gone, miffed because Drake had spurned his offer.

Even the Major seemed in cahoots against her. He

had given Drake his own office since he was such a draw to the resort, which allowed him to see even greater numbers of clients.

Strangely, now that Gina worked even more with Drake, she seemed to see less and less of him. He was busy with his patients, especially Annabelle who seemed to require a great deal of his time. And if he wasn't seeing a patient, he was writing notes or reading books. The only chance she really got to talk to him was at dinner each evening.

Esme had set aside a private table for them in the dining room to discuss the day's cases. It was the one time they were free of their chaperones, since they had convinced the Major that they needed the privacy to discuss Drake's patients. And since the table was in clear view of the other guests, the Major had agreed.

She joined Drake in the dining room, and thought even Mrs. Biddle couldn't be worried about them being together now. He had papers and books spread out all over the table and was studying them with such concentration that he didn't even notice her arrival.

Usually, Gina wouldn't care if a guy rose when she entered. Heck, she rarely noticed. But she had gotten so used to Drake's reflexive courtesy that the lack of it annoyed her, and she refused to sit down until he acknowledged her.

But she wasn't going to wait either. She waved her hand in front of his face and Drake jerked back to the amusement of the other diners.

"I beg your pardon," he said, rising. "I didn't see you there."

"I know," Gina said as he held her chair for her. It was kind of humbling. He hadn't proposed marriage for at least a week either, and she wondered what she had done wrong. Though she refused him every time, she had gotten kind of used to the proposals.

Bridget, who had become their regular waitress, hurried over to take their order. A few of the other girls resented Gina's elevation from dog handler to receptionist for the resort's most eligible bachelor, but not Bridget. She was always cheerful and nice. And she had helped soothe Sasha when Gina had resorted to eating only one course each evening. If she hadn't quit eating the rich food, she wouldn't be able to fit into her uniform anymore.

Bridget took their order and left. But before Drake could bury himself in his notes again, Gina said, "Can we have one night off?"

"Off?"

"Yeah, you know, one night when we don't discuss other people's problems. One night when we can just eat and talk like normal people."

He smiled at her, his eyes twinkling, and said, "All right. I think we can do that. What do you want to talk about?"

That twinkle for one thing. Ever since he'd caught her searching his room, he'd apparently decided she was there to provide entertainment. So instead of being annoyed by some of the things she did, he seemed supremely amused. It bugged the hell out of her, but discussing it wouldn't do any good—he'd just twinkle at her some more.

"I don't know," she said. "Anything but other people's problems." Especially Annabelle's. "How about yours?"

"But I don't have any problems . . . save for your contention that I'm going to die soon."

His smile didn't even falter when he said that.

"It's not funny—it's true."

He shrugged. "What would you have me do? Wear sackcloth and ashes until I reach the date of my supposed demise?"

"No, what I would have you do is leave this resort," she said between clenched teeth.

"Well, as you so quaintly put it, that ain't gonna happen."

Gina sighed. She'd known what his reply would be, yet she had had to try anyway.

"How about you?" Drake asked suddenly.

"What about me?"

"Let's discuss your problems."

"I don't have any, either—except for you refusing to believe me." And the fact that she hadn't found the pistol yet. It hadn't been in the Rutledges' room—she and Rupert had checked when Drake had backed out on her.

"Well, now that we've done the obligatory accusations, can we talk about something else?"

Amusement again.

"Okay," she said grumpily. "Like what?"

"Like you—I'd like to know more about you. Your childhood, your interests, that sort of thing."

Flattered by his obvious sincerity, she opened up as they ate dinner. Drake was a good listener, and she found herself telling him about the father she had adored and the mother who was never satisfied with what she had—especially not with her daughter. Her father had served as a buffer between them until he died, then nothing Gina did was ever right.

"I think that's why I agreed to marry Jerry," she said. "Mother wanted it so badly, and he was the first guy I dated who she actually approved of. Besides, she liked the idea of being mother-in-law to one of the most successful men in Richmond." She grimaced. "His family's money didn't hurt, either."

"That's not a very good basis for marriage."

"I know—and it would have been a horrible one. Thank heavens I realized that before we walked down the aisle together. Jerry actually did me a favor, though Mother wouldn't understand that."

"Perhaps your mother—"

He broke off as Chloe and Letty approached their table and rose to greet them warmly. Though the two girls had originally been set upon them as chaperones, their increased confidence under Drake's tutelage had turned the four of them into friends.

Drake invited the girls to join them, and Chloe said, "Just for a few minutes. Did you hear the news?"

"What news?" Gina asked.

"The Chesterfield is having a Halloween ball," Letty said.

"That's right, I'd heard about that," Gina said, though she didn't expect to attend.

"Even better, they're bringing in Madame Rulanka at midnight," Chloe whispered in thrilling accents. "She just arrived today."

"Who's she?" The name sounded vaguely familiar. . . .

"You've never heard of her?" Letty exclaimed. "She's one of the most renowned spiritualists in the world."

Gina wasn't any wiser, but didn't want to display her ignorance by asking what a spiritualist did.

But Letty must have caught her incomprehension, for she added, "You know—a medium. She communes with spirits, people who have passed on to the other side."

"Oh, a psychic."

"You don't really believe in that, do you?" Drake scoffed.

Chloe's eyes widened. "Why, yes. Don't you? After all, you showed us there's a lot more to the human mind than we know. Why shouldn't we be able to speak to those who have passed on?"

Thus appealed to in his own specialty, Drake said, "I have to admit the possibility is intriguing, but how do you know this Madame Rulanka isn't a fake?"

Naive Letty said, "Oh, Major Payne wouldn't bring a *fake* to the resort."

"Not if he was aware of it, but what if she has him fooled?"

"Well, Mama took me to see her last year," Chloe said, "and Madame Rulanka convinced me. She'll convince you, too. See if she doesn't."

"She has a point," Gina said. She hadn't believed either until Drake's ghost snuggled up to her. "How do you know until you've experienced it yourself?"

Drake raised a skeptical eyebrow. "I have no intention of attending such an event."

"Oh, but you have to," Letty exclaimed. "You have to tell us what happens."

"Aren't you going?"

Letty's face fell. "No, we're leaving tomorrow. That's why we really came—to say good-bye."

"Both of you?" Gina asked in surprise.

"Yes." Chloe giggled. "Mama finally figured out that Mr. Manton isn't looking for a wife, so we're leaving. We've been here a lot longer than we planned, anyway."

"We, too," Letty said sadly. "And since Mrs. Harrington is leaving . . ."

Ah, that made sense. Mrs. Biddle no longer felt the need to stay and compete. "I'll be sorry to see you go." She had enjoyed their company, once they were away from their mothers. "But what shall we do without our chaperones?"

The girls exchanged glances, and Chloe spoke. "I asked the Major about that." She giggled. "He said you've been very circumspect and since our mamas are leaving, too, you won't need chaperones anymore."

Drake smiled. "So it was merely to appease them. I thought as much."

"Yes," Letty said, "but we aren't complaining. If it hadn't been for chaperoning you, we would never have learned the benefits of mesmerism."

"And what shall I do without my best subjects?" Drake asked in mock horror. "I'll be ruined."

"Nonsense," Chloe said. "You'll find others. Or just use members of the audience—that's worked very well for you."

Gina grinned. How far they had come. Two months ago, they wouldn't have dreamed of contradicting him. Now they did it freely.

She exchanged hugs with the girls, and they hurried away to finish packing.

"So," Drake said with a smile. "Are you going to the ball?"

"No," she said, trying not to let her wistfulness show. Though it was open to the public and they expected quite a few townspeople to be present, as an employee, Gina couldn't attend without being invited by a guest. But she didn't want to seem as if she was hinting, so she hedged. "I don't have anything to wear—it's a costume ball."

"If I could arrange for a costume, would you attend with me?" he asked.

She stared at him in surprise. "You *want* to attend?"

He had avoided people and social events the entire time he'd been here.

He shrugged. "I think it is time I rejoined society. Will you go with me?"

She really wanted to, but . . . "It might look odd if you take me. Shouldn't you go with someone else?"

"But I want to take *you*," he said softly.

Her heart pirouetted with pleasure.

"Besides," he added, "no one will think it odd if I reward my trusted employee with one night of merriment . . . especially since our two greatest critics will be gone by then. So, will you come?"

"Yes," she said and couldn't help but beam at him.

"Good—I'll arrange costumes for both of us." He smiled. "But it will seem very odd without our chaperones."

"Yes, it will." To tell the truth, she'd been wondering if they were even needed. Not that she wanted him groping her on the sly or anything, but she couldn't help but remember the night they had made love. She had yearned for that closeness ever since— the warm touch of his hand, the cleverness of his mouth, and the marvelous feeling of being thoroughly cherished.

Wondering if he felt the same, Gina glanced at him from under her lashes. "The Major thinks we don't need chaperones anymore."

A small smile played around Drake's mouth. "The Major is wrong."

"Is he?" she asked, knowing she was playing with fire.

"You know he is," Drake said. "Did you think I had forgotten the night you spent in my arms, the night we were as one?"

Her senses spiked cold with pleased surprise then

went warm with longing. "No," she said in a small voice. In fact, the memory was playing havoc with her body as moisture began pooling within her. Maybe it wasn't such a good idea to have this conversation here. "I haven't forgotten either."

"Would you like to share my bed again?" he asked softly.

Gina stared at him in shock. Somehow, it felt very wicked talking about this in public, in broad view of all these very proper ladies and gentlemen. And she certainly hadn't expected the gentlemanly Drake to come right out and ask. "Yes," she breathed.

"Then marry me."

The mood evaporated. So, he was on that kick again, was he? Angry, she glanced away. "You know I can't do that."

"Because you think you're going back to the future?" he asked wryly.

"Yes, because I *know* I am . . . and the fact that you won't live long enough to marry anyone."

He sighed. "It's too bad your delusion is keeping us apart."

"You're the one with the delusion," she snapped. And one of these days, she'd prove it to him.

But how? Letting him hypnotize her was out. And though he'd said he might believe her if his own ghost crawled into bed with him, she couldn't arrange that.

Then it struck her. *She* couldn't . . . but maybe Madame Rulanka could. Or something similar, anyway. And Gina just remembered where she'd seen the woman's name before—on the same page as the article about Drake's demise.

Brilliant—it was the perfect way to convince him. And he'd given her the idea himself.

* * *

Since Rupert was being difficult about helping her again, it took Gina a couple of days to track down the room where Madame Rulanka was staying. Because the spiritualist had insisted she needed privacy, the Major had hastily converted one of the nearly completed tower suites for her use, and the woman had the entire tower to herself.

Just as well—that way Gina would be less likely to be seen. Leaving Scruffy in her room, she slipped off to the tower.

When she reached the room, she heard raised voices beyond the door. She raised her hand to knock, but the door opened and a tearful young woman burst out of the room and ran off.

A tall, cadaverous-looking man came to the door and shouted, "Imbecile!" after her, then glared down at Gina. "What do you want?"

"I want to see Madame Rulanka."

He sniffed. "I'm sorry, but the world's greatest spiritualist does not give private seances to . . ." his gaze flickered in disdain over her uniform ". . . servants."

He tried to shut the door, but she wedged her sturdy shoe inside. "I don't want a seance. I want to talk to her on a different matter."

From inside the suite, a woman called out, "Who is it, Rath?"

"Nobody," Rath said with a scornful look at Gina. "Merely a servant."

"A servant?" A middle-aged woman came to the door, peering out at Gina.

Was this the famed Madame Rulanka? She appeared altogether ordinary—the very picture of a respectable matron, though her gaze was shrewd as she looked Gina up and down. "I might have need of a servant. Come in, child."

Gina wasn't sure what the woman had in mind, but if it would get her past the spectral Rath, she was all for it. Sliding past the man, she seated herself on the settee at the woman's invitation.

"Now, why did you come to see me?"

So this *was* Madame Rulanka. Gina slid an apprehensive glance toward Rath, but it was obvious the man wasn't going to budge.

"Don't mind Rath," Madame said. "He's just a little overprotective. There are so many who need my help, you see. It has become necessary to sort the idly curious from the true seekers."

"I see."

"What was it you wanted of me?"

Gina paused, not sure how to put this without insulting the woman. "Well, I understand you are to give a performance here on Halloween night?"

"I shall commune with the spirits, that is correct."

"Well, I was wondering if you could see your way clear to communing with one *particular* spirit."

Madame's eyebrow rose. "I do not command them, I merely open myself to the cosmic vibrations and hope they appear."

Yeah, right. She was going to get nowhere if Madame Rulanka persisted in this act. "May I speak frankly?"

Madame's expression was wary, but she said, "Please do."

"Well, I happen to know that you're a fake."

Rath rose to tower over her menacingly and Madame's expression turned frosty.

"No, it's okay," Gina assured them. "I don't care if you're a fake or not. And the fact that you are just makes it easier for me."

"You have insulted Madame," Rath said. "You must leave."

"No, wait, I can prove it. I know your entire schedule . . . and I know exactly where and when your methods are going to be unmasked within the next few months."

"You are calling me a fraud, yet claim to know the future?" Madame said in a disbelieving tone.

"Just this one small part of it. You see, I have proof."

"What proof?"

"A newspaper article, written on the date you are exposed." Quickly, Gina explained how she had come in possession of the article and the whole time travel bit.

"Shall I throw her out now, Madame?" Rath asked.

"It is an absurd tale, yet she seems altogether rational . . . and her aura sparkles with truth." Madame paused, regarding Gina thoughtfully. "Messages come to us in many and mysterious ways. I cannot disregard this one. Tell me, child. What are the cities in which I am to appear?"

Gina had memorized them from the article, so she named off the rest of their stops through the end of the year.

"Quite right," Madame said. "And I don't make my schedule public, so this lends veracity to your claims. Now, which engagement is to be my downfall?"

"Oh, no, I'm not telling you that until you agree to what I want."

"And that is?"

"I need to convince a man that I really am from the future and that he is going to die when and how I predicted." She grinned. "I figure he'll believe it if he sees his own ghost." Quickly, Gina explained what she wanted her to do.

"I believe I can arrange that," the spiritualist said. "Sometimes the spirits are not accommodating, and need a little . . . assistance. This may be just such a time. Now, may I see this newspaper article you spoke of?"

"No, I think I'll hold on to that until after the seance," Gina said.

Madame scowled. "Without proof, why should I help you?"

"Until you help me, why should I show you the proof?"

They regarded each other stonily for a few moments as Gina searched for a way to break the impasse.

Finally, Madame Rulanka said, "I have a proposition for you. One of my staff has just left, and I find myself temporarily in need of help." She paused, then added, "Discreet help."

Gina could be discreet when she wanted. "What do you need?"

"The spirits do not always come when I call. To make it more . . . enticing for them to appear, it is necessary to glean certain information about the hotel guests and members of the town."

The woman wanted her to tell everyone's deep, dark secrets so she could divulge it onstage? The idea made Gina feel slimy. But instead of refusing outright, she said, "I can't help you there—I don't know anything."

When the woman looked doubtful, Gina added, "I don't get out much."

"Then you shall make it your business to find out," Madame insisted. "Having good information will allow the spirits to be more accurate . . . and make the ghost of your mesmerist that much more believable.''

She had a point, but Gina wasn't about to divulge the secrets she'd heard in Drake's office. She couldn't betray his trust—or the patients'—that way.

But maybe she could give the woman a few tidbits about other people . . . things that were already common knowledge. "Okay," Gina said. "I'll see what I can do. Then, afterward, I'll tell you which town you'll be unmasked in. Is it a deal?''

"Yes, we are agreed.''

They shook hands, and Gina went off to figure out what she could tell Madame Rulanka without hurting anyone or compromising her own integrity.

Chapter Twelve

Halloween dawned crisp and cold, and the entire resort held an air of excitement as people rushed to and fro, getting last-minute trimmings for their costumes and consulting with each other on the intricacies of keeping their identities secret until the right moment.

Gina became caught up in it, too, as the patients seemed to talk of nothing else. When the fourth one in a row asked her what her costume was for that evening, Gina said, "That would be telling, Mr. Feeney. You'll just have to wait and see."

Then, after he left, she turned to Drake and asked, "Just what *are* we wearing tonight?"

He smiled. "As you so aptly put it, that would be telling."

It wasn't like Drake to be so coy. Then it struck her. "You don't know, do you?"

His expression turned rueful. "Not exactly, no. But

we *will* have costumes, I promise you. Jack O'Riley is arranging it.''

Uh-oh. What would a tipsy porter consider appropriate costuming? ''When will we find out what they are?'' If he'd chosen something hideous, she wanted the opportunity to come up with something else, quick.

''They should be in our rooms now,'' Drake assured her. ''Just one more patient and we can go see the worst.''

When Gina returned to her room and the costume, she was pleasantly surprised to see it wasn't bad at all—some sort of filmy violet dress.

She heard a knock at the door and Bridget poked her head in. ''Isn't it grand?'' she asked in her lovely Irish lilt.

''It's lovely,'' Gina agreed. ''Your father did a wonderful job. But . . . who am I supposed to be?''

''Here's the rest of it,'' Bridget said and brought in a tall cone-shaped hat about three-and-a-half feet tall, the same color as the dress. It had a long wisp of violet silk attached to both ends in a long arc.

''I'm a dunce?'' Or a Conehead. . . .

Bridget grinned. ''No, you're Juliet . . . and Mr. Manton is Romeo.''

Juliet? Obviously, she and Bridget hadn't seen the same movies if this is what she thought Juliet would wear. *I wonder what silly thing Drake is looking at now?*

Bridget sighed. ''Isn't it romantic?''

So Jack O'Riley and his daughter were playing matchmaker now, were they? ''Not really,'' Gina said dampingly. ''I'll be too worried about whether this hat is going to fit through the doors, catch on the chandeliers, or knock me off-balance onto my bu—

backside. Maybe I'll just leave it off." It would certainly be safer.

"Oh, no," Bridget said in dismay. "You can't. Da looked long and hard for just the right costume. You have to wear the hat or you won't be Juliet."

The girl looked so devastated that Gina found herself rashly promising to wear the dumb thing throughout the entire ball.

Bridget beamed. "And I'll come back this evening to help you with it."

"Weren't you invited to the dance?" Surely some guest or local had seen the advantages of squiring sweet, pretty Bridget.

"No, I have to serve. But Miss Sparrow said we could all come see Madame Rulanka later."

So Gina agreed and Bridget came back that evening to help her into the costume. It wasn't really that difficult, since it was a simple empire-waisted gown, but Gina couldn't deny the girl the obvious pleasure it gave her.

Once she had it on, Bridget regarded her with delight. "You're beautiful," she said in awe.

Gina smiled. Though she couldn't see much of herself in the small mirror above the washstand, she could tell that the violet silk complemented her dark hair and skin tone, making her look better than she ever had in her life. But something was wrong. . . .

Her hair. Piled on top of her head like this, it looked ridiculous with this costume. Ruthlessly, she pulled out all of the pins and let her hair fall to her shoulders. Sighing with relief, she scratched her head. Boy, that felt good for a change.

She brushed it out, and Bridget's eyes grew wide. "Never say you're going to wear your hair down like that."

"Sure, I am. Why not? Don't I look more like young, innocent Juliet this way?"

"Yes, but the Major . . ."

Gina gave a negligent wave of her hand. "Who cares about the Major's antique policies tonight? This is a costume ball and I need to be in character. Besides, I won't be in uniform, so why should he care?"

"I don't know. . . ."

"It will be okay—trust me. Now, help me with this mask, will you?"

Bridget tied the mask in place and Gina was glad to learn she could still see out of the silly thing.

"Now the hat," Bridget coaxed.

Gina eyed the low ceilings doubtfully. "I don't think there will be room for all three of us in here."

Bridget giggled. "Then come out into the hall."

Once in the hall downstairs, there was a lot more room to accommodate the headdress so Bridget put it on. In fact, she used so many pins to secure it that Gina was sure it wouldn't come loose even in a gale-force wind.

"There," Bridget declared in satisfaction. "Now, let's meet Romeo."

She and her father must have arranged this ahead of time, for Jack and Drake were waiting for them at the end of the hall, in the large space where the west wing joined the main section. Jack looked puffed-up with self-congratulation, and Drake looked . . . uncomfortable.

His costume was almost as strange as hers. He wore dark purple stockings and some kind of puffy purple and violet striped shorts, topped with a matching short jacket and a floppy beret-style hat with a feather sticking out the side. She might not have known it was him save for those magnetic eyes glinting at her from behind his purple mask and the telltale streak in his hair.

But by far, the most interesting part of his costume was the huge codpiece decorated in large, fake amethysts and diamonds. Talk about family jewels. . . .

Gina suppressed a laugh. Whoever had put these costumes together had little regard for historical accuracy.

Strangely enough, he looked great. Who knew he had such fabulous legs? "Well, hello, Romeo," she said teasingly.

Drake's gaze traveled up and up, his mouth parted in astonishment as he took in the full extent of her cone head. "Juliet," he acknowledged in an amused voice.

Jack beamed at them. "Now, don't ye two look marvelous."

Well, she had to give Jack credit, he had certainly tried to do his best. "Thank you for finding these for us," Gina said politely.

"Think nothin' of it," Jack said with a wave of his hand. "Just have a good time at the ball. Go on, now."

He waved them on like a fairy godfather with an invisible wand, and Drake offered her his arm. "Shall we?"

"Of course," Gina said, taking his arm. Then, once they were out of earshot, she said, "Don't I look ridiculous?"

He laughed down into her face. "No more so than I."

"I don't know . . . that codpiece is rather impressive," she said, grinning. "All the ladies will be envying me tonight."

He laughed with her. "I wanted to leave it off, but Jack was so insistent, I didn't want to spoil his fun."

"Well, that's what you get for leaving the costume choice up to someone else."

"Yes, I shall remember that in the future. My one consolation is that your headgear is far more absurd than mine."

"Yes, it is, isn't it? I'm afraid if I dip my head, I'll impale someone or strangle them with the loop of silk at the end."

He bowed gallantly. "Then I shall endeavor to protect the other guests from the dangers of your chapeau."

With that, they entered the ballroom, laughing when Gina had to bend almost to her knees to avoid catching her headdress on the doorway. Luckily, the chandeliers appeared to be high enough to be out of range.

And she was glad to see that their costumes weren't the most fantastic in the room. A five-and-a-half-foot goggle-eyed fish walked by on the arm of a fishing rod, and a canary in a gilded cage stood over in the corner, talking to a six-foot peacock.

Most of the costumes were more staid, however. She saw several Napoleons and Cleopatras, and others she was sure were supposed to represent historical or mythological characters . . . though she couldn't figure out who. And most people were recognizable despite their costumes and masks.

The Major was here in some sort of antique uniform, accompanied by Miss Sparrow, attired discreetly in a birdlike costume that looked nothing like her namesake. In her soft yellow dress and fluffy, feathery hat and mask, she looked like a newly hatched chick.

Drake leaned down to whisper, "Shall we get something to drink?"

"Sure," Gina said. Even making their way through the crowd to the refreshments was fun as she tried to identify costumes and faces. There were the Rutledges, apparently attired as Zeus and Hera. His costume might be appropriate, but Gina couldn't imagine Annabelle as queen of anything, especially not the gods. Even now, she seemed to hover uncertainly in Zeus's vicinity.

Drake procured them each a glass of champagne, and they sipped it as they people-watched, pointing out the absurd and the just plain strange costumes to each other. Everyone seemed to be having a great time, especially on the dance floor.

"Would you like to dance?" Drake asked.

Gina shook her head with real regret. "I don't know how." She had never learned ballroom dancing, but if the band struck up a top fifties hit, she was ready to boogie.

As one song ended and another began, Drake removed the glass from her hand and set it on a nearby table, saying, "For this one, you don't need to know how. Just follow my lead."

He swept her onto the dance floor so fast, Gina didn't even have time to protest. With one arm firmly around her waist and the other holding her hand, Drake led her around the floor in a waltz. She stumbled a couple of times, but soon got the hang of the rhythm, the champagne helping to loosen her up.

"You see," Drake murmured. "It isn't so difficult."

No, it wasn't. And now that she had relaxed, she even found herself enjoying it. Though in her time, slow dances meant being plastered against your date's body, she rather thought she preferred the old-fashioned waltz. Drake's strong arms made her feel safe, his gaze was warm, and the slight distance between them only added to the tingling anticipation of being so close . . . yet so far. She found it surprisingly sensual.

Enveloped as she was in a fog of intoxicating champagne and rising desire, she lost all awareness of the people around her and felt the world fade away. There was nothing but the two of them, yearning toward each other, basking in the glow of heady awareness and a magical enchantment.

He drew her closer, riveting her with those mesmerizing eyes. Lost in his gaze, she tilted her head back with a sigh and her lips parted as . . . her head was suddenly jerked down and sideways.

Gina grabbed for the cone, which felt as if someone had just tried to wrench it from her head. "Ouch." What a rude awakening. Leaning uncomfortably backward, she realized she was tethered to something by the silk on her hat.

"Damn it," she heard a man say in an exasperated voice behind her. "Let go of me."

Drake steadied her and spoke to the man behind her—a short Napoleon. "Wait—you're caught in her hat."

Gina twisted slightly to see and sure enough, the silk had managed to wind itself around Napoleon's neck. It wound even tighter when she turned her head to say, "Oh, I'm sorry."

A titter of laughter followed, but Gina didn't find it at all funny. It hurt.

"You stupid fool," Napoleon muttered, and Gina recognized his voice this time—it was Shorty Callahan. And, as usual, he had his friends in tow. Though she thought if she had friends like that, she'd find a new set. Like the last time, they laughed and jeered at his predicament.

She felt Drake stiffen. "That's no way to speak to a lady."

"Then get her offa me," Shorty insisted vehemently and tugged on the silk, nearly ripping the hat from her head.

Gina winced and Drake commanded, "Hold still."

As he freed Shorty from the length of violet silk, Shorty glared at Drake and muttered, "You! I shoulda known. It wasn't enough for you to humiliate me once, but twice?"

Drake ignored him as he helped Gina straighten her hat. Gina felt only relief, but Shorty was still ticked. "I'll get you for this," he threatened, but allowed himself to be pulled away by his friends. "You'll be sorry," he shouted.

Now that the incident was over, the rubberneckers turned away and Drake held out his arm to escort her from the dance floor.

Esme hurried up with a concerned expression. "Are you all right, dear?"

"I don't know. Do I have any hair left?" It felt like most of it had been pulled out by the roots.

"It looks intact to me," Drake said.

"Good—then I need to take this torture device off."

Esme led her to the ladies' room and helped her pull out the umpteen pins Bridget had used. Finally, Gina took the offending headgear off with a sigh. "There, that feels better." But jeez, talk about hat hair. . . .

Esme clucked. "I don't know how you get yourself into these predicaments."

As Gina tried to restore some semblance of order

to her hair, she said, "I don't, either. But this one was Bridget and Jack's idea."

"I see," Esme said, eyeing the hat with a disgruntled expression. "Well, you go back to the ball and I'll get rid of . . . this."

"You won't damage it?" Jack and Bridget had meant well, and she didn't want them to get in trouble for a ruined costume.

"No, I'll just have one of the girls return it to your room."

Gina smiled. "Thank you."

"You're quite welcome. Now, run along and enjoy your dance with Mr. Manton. And Gina," she said in a bemused tone, "do try not to get into any more trouble, won't you?"

"I'll try not to," Gina said, but she couldn't guarantee anything. It wasn't something she seemed to have any control over.

Drake was waiting for her, and led her back into the ballroom. They danced a few more waltzes, but it wasn't quite the same since Shorty had ruined the mood. Then, at midnight, the band played a flourish and everyone unmasked. There were exclamations throughout the room, but Gina, for one, had figured out who nearly everyone was anyway and was just glad to get the mask off.

Then the Major called for everyone's attention. "Ladies and gentlemen, it is my great pleasure to present, at popular request, the famed Madame Rulanka. Those who wish to see the spiritualist contact the dearly departed, please make your way to the theater now. Those of you who wish to keep on dancing, please do so. The band will be more than happy to accommodate you."

About three-quarters of the crowd headed off

toward the doors but when Gina tried to follow them, Drake stopped her. "Let's stay," he said softly.

"But I want to see Madame Rulanka. I've heard so much about her."

"Wouldn't you rather dance?"

She would, but she'd put so much time and effort into convincing the spiritualist to set up this little demonstration that she didn't want to go back on it now. And, with Rupert's help, she'd been able to glean the sort of gossip the woman seemed to want without hurting anyone. "Oh, no, I really want to see her. Besides, I promised Letty and Chloe I would tell them all about it, remember?"

He frowned, but before he could say anything else, she fumbled for another excuse. "And I can't go without an escort, or the Major will be furious." It wasn't exactly the truth, but she had to find some way to get him to the performance. "Please, won't you come with me?"

Though his expression showed he wanted nothing to do with it, Drake, ever gallant, agreed. He once more offered her his arm and Gina exulted inside. This time, her scheme would work. It had to.

Drake didn't know what scheme Gina had up her sleeve, but it was obvious she was up to something. He just regretted that they had to leave the ball. It had been a long time since he'd attended anything so frivolous, and he'd enjoyed it—especially with Gina. Holding her in his arms, chatting with her about inconsequential things, and sharing her simple plea-sure in the dance had been sheer joy. So why did she have to cut it short to listen to some crackpot with a crystal ball?

Once everyone had been seated, the strains of a violin filled the theater. They all hushed as a tall, thin man walked onstage playing blood-stirring gypsy music. The curtains opened with a dramatic whoosh upon a middle-aged woman dressed in gold and scarlet with a colorful scarf wound around her head. She threw her arms wide in recognition of the applause that filled the room, then seated herself at a small table onstage.

Drake guessed she was supposed to represent a gypsy, and she certainly seemed to have most of the audience convinced—or at least willing to suspend disbelief—as they murmured with satisfaction at her appearance.

The man brought the music to an aching finality, then lowered his violin to say in a deep, resonant voice that filled the small space, "You have a rare treat in store for you this evening. Madame Rulanka, Queen of the Gypsies, famed spiritualist and medium, has deigned to grace these premises with her presence."

Drake snorted. Queen of the Gypsies, indeed. But Gina elbowed him in the side, saying, "Shh."

Other murmurs broke out, as well as a few giggles, at his announcement, and the man boomed, "Silence! We must have silence if the spirits are to appear."

He went on to explain that the veil to the spirit world was at its most tenuous tonight on All Hallow's Eve, and that the audience would be most likely to experience an appearance . . . but only if there was complete quiet.

A hush fell over the room and the man gestured dramatically toward Madame Rulanka who had placed her hands flat on the table and thrown her head back. The lights dimmed to complete blackness, and the only thing visible was the spiritualist.

She went through some rigmarole about calling to the spirit world and asking them to answer. Drake suppressed another snort. He doubted if the "spirits" would disappoint her—she had too big an audience.

Sure enough, the vague form of a man appeared onstage to the wonderment of the audience—a man draped in white flowing draperies who seemed to float in midair. He moaned in blood-chilling accents as a trumpet appeared and floated nearby.

"Is that you, old friend?" Madame asked.

The so-called spirit moaned again.

"The former Tsar of Russia," she announced, and Drake heard an exclamation from the back of the room.

"S—Sire?" a man called out in quavering tones.

Drake craned his neck and was surprised to see the speaker was the hotel chef.

Madame threw her head back and said, "He wishes to speak to a favored servant . . . Sasha?"

Sasha made a sound that sounded almost like a sob, his gaze riveted on the stage and the glowing apparition.

"He says . . . He says you are not to grieve for him. He is in a better place now, though he sorely misses the feasts you used to prepare for him."

Sasha exclaimed volubly in Russian, then turned and left the theater, sobbing with joy. Well, there was one satisfied customer, anyway.

Murmurs spread throughout the audience, but quickly ceased as the man boomed, "Silence!" once again.

Then, after a short period of time, a small apparition appeared, close to the ground.

"Who is this?" Madame asked.

Then, apparently receiving an answer, she said, "Poopsie? Does anyone here know a Poopsie?"

The woman in front of Drake gasped audibly and cried out, "My little doggie?"

Apparently satisfied, Madame said, "He wants you to know that he misses you and he loves you . . . and he will be waiting to join you on the other side."

The woman sobbed out, "Thank you. Oh, thank you," as she buried her face in her handkerchief.

Drake glanced around. Didn't anyone else see this as ridiculous as he did? Apparently not—they all seemed completely enthralled as Madame continued to interpret for dead people. Oh, she was definitely a fraud, but at least she wasn't a mean one. Each message from the other side reassured those left behind or gave them hope for the future.

But he'd heard enough. "Let's go," he whispered to Gina.

"Not yet," she said, an odd tension in her body. "I want to stay for the whole thing."

He listened to yet another ghost give reassurance to her widowed husband, then a different female ghost appeared onstage.

"Who is this?" the spiritualist asked. A pause, then, "Charlotte Ruxton? Does anyone know a Charlotte Ruxton?"

Drake went rigid and cold with fury. How dared they bring his sister into this? Beside him, Gina gasped and gave him an apprehensive, sidelong glance. He tried to rise, but Gina had a death grip on his arm.

Madame continued, "Charlotte has a message for her brother." She paused, then added haltingly, "You must listen to the young woman who has come so far to warn you, or you will surely join your sister on the other side. Heed her well . . . it is not yet your time."

Not for him the reassurances of the dead. Oh no, for Drake there was nothing but a warning—a warning that echoed the many Gina had forced upon him since they'd first met.

This had to be her doing. He trembled with outrage. Damn her and damn Madame Rulanka. "This time, you've gone too far," he hissed.

Wrenching his arm from Gina's hold, he stormed out of the theater without looking back.

Chapter Thirteen

Gina sat stunned for a moment as Drake left the theater. His lapse into bad manners—for whatever reason—was just so out of character, she found it difficult to comprehend. But she quickly regained her composure enough to take off after him, though she was careful to maintain a ladylike pace. Most people were intent on the stage and Madame Rulanka, but she couldn't count on the Major ignoring an infraction. He seemed to be able to spot them with his eyes shut.

Once outside the theater, she abandoned caution and hurried to catch up. "Drake, wait," she called.

He didn't even pause as he strode rapidly away from her, his back rigid and unyielding. He must really be ticked off.

She couldn't blame him after what had happened in there, but it wasn't really her fault. Madame Rulanka had gone over the line.

She chased him up the front part of the main section and down the north side. There were couples strolling everywhere after the ball so she didn't want to yell at his retreating back and make a scene any more than she had to—word would get back to the Major, then she'd really be in trouble. And people were staring hard enough at them already.

Instead, she waited until he reached the junction between the north and west wings before she put on a burst of speed. Darting in front of him, she caught his arm so he would have to stop. "It wasn't me," she panted out. "I didn't do it."

His eyes had turned flat and angry. "You expect me to believe that?"

"Yes, because it's true."

"Let me get this straight," he spit out. "Did you or did you not give Madame Rulanka information on resort guests and employees?"

"Well, yes, but—"

"And did you or did you not ask her to warn me to leave the resort?"

"Yes, I did that, too, but—"

"That's what I thought." He jerked away again and took off toward the west wing and his room.

"Drake, wait, let me explain."

Again, no response except for the eloquent rigidity of his back.

She ran ahead of him and stopped at his room, splaying herself in front of his door so he couldn't enter without hearing her out first. "I didn't tell her about Charlotte."

"Don't even mention her name," he gritted through clenched teeth.

"No, it's true. I didn't tell Madame Rulanka anything about your sister. All I did was ask her to warn you off, using your own ghost."

Annoyed confusion flitted over his features. "My own ghost?"

"Yes, remember, you said you might be convinced that I was telling the truth if your own ghost crawled into bed with you?"

His face hardened again. "I was being facetious. Surely you didn't expect me to believe that?" He answered his own question. "Of course you didn't— that's why you brought Charlotte into it."

"But I *didn't*."

"Then how did that fraud know about my sister?"

Gina had been wondering that herself. "I don't know—I guess she had other sources."

"You are the only one here who knows about Charlotte."

She knew it looked bad, but . . . "Well, I didn't tell anyone. Look, she must have found out from someone else." Then she remembered something else. "She mentioned Char—your sister's last name. I didn't even know her married name—you never mentioned it."

"You probably had your newspaper friends look it up."

So he was on that kick again, was he? "I don't *have* newspaper friends," she reminded him. "Though Madame probably does."

He just regarded her coldly, and she regretted ever thinking she didn't like his amused twinkle. *Can I have it back now, please?*

He reached for the keyhole under her outstretched hand and unlocked the door.

"You've got to believe me," Gina pleaded.

"How can I, after all the stunts you've pulled? Trying to scare me off, setting me up to tour the West, pretending to be a ghost ... ? Those were bad enough, but this? I thought better of you." With that, he pushed open the door, shunted her aside and entered his room, shutting the door in her face.

His disappointment was even harder to take than his anger. As Gina regarded the closed door, she wished she'd never even met Madame Rulanka. She'd give anything to be back on easy terms with Drake, to not have him so angry with her. What could she do to make him believe her? Heartsick, she pounded on his door in sheer frustration.

It didn't do any good. Nothing but cold silence came from behind it. And the hallway was beginning to fill. The show must be over. Well, she didn't care. She would stand here and pound on his door all night if that's what it took to get him to listen.

She raised her fist again, but a hand caught hers before it connected with the door. In surprise, Gina realized the hand belonged to Esme—the demure yet strong housekeeper.

"Do you really want to make this kind of scene?" the housekeeper asked softly, looking incongruous in her chick costume. "Word might get back to the Major and I won't be able to protect you."

"Who cares? I probably don't even have a job anymore the way Drake is acting."

"Well, you won't have one at all if you continue in this way." Then, more gently, she added, "Why not give him some time to calm down?"

Gina sagged. Esme was right—and it wouldn't do

any good to pound on Drake's door anyway. He'd just ignore her.

Esme led her away, toward the servants' quarters at the other end of the wing.

"What am I going to do?" Gina wailed.

Esme patted her hand. "Don't worry, you'll think of something."

Unfortunately, Esme had more faith in Gina than she did in herself. "Is there something *you* can do?" The head housekeeper seemed to have vast, strange resources that Gina could only imagine.

"No, I'm sorry. I wish I could, but I have tampered enough in your life."

"Well, tamper some more! You and your hope chest got me into this mess. Can't you at least get me out of it?"

Esme regarded her sternly. "I was not responsible for this particular mess. You managed that all on your own."

There was some truth in what she said. Gina might not have told Madame Rulanka about Charlotte, but since she had passed on other information, it did look bad. Numbly, she allowed the housekeeper to lead her to her room, where she sank down on the bed to be comforted by Scruffy.

This was all Madame Rulanka's fault. If she had done exactly what Gina had told her to, Drake might still be speaking to her.

Wait—that was it. What if she could get Madame to tell Drake the truth about what had happened? Gina still had the leverage she needed, if Madame would agree.

Gina grabbed the newspaper clipping from its hiding place and rushed off to the tower. Now that the show was over, Madame was bound to be waiting for her to fulfill her part of the agreement.

Sure enough, this time Rath didn't even hesitate when she knocked on the door, but let her in right away.

Madame was still dressed in her gypsy outfit, but she looked tired underneath the heavy makeup. "Do you have the proof?" she asked, her hand outstretched imperiously.

"Yes, but first, tell me why you didn't stick to our agreement."

"What do you mean?"

"You were supposed to warn Drake away with his own ghost, not his sister's."

She shrugged. "Wasn't this more effective?"

Not from Gina's end. "Where did you learn about Charlotte, anyway?" Maybe if she could prove that Madame Rulanka had ferreted out Charlotte's name, Drake wouldn't be so mad at her.

"From Charlotte herself," Madame said calmly.

"What?"

The spiritualist regarded her with amusement. "I know I said that the spirits sometimes need help . . . but not always."

Was she saying what Gina thought she was saying? "But *I* gave you that information on Sasha and Poopsie."

"Yes, and several others," Madame said calmly. "But that was just to prime the other spirits, so to speak. Sometimes, they are quite willing to come forward to pass messages on to the living. The last few came through on their own—including Charlotte."

When Gina could do nothing but regard her numbly, Madame said, "I'm sorry if it wasn't what you wanted to hear, but I didn't even realize the spirit was addressing your mesmerist until he left."

Gina had no choice but to believe her—Madame obviously believed what she was saying. Even if she didn't, Gina doubted she'd ever get the truth out of her.

Madame held her hand out again. "The proof now, if you please?"

Numbly, Gina handed her the clipping, and Madame read it. "I see. Well, we shall just have to cancel our trip to Las Vegas in the New Mexico Territory, won't we?" She raised an eyebrow. "May I keep this?"

Gina shook her head and took the paper back. "I might need it again—to convince Drake."

As she left the tower suite, Gina felt totally defeated, all plans of proving herself to Drake lost. What could she tell him? That the ghost really *was* Charlotte?

Yeah, right. He'd really believe that.

She glanced down at the paper in her hand. Before her eyes, the article exposing Madame Rulanka as a fraud faded out, to be replaced by one lauding her success. Gina blinked in surprise, wondering if her eyes were playing tricks on her. But no, it had definitely changed—just like Marty's photo in *Back to the Future*. Spooky.

Well, it was nice to know she *could* change the future . . . but the article about Drake's death was still as bleak as ever.

When Mr. Feeney left, Drake tarried for a moment before leaving his office. In the week and a half since the Madame Rulanka debacle, his relationship with Gina had become very strained. It was an effort to remain civil each time he faced her, and, knowing she waited just outside the door, he didn't want to face her just yet.

A week and a half ago, his first, irate instinct had been to pack up and leave the resort, never to see her again. But once the flush of anger had faded, he realized that to do so would mean abandoning his patients . . . and giving Gina exactly what she wanted. She was the one who ran away from everything, not him. So, he stayed.

He had even planned to fire her and damn the consequences since her actions had shown she didn't deserve his consideration. But more than her livelihood was in question here. In his current position as mesmerist to the resort's influential guests, most of whom had nervous complaints, he needed to ensure some sort of stability. And causing a scandal by firing his assistant would not help that. Furthermore, explaining that he had done so because she had counterfeited his sister's ghost would not only make both of them appear more disturbed than his patients, but it would be difficult to prove.

And I wanted to marry this woman?

No, "wanted" was the wrong word. "Felt an obligation" was far more accurate. After the night of passion they had shared, he had felt honor-bound to offer her the protection of his name. Any fantasies he might have indulged in beyond that were just that—pure fantasy.

He had always dreamed of a wife who would be so much more than a mere ornament—a woman who would gladly warm his bed, bear him children, and enliven the many years to come with her warmth and wit. But Gina wasn't that woman. She had proven to be coldhearted and witless. How had he ever even considered her as his wife?

His one consolation was that there didn't seem to be a babe coming as a result of their union. So, he no longer felt any obligation whatsoever. He shook his head. He should have remained with his original vow to have nothing to do with women until he had fulfilled his promise to Charlotte.

He heard a soft knock on the door and Gina opened it tentatively.

He still couldn't help but tense at the sight of her. "Yes?" he asked coldly. "Is the next patient ready?"

"No, Mrs. Rutledge sent a note saying she is ill."

"Then we are done for the day," he said in a dismissive tone. He bent to gather up his notes, but Gina remained. "What is it?" he snapped.

She advanced a little farther into the room. "Please, I just want to—"

"Is this about a patient?"

"No—"

"Then I don't want to hear it." He'd heard enough protestations about her innocence. If he didn't believe them then, what made her believe he would now?

She bit her lip. "But what about Shorty's threats?"

"What about them?"

"He's been heard all over town, saying he's going to get you for embarrassing him twice."

Drake sighed. "I'm not worried about Shorty Callahan. He's all bluster. And if he hasn't followed through on his threats now, I doubt he ever will."

"He will if he gets drunk enough and works up the courage. After all, the newspaper article—"

"That's enough," Drake barked out. Damn it, could the woman think of nothing else? "I am well able to take care of myself." When she opened her mouth in an obvious protest, he added, "I want to hear no more on this subject."

She pouted. "All right, but how about Annabelle? Will you talk about her?"

"What about her? Is she very ill?" He had assumed it was just some sort of nervous female complaint— the sort a woman like Mrs. Rutledge was very susceptible to.

"No, I don't think she's ill at all. I think her husband made her send that note."

"And why would he do that?"

"Because there's been talk about you two."

"What sort of talk?" he asked in a warning tone. Was she going to mention that blasted article again?

"I've heard some men in the waiting room making comments to him ... comments about you seeing Annabelle all alone."

"I see many of my patients alone."

"But none of them are as beautiful ... or have such a jealous husband."

He scowled. He hadn't allowed Gina in on Mrs. Rutledge's sessions, fearing the woman would be too intimidated to talk freely. "If this is just a ploy to get me to let you in on her sessions, it isn't going to work." Gina still had this absurd notion that he was going to run off with Mrs. Rutledge.

She looked a little guilty. "Well, I do think I could help you with her, but that's not the reason I mentioned it. I think Mr. Rutledge is starting to suspect something is going on—and he told me he hasn't seen any improvements in her yet. I don't think he wants her to come back.''

"And why are you so concerned about Mrs. Rutledge all of a sudden?" Gina had done nothing but try to get him to drop her since he began seeing her.

"Well, it's like this. I know you aren't going to give up on her, so I figure I can help you cure her that much faster by setting Mr. Rutledge's mind at ease and helping you figure out a way to give her some backbone.''

Her arguments made sense. Setting aside his problems with Gina for his patient's benefit, he decided to discuss the case with her again. He had missed Gina's insights these past two weeks, and missed discussing the patients with her. Perhaps she would have some idea how to handle the woman. "It isn't that easy.''

He gestured her into a chair and seated himself. "You and I might think Mrs. Rutledge needs backbone, but *she* needs to be eased into that realization. After all, her reason for coming to see me is to correct those bad habits her husband frowns upon.''

Some of Gina's tension seemed to evaporate. "Have you been able to get her to open up about these bad habits?''

"A little. The problem is that she just can't seem to please her husband.''

"Isn't that her husband's problem more than hers?"

If it weren't for Charlotte, he might question Gina's interpretation, but after seeing how Charlotte's husband had browbeaten her into a sense of worthlessness, he couldn't deny that it was primarily her husband's fault that Mrs. Rutledge felt this way. "Perhaps, but that doesn't change the fact that she is in despair because of her husband's actions.''

And that very despair had caused Charlotte to take her life. He couldn't risk another death on his hands . . . not if he could prevent it. "She believes his opinion of her."

"So, we need to find a way to convince her she's not worthless and show her how to appease her husband, while making him comfortable with the fact that she's seeing you?"

"Yes, I supposed you could say it that way."

Gina frowned thoughtfully. "That's a tall order. Well, we can fix the last part by letting me sit in on your sessions." Before he could say anything, she held up a hand. "I'm not doing this to keep an eye on you—I really think it's necessary to make Mr. Rutledge agree to more treatment."

Unfortunately, she was right. "All right. I'll speak to Mr. Rutledge." Though he would find some other way to explain why Gina would now be sitting in on the sessions.

"Good," Gina said with a sigh. "Then maybe we can give her some ideas on how to appease her husband without groveling."

"We can work on that," Drake agreed. "But her primary problem is the first one you mentioned—convincing her she isn't as worthless as he makes her out to be."

Gina nodded, then said tentatively, "Maybe you could share Charlotte's experience with her . . . ?"

Rage erupted within him once more. "I told you never to mention my sister's name again."

She looked hurt at his outburst and Drake steeled himself against the pain in her eyes. He had no reason to feel guilty—Gina deserved anything he could heap upon her. In fact, he ought to be congratulated for being so forbearing as to speak to her at all.

He rose, preparing to leave. "Now, if there is nothing else?"

An answering spark of anger appeared in her eyes as she rose as well. "Oh, but there is. You may not want to hear this, but I'm telling you again that I had nothing to do with your sister's ghost appearing onstage."

"You're quite right. I don't want to hear it."

"But it's the truth!"

"The truth?" He sneered. "I doubt you have even a passing acquaintance with the truth."

Gina's fists clenched and she looked as if she would like to hit him, but refrained. "That was a nasty thing to say."

"But not undeserved."

"Yes, it was," she shouted back, her chest heaving with emotion. "And I'll prove it."

"Really?" he drawled. "How?"

"What would it take to convince you that I am who I say I am, that I didn't tell Madame Rulanka about Charlotte?"

He flicked a speck of dust from his sleeve. "I doubt you could provide any proof I would believe."

"Oh, yeah? How about if you mesmerize me? Would you believe me then?"

He froze. Why was Gina finally agreeing to let him mesmerize her? She must think she could fool him somehow. Well, he had ways of ascertaining if a person was truly mesmerized. And once he had her under his spell, he could learn once and for all the real reason why she was so eager to get him out of the resort.

He kept his voice even as he said, "I might . . . if I believe you are well and truly mesmerized."

"Then meet me here tonight after dinner," she snapped. "If you think you can handle the truth."

"Oh, I can handle it," he drawled. And he dearly wanted to know exactly what it was.

Chapter Fourteen

Eager to learn the truth about Gina's background and reasons for urging him to leave the resort, Drake arrived early to their meeting. As he played idly with the spinning disk, he wondered if he would finally get to the truth . . . and if he wanted to.

He had started out thinking of Gina as an impertinent servant, then was gradually charmed by that impertinence and captivated by her unreserved lovemaking to the point where he had been considering making her his wife. That, of course, was followed by her betrayal and his realization that she was nothing but a traitor.

The many faces of Gina. . . . What face would she display now?

She arrived and slipped in the door, closing it behind her. He held a chair for her, and once she was seated, she looked so nervous that his mesmerist instincts kicked in. "Don't worry—this won't hurt a bit."

She gave him a wary glance. "So you say."

Seating himself, he asked, "What is it you're so worried about?"

"I don't know what you're going to find when you go poking around in my mind."

That conjured up an interesting image, but he hurried to reassure her. "I simply want to learn the truth."

"But what if you ask questions that aren't related to it?"

How curious. What did she have to hide? "What are you afraid of?"

She frowned. "I don't know." She paused, then added, "It's hard to explain, but the main thing is, my thoughts and feelings are private. I don't want them laid out for just anyone to see."

By anyone, of course, she meant him since no one else would be present. He had run into this sort of resistance before, but he hadn't expected it with Gina who was so open and frank in other ways. "What can I do to help you relax?" he asked softly.

"Give up your idea of mesmerizing me?" she asked hopefully.

"No, I don't think so. Not if you want to convince me you're telling the truth."

Her face fell. "I was afraid of that."

"So how can I help you relax?"

She thought for a minute, then said, "I would feel more comfortable if you promise to stay within certain boundaries."

"All right. What boundaries?"

"Well, I don't want you asking anything that's none of your business. Stick to asking about the reason I'm here and what really happened with Madame Rulanka."

"And why you want me to leave the resort, of course."

She waved her hand dismissively. "Of course—that ties in with the reason I'm here."

"But how will I know if I'm going outside the boundaries? To get at the truth may require some judicious questioning."

She fixed him with a warning glare. "Just make sure it *is* judicious. Use your judgment. If I wouldn't tell you something while awake, don't ask me the question while I'm under, okay?"

"All right." Now that he knew her fears, he felt safe in reassuring her that he wouldn't encroach beyond the borders she had established.

"And make sure I remember everything that happens during this session, too."

"Done." Raising an eyebrow, he added, "Now if you are quite through stalling . . . ?"

Her mouth twisted in a rueful grin. "I guess."

"Good." He ensured she was settled comfortably, but it was obvious she was finding it difficult to relax. Time for the spinning disk.

Focusing on the whirling patterns seemed to help her and though it took longer than usual, Gina eventually succumbed to his hypnotic commands and entered a mesmeric state.

Or, at least she seemed to. Drake didn't ordinarily doubt his patients, but in this case, it was best to be sure. Giving her the suggestion that she had lost all feeling in her left hand, he concealed a pin in his hand, and pricked her thumb. Though a small drop of blood beaded at the site, she evinced no reaction. She must be truly mesmerized.

With a sigh, Drake regarded Gina. It was a heady feeling, having her under his control, her mind open to anything he might suggest. Odd that she had given him no prohibition on planting suggestions in her mind, only in delving within her thoughts and feelings.

Keeping that in mind for later, he formulated his questions carefully, starting with the simplest first. "What is your name?"

"Regina Marie Charles."

So she hadn't lied about that, anyway. "Where are you from?"

"Richmond, Virginia."

So far, so good. Now for the test. "What year were you born?"

"Nineteen seventy-three."

Impossible. Yet she still seemed to be in a mesmeric trance. How could she lie? Incredulously, he said, "This is eighteen eighty-five. How do you explain the fact that you were born over eighty years after this date?"

"I time traveled."

"How is that possible?" he muttered to himself.

Apparently under the belief he was addressing her, Gina answered, "I don't know."

He still couldn't believe it. Wondering if her story would stay consistent, he asked, "How was the time-travel accomplished?"

"I don't know," Gina repeated.

That simple answer was telling . . . and disturbing. Mesmerized subjects were very literal. If Gina had been awake, she would have understood the intent of his question and answered appropriately. Since she hadn't, she must be telling the truth.

But how could he believe her? He rephrased the question. "Describe the events surrounding your trip from the future to the present."

"I went with you and Scruffy to the ruins—"

"With me?" he asked, interrupting.

"With your ghost," she said in a matter-of-fact tone. So she still believed that. "Please continue."

"I went with you and Scruffy to the ruins of The Chesterfield and you found a hope chest. You called me over to look inside. I opened it, and found a bunch of junk."

"What kind of junk?"

"A badge with a point broken off, a damaged brass nameplate, a broken chain, a pair of rusted handcuffs, and a dueling pistol with the grip half-melted."

"What happened then?"

"I picked up the pistol, felt very dizzy, and the next thing I knew, I was back in the past, with Esme Sparrow bending over me."

He frowned. Her story was consistent, but it was also preposterous. So, what about the rest of her story? "And why do you want me to leave the resort so badly?"

"Because if you don't, you will die on December 22 in a fire with your lover, Annabelle Rutledge."

"Ridiculous," he exploded. "How could you possibly know this?"

"Because the article said so," she reminded him.

This was getting him nowhere. "Annabelle Rutledge is not my lover," he stated firmly. Maybe if Gina heard it in the mesmeric state, she'd finally believe it. The only woman he was even attracted to was Gina, and she had betrayed him.

Curious now, he asked, "And if I leave the resort as you wish, what will happen then?"

"Then I will have accomplished my task and can go home."

For some odd reason, that bothered him. She only

cared about saving his life so she could go home? "Why would you want to go back?" Especially since she had been treated so badly there.

"It's home," she said simply. "It's where I belong."

"What is waiting for you there that is so important?" Certainly it wasn't her mother or her fiancé—both had proven to be unworthy of her.

"Television, microwave ovens, cars, computers, movies, hot showers, shopping malls, drive-through hamburger stands, ice cream—"

"That's enough." As Gina obediently fell silent, he realized he hadn't understood half her words, though they had been filled with a longing that made them ring true. Could she really be from the future? Or did she just possess a very active imagination?

He decided to switch tacks and get to the truth about Charlotte's appearance at the seance. "Who told Madame Rulanka of Charlotte's death?"

"Charlotte."

"What?" Her answer made no sense. "Impossible."

When Gina didn't elaborate, he said, "Explain, please."

"Madame Rulanka said Charlotte's ghost contacted her."

"And you believed her?"

Gina wavered for moment. "I'm not sure."

"And what did you tell Madame Rulanka about Charlotte?"

"Nothing."

He asked the question in several different ways, but her answer was always the same—Gina had told Madame Rulanka nothing about Charlotte, and Madame claimed Charlotte had appeared on her own. In the face of Gina's indecision about whether to believe in Charlotte's ghost herself, he was inclined to believe her. In this, anyway. Madame had clearly found out about his sister elsewhere and merely claimed Charlotte had appeared as a ghost to confuse Gina.

A great burden lifted from his shoulders. Gina hadn't betrayed him or Charlotte's memory after all. She really was telling the truth—about this, anyway.

And now that he had learned what he needed to know, he was finished with Gina and ought to bring her out of the mesmeric state. He toyed with the idea of implanting some suggestions in her mind to help her with some of her delusions, but decided it would be unethical since she hadn't agreed to treatment. Reluctantly, he brought her out of her trance, telling her she would remember everything that had happened.

Gina sat still for a moment, obviously searching her memories to see if he had abided by their agreement. Apparently satisfied that he had, she sighed in relief. Smiling, she asked, "Do you believe me now?"

"No, I'm afraid not," he said as gently as he could.

"Why not?" she demanded. "You heard it—my story was the same."

"Yes, that's the problem. If you continue to believe this delusion even in a trance, your problems must go a lot deeper than I expected. You need help, Gina, but I fear it is beyond my capacity to give."

Gina couldn't believe her ears. She just stared at him, speechless. He didn't even believe the truth when he heard it. What would it take to convince him? "I have proof. Remember the article about your death?" She pulled it out of her pocket and shoved it at him.

He declined to take it. "We've been over this before."

"That's not what I meant. Do you remember the article next to your obituary?"

"I believe so. What's your point?"

Ignoring his question, she persisted. "Humor me, here. What was the article about?"

He frowned. "I believe it was about a spiritualist being unmasked as a fraud."

Good—he remembered. "Yes, it was about Madame Rulanka."

"I'm not surprised," he said dryly.

"But I showed her that article right after her performance," no need to reveal why, "telling her what city she was going to be unmasked in, and as soon as she decided to cancel her engagement in that city, the article changed."

His skeptical eyebrow rose. "Changed to what? A ghost of itself?"

"Very funny. No. Here, see for yourself."

She thrust the paper at him again, and this time he took it.

He skimmed the article. "Are you saying that the article changed to praising this fraud when you told her about the original article?"

"Yes, I saw it myself. It changed right before my eyes." When he didn't say anything, she said, "You do believe me, don't you?" He had to.

He shook his head sadly. "No, but I believe you are more ingenious than I ever gave you credit for. This is obviously not the same paper, but a clever reproduction."

"But it has the same tear as before—the tear you put in it. Look," she insisted, pointing at the jagged rip in the corner.

He fingered the edge, then said, "Nice touch. I assume you tore this one to match the other."

Damn, but the man was stubborn. Now thoroughly exasperated, Gina snatched the paper out of his hand. She folded it and put it back in her pocket, then decided it was time to pull out the big guns. "Okay, bud. I didn't want to do this, but we're just going to have to talk to Esme about this."

"Miss Sparrow?" he said incredulously. "Why would you want to bring her in on your delusion?"

"Because it's not a delusion. It's the truth—and she'll verify it. You'll believe me if Esme says so, won't you?"

"Miss Sparrow is too sane and practical to believe in time travel, ghosts, and other such nonsense."

"So if she corroborates my story, you'll believe it?" Gina persisted.

"All right," he conceded. "If Miss Sparrow validates your story, I will have no choice but to reconsider. However," he paused and looked at her sternly, "you must promise me something in return."

"What?"

"If Miss Sparrow doesn't corroborate your story, you must agree to seek professional help."

Gina swallowed hard. What kind of help did he have in mind? "Not a mental institution," she said. "Just seeing a doctor, you mean. Right?" If for some reason Esme chose not to confirm her tale, she didn't want to be stuck somewhere else come December 22.

"I'm not leaving out the possibility of an institution," he said firmly. "If you become a danger to yourself or others, it may be necessary."

So, he thought she was nuts. Well, she'd known he felt this way all along, but the realization that he would have no hesitation in shutting her up in one of those hellholes hurt. "How could you think of doing that to me? I wouldn't wish that fate on my worst enemy."

"Nor would I," he asserted, "unless it were absolutely necessary. So, are we agreed?"

She wasn't at all sure Esme would be willing to tell all she knew about the time travel. But if she didn't, Gina was sunk. Standing, she said, "Agreed. Okay, let's go." Sheesh, what she had to go through just to save this stubborn man's life.

"Go?"

"Yes, let's find Esme. I want to get this over with now."

"If you insist," he said with a sigh, though it was obvious he thought she was about to be disappointed.

She just hoped he was wrong.

They found Esme still at work, taking care of a few last-minute details for the day, and pulled her aside into a vacant sitting room where they all stood in a circle facing each other.

Folding her hands primly at her waist, Esme said, "Now, what is this all about?"

Drake spoke first. "Miss Charles has told me a rather unusual story regarding her origins and she insists you will be able to confirm it."

Esme gave her an admonitory look and Gina's heart sank. Before Esme could open her mouth and condemn her to life in an antiquated mental institution, Gina blurted out, "I had to tell him. He won't believe me any other way."

Drake glanced uncertainly at the two of them. "You mean she already knows this story?"

"Yes, of course," Gina said in exasperation. "I told you once before—it's her fault I'm here at all." Turning to Esme, she said, "Tell him."

When Esme did nothing but stand there looking

uncertain, Gina added, "Please? If you don't, he's going to lock me up in a mental institution forever and I'll never be able to accomplish my task."

Esme sighed, then indicated they should all sit. "All right," she said briskly. "What would you like to know, Mr. Manton?"

Gina began, "Tell him about the—"

"No," Drake interrupted. "I wish to hear Miss Sparrow's version without your interference."

"Okay," Gina said, not without trepidation. "So long as it's the real story."

Esme gave Drake a stern look. "First, I must have your word that none of what you are about to hear will ever be repeated to anyone outside this room."

Gina relaxed. If Esme was extracting this promise from Drake, it must mean she was about to tell the truth.

"Agreed," Drake said. "Now, if you will explain how Miss Charles came to be here?"

"She arrived at The Chesterfield on the summer solstice."

"From . . . ?" Drake prompted.

"From the future."

Whew. Gina's shoulders slumped in relief. For awhile there, she had been wondering if Drake was right and she was crazy. But Esme's simple statement had exploded Drake's theory all to hell. He looked a little shell-shocked, too, as he stared at Esme with his mouth open.

"Are you quite all right, Mr. Manton?" the housekeeper inquired solicitously.

Gina suppressed a giggle. Esme's matter-of-fact tone seemed wildly at odds with the words that had just issued from her mouth. Drake had to believe her now.

"I beg your pardon," Drake said slowly. "Did you just say that Miss Charles was from the future?"

"Yes," Esme said simply.

"Did she tell you to say that?"

"Of course not," Esme said reprovingly. "No one could coerce me to say something that isn't true."

"Of course not," Drake murmured, still looking stunned. "Then how do you explain this extraordinary assertion?"

Esme smiled at him. "Quite simply, I don't. I never explain myself."

Gina suppressed another laugh and silently wished Drake luck in getting anything out of Esme. Gina had been trying for months without success.

Looking taken aback, Drake visibly regrouped. "Then perhaps you could tell me about Miss Charles's task?"

"I don't think that's necessary. I'm quite certain Miss Charles has explained it admirably herself."

"Then the article is true? I really am going to die on December 22?"

Esme primmed her mouth at him. "It is the most likely possibility at this juncture . . . though not entirely immutable."

Drake shook his head slowly. Gina knew how he felt. Dealing with the reality of time travel and ghosts was hard enough, but knowing the time and method of your own death must be really creepy.

"So, there is also a possibility I may not be killed on that date?"

Displaying annoyance for the first time, Esme said, "Miss Charles showed you that it is possible to change your fate, as she did Madame Rulanka's. But if you do nothing, your fate will remain the same."

Now, how had Esme learned of Madame Rulanka's

changed history? Never mind, Gina didn't want to know—the housekeeper's knowledge was too spooky already.

Drake frowned. "I find this very difficult to believe."

"That's quite obvious," Esme said testily. "I should not be speaking of this at all, but you have been so intractable, it seemed necessary."

He glanced at Gina. "How do I know you are not saying this to keep Miss Charles from going to an institution?"

Esme considered that for a moment. "I suppose you don't. However, why would I jeopardize my own freedom to confirm her story? If she is judged insane, would I not be risking the same judgment?"

Good point—and Gina could see Drake thought the same. But he was obviously still not convinced.

"I would still like some sort of proof," Drake said firmly.

Esme's eyebrows rose. "Really, Mr. Manton. You have my word. What other proof do you need?"

He looked a bit taken aback, but rather than be rude and answer her question, he turned to Gina. "Where is this pistol that is supposed to have sent you back?"

"I told you—I don't know."

"And the hope chest?"

"I don't know—I haven't seen that either."

"It is in my room," Esme said.

Turning to Gina with an intent look, Drake said, "You've never been in Miss Sparrow's room?"

"Of course not," Esme said. "That is the only place where I can be alone. I don't encourage the girls to visit me there."

Gina grinned. *Don't allow the girls to visit is more like*

it. "That's right," she confirmed. "I've never been inside."

"Then describe the chest to me," Drake ordered.

Gina wasn't quite sure where he was going with this, but she did as he asked. "It's wooden, with brass handles, carved flowers all around and her initials on the front. Oh, and there are little drawers at the bottom." Curious, she asked, "Why do you want to know?"

He turned to Esme. "If possible, I would like to see this chest with my own eyes. May I?"

Esme hesitated, then said, "I suppose, if it will help convince you." She rose and headed for the door. "Follow me."

As they followed her, Gina wondered what kind of room the odd housekeeper would have. When Esme unlocked the door and ushered them inside, Gina was disappointed to find it altogether ordinary. Oh, it had more comforts than the girls' rooms did, and was a bit more frilly than she had expected of the no-nonsense housekeeper, but there was nothing otherworldly about it.

Drake seemed to notice none of it, though. Instead, his attention was riveted on the chest at the foot of her bed. Even Gina was surprised to see that it was exactly as she had remembered, only much newer-looking, of course.

He knelt to raise the lid, and Gina cried, "No, don't."

He stopped with an inquiring look. "Why not?"

"Because the last time I opened that chest, it sent me over a hundred years back in the past."

Drake hesitated and gave Esme a questioning look.

"It's quite all right," she assured him. "The time

portal only activates on the solstices, and there is nothing inside to worry about now.''

Oh, that's right. Feeling a little foolish, Gina just shrugged as Drake raised his eyebrows. "Go ahead," she said. She wanted to know what was inside, too.

She crowded close behind him as he opened the lid, wondering what they would find, if anything. She expected it to be empty, but there was clothing inside.

Looking perplexed, Drake said, "Where are the handcuffs, the badge, and the other things?"

Esme merely smiled. "Is that what she found? I wouldn't know—they haven't been placed inside yet."

At Drake's confused expression, Gina added, "I saw them in the future, remember? I guess they get put in the chest sometime between now and then."

He nodded slowly, and she hoped that confused expression meant he was finally beginning to believe her.

"What's this, then?" he asked, poking at the clothing inside.

Gina took a closer look. "Oh, those are my clothes."

"Yours?"

"Yes—that's what I was wearing when I arrived here. From the future," she reiterated, just to push her point home.

Giving her an odd look, Drake lifted her jeans from the chest and examined them closely. Though jeans weren't unheard of in this time, they didn't have the sophisticated manufacture of hers. The stitching and zipper seemed to fascinate him and the Velcro on her tennies even more so.

Gina watched him with a small smile on her face. "So do you believe me now?"

He handed the jeans to her with a faraway expression. "I don't know. . . ."

Feeling something hard in the pocket of the jeans, Gina fished inside and came out with a quarter. Handing it triumphantly to Drake, she said, "Here, read this."

He peered at it. "United States of America," he read. "Quarter dollar."

"No, the other side."

He turned it over. "In God We Trust, nineteen ninety-one."

He stood there stunned, just staring at the quarter for a few minutes as Gina silently urged his skeptical brain to believe in the evidence of his own eyes.

"It's true," he murmured, his eyes full of wonder. "You really are from the future."

Gina rolled her eyes. "Sheesh, it's about time."

And now maybe she could convince him to leave the resort to save his skeptical hide.

Chapter Fifteen

Drake handed the coin to Gina and turned blindly to leave. He didn't know where he was going, he only knew that he had to be somewhere else—anywhere else. With his world turned upside down, he needed to think about it, put it into perspective, find some way of dealing with it.

As he stumbled down the corridor to his office, he was vaguely aware of Gina following him, though she was part of what he was fleeing. He dropped into a chair and buried his face in his hands, his head whirling.

It was difficult to believe something so impossible, yet he had no choice. His own scientific studies had proved time and time again that Occam's Razor was valid—the simplest explanation, no matter how ridiculous, was usually correct. So, rather than believe that Gina and Miss Sparrow had gone out of their way to concoct an elaborate charade with increasingly complex props for no discernible purpose, he had no choice but to believe they were telling the truth.

Once he did that, everything else fell into place. All he had to do was believe this one absurd thing—that Gina had traveled through time—and everything else followed with perfect logic.

"Drake, are you all right?" Gina asked, concern in her voice.

No, he wasn't all right. She had just forced him to believe the impossible. Not only that, but she had predicted the date and manner of his death. "You were telling the truth," he said in wonder.

"Yes, I was."

She would have been within her rights to chastise him for not believing her, but she looked more worried than upset. "I'm sorry I didn't believe you."

"It's all right," she said soothingly. "It's difficult even for me to believe."

All of a sudden, he felt an overwhelming urge to know more. He raised his head. "Do you still have the article with you?"

"Yes."

"May I see it?"

She drew it out of her pocket with an apprehensive expression and handed it to him. He smoothed it out and read it again, this time treating it as a factual account instead of mere fiction.

"You see?" Gina said. "You must leave the resort right away."

Drake shook his head slowly. "This part about Mrs. Rutledge can't be true. I would never have an assignation with a married woman." Especially one so timid who reminded him of his sister. "Surely you know that."

"That's what your ghost said, too." But she didn't sound convinced.

"So, if this one thing is wrong, perhaps the rest of it is as well."

She shook her head. "I'm sorry, but that doesn't make sense. Even if they have that one part wrong, I doubt they would misreport two deaths by fire."

Unfortunately, she was probably right. "True."

"So, you'll leave now?" she asked hopefully.

Leave the resort to save his own skin when he was still needed here? "I cannot—not until I have helped Mrs. Rutledge. I can't abandon her to the same fate that claimed my sister, not if I have the means to stop it. And now that her husband has agreed to let her continue to see me . . ."

"That again?" Gina exclaimed in exasperation. "But if you don't leave, you'll die. And you'll never be able to join your sister—you'll remain a ghost, wandering around Hope Springs for the rest of your life . . . er, death. Whatever." She waved a hand impatiently. "Besides, you're risking Annabelle's life, too."

"But I risk it just as much if I abandon her to her husband."

"Are you *crazy*? She's the one person you must avoid at all costs. If you're never with her, then you can't die together."

"Actually," he corrected her, "I must only avoid her on December 22. I'm not in danger until that date, right?"

She regarded him doubtfully. "I'm not so sure it's that easy."

"Then I shall just have to carry a bucket of water around with me at all times."

She scowled. "That's not funny. But it's not a bad idea. . . ."

"I don't understand your concern. You've done your best to accomplish the task you were sent here to do, and I appreciate it. But if everything is as you say, you will be allowed to go home either way, whether I live or not."

Angry sparks flashed in her eyes. "But I don't want to go home if you're dead."

He stared at her, puzzled. "Why would my death make you want to stay here?"

"That's not what I meant at all," Gina said, looking flustered.

"Then what did you mean?"

"Oh, never mind." Suddenly, her face brightened. "I know—why don't you come with me?"

"Go with you? To the future?"

"Sure, why not? You'll love it there."

He frowned, not quite as sure of it as she. "I don't think so."

"Why not?"

"What would I live on? How would I support myself?" From everything Gina had told him, his skills would be obsolete in her time. "No, I'm better off staying here, in my own time."

"Fine," Gina snapped. Then, with a glare, she flounced out of the office, muttering under her breath.

As Drake watched her go, he realized that he should have recognized before now how very different Gina acted from the women of this time. But if this was how women acted in the future—stubbornly independent and outrageously frank—he wanted no part of it.

On the contrary, a small voice whispered. If Charlotte had been born into such a world with such an attitude, perhaps she would still be alive today.

It was now mid-November and Drake had come little closer to helping Mrs. Rutledge deal with her husband. He knew it could take years before she was cured, but he didn't have years. He had only five weeks left before the date arrived that was now burned into his brain.

Between Mrs. Rutledge's slow progress, his own looming death prediction, and Gina's unrelenting pressure to leave, Drake was nigh unto needing the help of a mesmerist himself. To save his own sanity, he had finally convinced Gina to ease up a little, but the stubborn woman insisted on having the last word. She had plunked down a bucket of water in his office, and checked it ostentatiously each morning to ensure it was full.

She had intended it to remind him of his coming doom, but he found it rather amusing. To humor her, he decided to leave it where it was. Besides, it couldn't hurt. . . .

Drake checked his watch. It was time for the last appointment of the day, Mrs. Rutledge. He had increased her sessions to twice a week, but even that didn't seem to help a great deal. She had become more forthcoming and seemed to trust him, but had made little progress in dealing with her husband. At Gina's insistence, he had agreed to be a little more forceful this time, in hopes that would yield results.

Gina ushered Mrs. Rutledge into the office then sat in the corner as usual. Gina had promised to keep quiet while playing this propriety role, but that didn't keep her from taking notes and giving him her plain-spoken opinion after each patient's session.

And, to tell the truth, he didn't mind. Sometimes she caught things he didn't or had an insight that gave him a fuller understanding of his patients' problems.

But when she had tried to convince him to install a small couch for his patients to lie on, he put his foot down, fearing his female patients would become alarmed if they had to lie down in the presence of a man. Instead, he seated Mrs. Rutledge in the comfortable chair they had compromised on. How odd—even after all these sessions, the woman still seemed a bit nervous in his presence.

"So," Drake said in a calming tone, "how did the past few days go?"

Mrs. Rutledge plucked uneasily at her skirt. "Well, Clyde says—"

"I'm not interested in what Clyde says," Drake interrupted. "I'm interested in what *you* say."

"But he's my husband. I must honor and obey him." She looked uncertain, which he had to admit was an improvement over the fear and excessive timidity she had originally displayed.

"Of course you must," Drake soothed and ignored the gagging sounds Gina made in the corner. "But he's not the one I'm trying to help. You are. So, I need to know how you feel and think." Though he wished he could get the man into his office—Clyde was really the one who needed help.

"Oh," she said in a small voice. "I see. But I need to tell you what Clyde thinks first. Is that all right?"

Gina sighed in frustration, but Drake ignored her and nodded at Mrs. Rutledge. At least he had made some progress if she were able to question him this way. "Yes, of course."

"He—he says it's not working fast enough."

"What isn't?"

"Breaking my bad habits."

Drake suppressed a groan of frustration. Even after all this time, he hadn't been able to convince her that it was her clod of a husband with the problem, not her.

Drake felt so inadequate. Nowhere in all his readings had he found advice on how to help a woman stand up to her husband. Nor had it even been hinted that such a thing was desirable. What should he do? Perhaps, as Gina suggested, he had been too subtle. Time to spell things out a little more clearly.

"Your only fault," Drake said softly, "is a tendency to believe everything your husband tells you."

He could tell she wanted to believe, but it was difficult to overcome years of abuse. "But I must, or he becomes very angry."

The apprehension in her eyes sparked a question in his mind. "Angry, how?"

She averted her gaze. "He yells at me and . . . and he throws things."

And that must be very difficult for such a sensitive soul. "Does he do anything beyond that?" he asked gently. "Does he hurt you?"

She shook her head violently. "No!" But she wouldn't meet his gaze as she rubbed her left arm.

Anger surged through him, but before he could pursue this line of questioning, Gina bolted out of her chair with a militant expression and yanked up the sleeve on Mrs. Rutledge's dress to reveal several bruises. "Then how do you explain that?" she demanded, pointing at the area the woman had been rubbing.

As Mrs. Rutledge shrank away from her with a small

sound of distress, Drake glared at Gina and motioned her back to her seat. He had been leading up to the same question, but he hadn't planned on being quite so blunt about it. Gina glared back, but complied.

"He didn't mean to," Mrs. Rutledge said defensively, smoothing her sleeve back down over the evidence of her husband's ire. "He doesn't know his own strength."

"And has he hit you?" Drake asked with a warning glance at Gina.

Mrs. Rutledge shook her head, but she wouldn't raise her head or meet his gaze.

"He has, hasn't he?" Drake made it more of a statement than a question.

"Only a few times," the woman said with a pleading expression. "And only when I made him very angry with my wicked ways."

Drake could tell Gina wanted to jump in again, but he didn't need any help in handling this. He gave her another warning glance. "What wicked ways?" he asked softly.

"Speaking to strange men," she whispered. "Reading novels, and . . ." she covered her burning cheeks with her hands, ". . . being vain." A sob escaped her lips. "I'm so ashamed."

Further questioning revealed that the strange man in question had only been asking for directions, and her only vanity lay in taking a justifiable pride in her appearance and wanting to look nice for her husband.

"There's nothing to be ashamed of," Drake assured her.

"But Clyde says—"

"Never mind." Drake was quite tired of what Clyde said. He wanted to tell her that her husband's opinions were irrelevant, ignorant and stupid, but she would never believe him. "Clyde is blinded by jealousy," he said softly. "Can't you see that?"

"Yes, I—I suppose—he even accused me of having a lover, which he has to know isn't true . . . but what can I do about it?"

Just admitting that her husband was part of the problem was a huge triumph and Drake shared a brief victorious glance with Gina. "Unfortunately, there's nothing you can do to change him, only yourself."

"I've tried," she wailed, finally showing some spirit. "But I can't seem to please him, no matter what I do."

"That's more his problem than yours," Drake said, and Mrs. Rutledge regarded him as if he had just grown a second head.

Gina cleared her throat, much louder than necessary, and Drake took the hint. Now was the time to broach the subject they both had agreed upon. "Perhaps you might consider leaving him?"

Mrs. Rutledge gasped. "Leave him? You mean . . . go home to Mama for a little while?"

"No, I mean forever. Even . . . get a divorce."

He knew as he spoke the words that she would be appalled, and she didn't disappoint him. "How could I possibly? The disgrace . . . My family . . ." Then, as if it were relevant, she exclaimed, "I'm from Boston."

Maybe it *was* relevant. The blue bloods of Boston and the middle class who emulated them wouldn't dream of anything so lowering as divorce, no matter what the circumstances.

"I'm from Boston myself," he said, which gave him an idea that might help her. "Would I know your family?"

"I don't know," she said, seeming more confident

now that they were on a different topic. "My father is Robert Lawton—do you know him?"

"No, but I've heard of him." And there was nothing in the man's background to make Drake think he would abandon his daughter. "Wouldn't your family rather you be safe and happy, rather than battered and miserable?"

"But no one in my family has ever gotten a divorce," she said in shocked accents.

It was obvious she hadn't heard the important part of his sentence and had fixated on the one word that terrified her—terrified her even more, perhaps, than her husband.

It would be impossible to convince her to leave her husband now, but at least Drake had planted the seed in her mind. "Perhaps it needn't go that far," he said soothingly, ignoring the rude noise Gina made in the background. Especially if he were to contact her father and let him know exactly what had been going on with his daughter and her husband.

Mrs. Rutledge slumped in relief, and Drake said, "Instead, shall we work on making you less afraid of him?"

She looked undecided, so he added, "If you aren't afraid of Clyde, there will be no reason to leave him." It wasn't the real reason, but he needed to ease her into the idea of divorce, and to do that, he needed to help her find some self-assurance first.

"All right," she said hesitantly. "If you think that's best."

"I do," he assured her. She relaxed as he used the by now familiar passes of his hands and soothing words to help her slip easily into the mesmeric state. Once she was firmly ensconced there, he made her believe that Gina was her husband, to see how they interacted.

Gina rose and scowled down at Mrs. Rutledge. "You read too many novels," she scolded.

Her "wife" cringed, saying, "I'm sorry, but I love them so."

The sight riveted Drake with anger. He recalled Charlotte exhibiting similar behavior to her boor of a husband, though he hadn't recognized what it portended at the time. Now, however, he did, and he had to do something about it.

"No," he said gently to the cowering woman, though he wanted to throttle the man who had put her in this condition. "You are not a cowering slave. You are Clyde's wife, his helpmeet."

"His equal," Gina supplied. "No, his superior."

Well, he wouldn't quite go that far, but if it would help Mrs. Rutledge, he was willing to let it go. "He has no right to treat you badly, to bruise and beat you. You mustn't let him." But how could he provide an example to show her how to behave—a person she could emulate? He had no idea what her female relatives were like.

But of course—she had one right here. "When your husband speaks to you this time, pretend you are Miss Charles," he urged.

Gina's eyebrows rose, but she gave him a slight nod of agreement. The only side of Gina that Mrs. Rutledge knew was the confident way she acted around him, so it should work.

He nodded at Gina, and she turned to Mrs. Rutledge, reiterating her earlier statement. "You read too many novels."

Instead of cringing, this time Mrs. Rutledge said calmly, "Do I?"

"Yes, you know you do," Gina said, getting into her role as Clyde Rutledge.

"Then I shan't do it again."

Gina seemed a bit taken aback. She had obviously expected an argument, but was met instead with passive acceptance. She didn't seem to know how to handle it. Much as Clyde would react, Drake hoped.

But Gina gamely hopped in with several other accusations. Each time, Mrs. Rutledge answered calmly, turning her "husband's" accusations aside with calm and dignity. He could see the gracious, gentle woman she used to be before her husband had changed her, and it made him even more determined to help her.

Though her reserved handling of the situation wasn't the way Drake would have assumed Gina would react to the situation, this particular role seemed to work for Mrs. Rutledge.

So much the better. He didn't want her browbeaten—or beaten in any other way—before he had a chance to convince her to leave her husband.

Their time was about up, so he ended the session. But, fearing too much of a change would send warning signals to the angry Clyde, he didn't urge Mrs. Rutledge to remember what had happened during the trance this time. Besides, it might frighten her. Instead, he asked her to remember the confidence she had felt, and told her that when she needed it again in the future, she would remember just enough to give her the edge she needed.

Then, feeling rather pleased with himself, Drake ushered her out to where her husband waited, glad to see the waiting room was otherwise empty.

Gina watched him go, shaking her head. The woman was hopeless, if only he could see it. And though it was nice to finally be in Drake's confidence again, Gina wished she could recapture some of the closeness they had once had. Instead, he seemed to be getting closer and closer to Annabelle . . . just as the article promised.

Jealousy struck at the thought of Drake and Annabelle together, but Gina quickly pushed it aside. She couldn't let herself care about Drake, or anyone else in this time. In less than five weeks, she'd leave them all behind when she returned to the future.

Drake returned, rubbing his hands in satisfaction. "That went rather well, don't you think?"

"You're kidding, right?"

"I beg your pardon?"

Gina couldn't help being snippy. She agreed that the best thing to do was to encourage Annabelle to leave her husband, but since the wimp was unable to take care of herself, that meant Drake would probably have to leave with her. It was the only way to get Drake to leave the hotel, though it veered way too close to the article's accusation for Gina's comfort.

But she couldn't complain about that, so she picked on the first thing she could think of. "You need to be more forceful," she said in a quarrelsome tone.

His eyebrows rose. "Yes, I gathered you thought so from the rude noises you were making in the corner."

Gina shrugged, just a tad embarrassed. "Well, you won't let me talk, so that's the only way I could tell you what to do. You should have tried a little harder," she reiterated.

"But Mrs. Rutledge needs a gentle hand . . . surely you understand that."

"We don't have the time for it," Gina insisted. "We have to get you—and her," she added grudgingly, "out of the hotel as soon as possible."

"But she's not ready yet. What would you have me do? Kidnap her? I'd be no better than her husband."

"No, I just want you to live," Gina said in frustration. She couldn't bear the thought of him dying in that fire. And the threat was so real, she even imagined she could smell smoke.

Wait—that was no illusion. She *did* smell smoke.

She watched in horror as wisps of dark gray vapor curled in from beneath the door. Her heart stuttered like a jackhammer as she clasped a hand over her mouth and pointed.

As a distant voice yelled out a warning, Drake whirled around and grabbed the door knob. "Hot," he exclaimed, shaking his hand. He swiftly removed his coat and wrapped it around his hand, then opened the knob. A wall of flame roared up, flaring toward the ceiling.

As it reached greedy fingers toward Drake, Gina screamed. *Not now—it's too soon!*

Chapter Sixteen

Drake backed away, shielding his face with his arms. The flames subsided as fast as they had flared up and Drake saw that it wasn't nearly as bad as he had at first thought. The fire seemed confined to the doorway of the office, though the flames and smoke made it impassable. "The other door," he said.

Gina choked in the smoke behind him. "I just tried it. It's blocked," she said, fear in her eyes.

He had to do something. Wait—the water. He grabbed the bucket from beside his desk and hauled it to the door, but before he could dump its contents over the fire, he heard a deep voice bellow, "Ready, aim, fire!" and a deluge of water smacked them in the face.

He wiped the water out of his eyes to see the Major, Rupert, Jack, and a couple of bath attendants standing on the other side with empty pails. Filled, no doubt, from the nearby baths. Luckily, they had managed to get some of the liquid on the fire, and it fizzled out.

"Reload," the Major ordered and the others hurried off with the empty pails while Drake doused the surrounding area with the contents of his bucket, just in case an errant spark had escaped. When Jack and Rupert returned shortly, they zealously emulated him until the entire area was drenched.

Now, Drake could see that the fire had indeed been localized in the doorway, in a metal bucket of its own. Carefully grasping the handle with his ruined coat, Drake moved it out of the way so he and Gina could leave the smoke-filled room.

Though she was shaking with reaction and he wanted nothing more than to comfort her, they had too much of an audience. The commotion had attracted the notice of the guests, and the area was filling with people who had come to gawk.

The hotel employees were opening windows throughout the bathhouse to disperse the smoke, and were therefore too busy to disperse the guests until Miss Sparrow arrived with Jess Garrett, the police chief, in tow.

The chief quietly and efficiently shooed the guests out without ruffling sensibilities as Miss Sparrow gathered Gina into her arms to give her the comfort she needed.

Drake felt the need of comforting arms himself. Now that it was all over, the realization of how bad it could have been washed over him. Good God, they could have died. His knees turned weak and dizziness washed over him. It was entirely too close. To cover his weakness, he shakily leaned against a nearby wall and asked the police chief, "How did you get here so fast?"

"I was already at the hotel," Garrett answered. "Miss Sparrow sent a message asking me to check on a report of stolen jewelry."

"Lucky for us that you're here, then." And very convenient, too. Had the housekeeper somehow known he would be needed?

"Yes," Garrett said. "Let's see what we have."

As the Major sent the hotel staff to ensure no one was still lingering in the bathhouse, the police chief inspected the burned area. The door was blackened and scorched, and the paint and wallpaper next to it blistered and peeling. "The fire was here?"

"Yes," Drake answered. "The bucket was in front of the door."

They looked inside and found rags that had evidently been soaked in some flammable substance. "It was definitely set on purpose," Garrett muttered. "But the man who did this wasn't trying to burn down the hotel, or he would have used a more flammable container. It was probably a prank."

"A prank?" Gina exclaimed as she came over to join them. She seemed to have recovered from her fright and was now fighting mad. "It was more than that. Whoever did this also blocked the other doorway—we couldn't get out."

Garrett went around to check Gina's assertion, and they found that a chair had been wedged under the doorknob on the other side. Frowning, Garrett said, "This is a bit more serious. With one exit blocked by the chair and the other by fire, you wouldn't have any escape except from the second story window."

"We could have suffocated," Gina exclaimed. "Or died of smoke inhalation."

"Do you know who might wish the two of you harm?"

"I'll tell you who," Gina said. "It's that Shorty Callahan. He's made threats against Drake before."

Drake nodded. "Yes, we have reason to believe he may be an arsonist."

Garrett regarded them thoughtfully. "I've heard . . . rumors about Mr. Callahan, but nothing I have been able to confirm. Do you have proof?" When they shook their heads in the negative, he asked, "Did you see him in the hotel before the fire was set?"

"No," Gina said, "We were inside the office with the door shut. But that doesn't mean he wasn't here."

"Of course not," the police chief said, then asked the same questions of the rest of the hotel staff. No one had seen Shorty Callahan or anyone else who looked suspicious loitering around the bathhouse. Until someone had yelled fire, none of them had been there.

Garrett nodded. "I'll question the guests, then." Turning to the Major, he said, "You'll probably want to close off the bathhouse, at least for a day or two. The fire chief may want to take a look at the damage."

The Major wisely deferred to the police chief. "Of course. We'll need to clear out the smoke and repair the damage caused by the fire anyway."

"Aren't you going to arrest Shorty?" Gina demanded incredulously.

The police chief gave her a stern look. "Not unless we have some proof he is responsible for this."

"But—"

"However, you can be quite sure I will question him," Garrett added, overriding her objections. "And I will attempt to ascertain where he was at the time of the fire."

Before Gina could protest again, Drake said, "Thank you, Chief. I'm sure you'll do your best."

Gina glared at him, but she would have to be satisfied with that. Short of mesmerizing Shorty and wringing the truth out of him, there was nothing else they could do. And Drake sincerely doubted Shorty would ever allow himself to be mesmerized again.

After the police chief left and the staff reported that the rest of the bathhouse was empty, the Major drew himself up and boomed, "All right then, you heard the chief. Everyone out."

The few employees who were still left drifted away as the Major shooed them away like so many errant chicks. When Drake hesitated, the Major turned to him with beetled brows, obviously wondering why he wasn't following orders.

"I'd like a little more time," Drake explained. "I need to collect my papers and clean out my desk if I won't be able to get to them for a couple of days."

Major Payne grudgingly nodded, and Gina moved forward, saying, "I'll help."

Before he could object, Drake said quickly, "Thank you. It will go much faster with two people." He ushered Gina back into the smoky office, saying over his shoulder, "Don't worry, I'll lock up when we're through."

The Major gave them a suspicious glare, but pressing questions from the guests on the other side of the door claimed his attention, so he merely nodded and gave them a warning scowl.

Once the door closed behind the hotel manager, Drake felt relief that it was all over. And, knowing how shaken he had felt, he was surprised Gina hadn't succumbed to hysterics. But . . . was she really as tough as she appeared? He paused in the doorway as she busied herself with his papers. "That can wait," he said gently. "Are you really all right?"

He does care. Gina dropped the papers she'd been blindly pushing around and flew into his arms. "I was so scared."

"Me, too," he murmured, holding her close and stroking her hair.

Damn, it felt good. She needed this. "I thought I had done something wrong," she confessed. "I thought I somehow caused the fire to happen earlier rather than later."

He smiled down at her. "Well, you made a believer out of me."

"Does that mean you'll—"

He placed a finger on her lips. "Shh. Not now, please."

She nodded. She didn't feel like arguing anyway. She just wanted to be held, comforted. She snuggled into his rather squishy warmth, then looked up at him and wrinkled her nose. "You're wet. And you smell like smoke."

He smiled as he lifted a lock of her hair to his nose. "So do you."

In fact, the whole room stank of it, and she wanted nothing more than to get away from the reminder of fire. "What I really need is a hot bath," she said, longing for her tub at home with its endless supply of hot water and frothing, fragrant bubbles.

"I'll let you go then, so you can clean up."

She grimaced as he released her. "Thanks, but it doesn't sound all that great. All I have in my room is a washbasin . . . and tepid water. Makes it difficult to get the smell out of my hair."

"Why not use the bathhouse then?"

She shook her head regretfully. "Hotel employees aren't allowed to use the baths."

"I think you've earned it today." He smiled wickedly. "Besides, who will know? I'll lock up and no one will be able to get in. You can indulge yourself to your heart's content."

It sounded wonderful, but . . . "What if someone is still inside?" She hated the thought of being caught naked, vulnerable, and alone.

"The staff did a pretty thorough search, so I doubt anyone is, but I'll be your lookout if you prefer."

"It would make me feel better," Gina said. Though she put on a good face, she still felt a little shaky and definitely didn't want to be left alone.

"Then I would be most happy to be your lookout."

"Great," Gina said, and headed toward the open foyer and the entrance to the bathhouse.

He gestured her in with a wave of his hand. "Ladies to the right, gentlemen to the left."

"Oh, what the heck. I'll be a lady today." She headed toward the right and opened the first room she came to. With Drake's help, she figured out the antiquated spigot, but the water that came out was just barely warm and smelled funny.

"It comes naturally that way, from the mineral springs," Drake explained. "But for those who like it hot, The Chesterfield has the latest in luxury—a water heater."

He showed her how to light it, and they found a big supply of the linen cloths that passed for towels in this time, but no soap or shampoo.

"People don't usually bathe here," Drake explained. "They immerse themselves in the waters to cure their illnesses. But, occasionally, we have those who wish to bathe as well. Wait a moment."

As Gina unpinned her hair, he disappeared, then came back with a bar of Pear's soap. "I found it in the attendants' room," he said triumphantly.

Gina took the soap from him, knowing better than to hope for shampoo as well, and said, "Thank you. This is wonderful."

Smiling, his eyes sliding admiringly toward her unbound hair, Drake handed her a thin robe. "And you can put this on afterward."

She would have preferred thick, soft terry cloth, but it was better than getting back into her dirty uniform. Gina thanked him and when he just stood there, she asked, "Are you planning to stick around and wash my back?" It would sound like fun at any other time, but she felt too grungy to play right now.

He smiled and backed out, shaking his head. "I'll just be out here if you need me."

Once the door closed behind him, she sighed and turned on the water, figuring it should be hot by now. It was, and she gratefully stripped out of her soggy uniform, then stepped into the odd copper tub with a sigh. Ah, heaven.

She just soaked for a few minutes, enjoying the unaccustomed luxury until she couldn't stand her hair any longer. It was difficult to wash it this way, but she managed it, then cleaned the rest of herself.

When she finished, she felt a little guilty. Drake must be feeling just as dirty, but she'd left him sitting out in the hall, guarding her. Reluctantly, she got out of the tub and dried herself with the linen towels, then put on the robe. Raking her wet hair out of her face, she opened the door to find Drake waiting outside in a similar robe, his hair wet and slicked back, and looking squeaky clean.

"I used the room across the hall," he explained, "but I kept the door open in case you should call out."

"Oh," Gina said in disappointment with a longing

look back at the draining tub. "You mean I could've stayed there longer?"

"Did you want to?"

"Yes, I was just beginning to relax. But I used all the hot water."

He smiled. "Then come with me."

She followed him down the hall, admiring how the thin robe clung to the contours of his body. He led her to a door and opened it with a flourish.

"The ladies' bath," he said.

She reluctantly tore her gaze from his backside to look. Beyond was a large round pink marble pool taking up most of the circular room. The familiar mineral odor wafted up from the pool and steam rose faintly from it. "Wow, a giant hot tub."

"They keep it warmer, here," Drake said. "I think you'll like it." He gestured toward the pool and turned his back, obviously doing the gentlemanly thing. The pool looked so inviting, Gina couldn't help but succumb to its invitation. Who needed a swimsuit when it was just the two of them?

Slipping from her robe, she eased into the hot water and sighed, stroking to the middle. Ah, much better. She had never been skinny-dipping before, but if this was how it felt, she resolved to do it more often. The warm water caressed her body without the restrictions of clothing, making her feel a bit wicked.

At her sigh, Drake turned around and sat on the edge, his feet dangling in the water.

"This is great. Aren't you going to join me?" she asked, only her head visible above the warm water.

He looked startled, then nodded, his eyes dark and smoky. "I think I will."

To afford him the same courtesy he had shown her, Gina averted her eyes until she heard a splash.

She looked back to see Drake resting against the edge of the pool about five feet away, his arms outspread on the marble lip with his head back and relaxed as he floated in the welcoming water. My, my, he looked good—sleek, wet, and very, very sexy.

Tingles raced through her as she suddenly became very aware of him as a man. And as she bobbed up and down in the sensual pool, she felt the water move over her, caressing her in intimate places, places that yearned for Drake's touch.

How could he be so unaffected? Well, if it were up to her, he wouldn't be for long. She glided to the edge of the pool, out of reach yet still within full view, and copied his position. "Isn't this wonderful?" she asked in a low, throaty voice.

"Umm," Drake murmured. He opened his eyes lazily, and she knew the exact moment when he caught sight of her, for he froze, staring. "Wonderful," he breathed.

By emulating Drake's position with her arms outstretched on the lip, her breasts were visible, bobbing up and down, her aroused nipples peeking out with each gentle lap of the water.

As his eyes turned dark and smoldering, Gina's insides turned molten with longing, a deep heat that had nothing to do with the water and everything to do with Drake. She held her breath, wondering if she was going to have to make the next move or if he had figured it out yet.

Thank heavens, he was a fast learner. He pushed away from the side and stroked toward her, his gaze never leaving her face and breasts. Breathless, Gina couldn't wait any longer. She, too, pushed away from the edge to meet him halfway. As they met, skin to skin, she wrapped her arms and legs around him, gasping with the pleasure of her breasts against his chest, his hardness resting against the cleft between her legs.

Their mouths met in a hot, wet, hungry kiss that made her dizzy. Eons later, after nearly drowning in his kisses, she drew back, gasping for breath, and said, "More. I want more."

Reaching between them, she grasped him and tried to guide him inside, but he gasped, "Wait."

"Why?" She could tell he wanted her as much as she wanted him.

"Let's move to the side," he said.

Good idea—more leverage. They hurriedly moved to the side, and Drake positioned her with her back against the pool wall, raising her slightly so her nipples crested the water. Filling his hands with her breasts, he licked and sucked and nipped until she thought she would go crazy.

It didn't help that the lapping water was bringing the rest of her body to aching awareness as she floated free from the waist down. The only thing that kept her from floating away were Drake's hands on her breasts, and the cage of his legs holding her inside. Every once in awhile, she could feel his penis brush against her inner thighs and it was driving her crazy. She knew where she wanted him, and it wasn't poking at her legs.

She reached for him again, and this time he let her grasp him firmly. But instead of guiding him inside where she wanted and needed him, she prolonged the agony by stroking him, loving the feel of him in her hands.

He moaned with pleasure and glided his own hand down between her legs, sliding one finger inside her to drench himself in her moisture and titillate her overly sensitive nub.

Gina gasped as dizzying pleasure rolled over her, but she refused to succumb. Instead, they stroked and fondled each other as their eyes locked, their chests heaving.

But she couldn't hold back forever. All too soon, the sensations peaked, sending wave after wave of pleasure washing over her. It was too much. . . . She threw back her head and screamed with exultation, the only way she could release the sheer, raw emotion he engendered in her.

But there was no time to savor it as Drake thrust into her, their pelvic bones meeting as he seated himself to the hilt.

God, that feels good. It felt even better when he slowly began to rock within her, his eyes half-lidded as his dark, mesmerizing eyes spoke their need. She wrapped her legs around his waist, and his eyes closed as his face reflected his sole purpose. He drew her even closer, going faster now. His breath came in heavier and heavier gasps, and he buried his face in her neck as he thrust even harder despite the barrier of the water.

Watching his excitement had rekindled her own, and when Drake finally peaked with an exultant cry, she found herself following him over the edge, pulsing and quivering with exquisite completion.

They just floated there for a moment, holding each other and trembling with the aftermath of their love-making. Gina recovered first and lovingly caressed Drake's wet hair. "That was awesome," she whispered.

He gave her a gentle but thorough kiss. "You do

have a way with words," he murmured. "That was, indeed, awesome."

Yes, awesome and awe-inspiring as well. For Gina had realized something else. Drake was the only man who had ever truly made love to her—not acting merely on lust, not just slaking a need, but truly making love.

And when she realized that, she also finally recognized that she had fallen hopelessly and completely in love with him.

But her joy turned to ashes as she realized she could never have him, for come December 22, she would be going back home and he would be staying here—dead or alive.

Chapter Seventeen

Two weeks after they made love, Gina was still regretting it. Oh, not the actual act itself—that was wonderful. But the realization she'd come to still had the capacity to unsettle her.

Every time she was around Drake, she feared her newly discovered feelings would show on her face or in her manner, so she took extra care to be more flippant than ever. It was necessary because, though the event had been momentous for her, it was obvious he hadn't felt the same.

In the aftermath, they had floated in the marvelous giant hot tub for awhile and talked about various things, including the fact that women in the future were far more open about things like sex. Gina had initiated the discussion to assure him that she wasn't a loose woman by the standards of her time, but it had backfired.

He seemed relieved at being absolved of guilt for

bedding her, and it had the added consequence that he didn't seem to feel the need to renew his marriage offers.

Too bad. Though Gina had a very bad brush with one fiancé, the thought of marrying Drake didn't seem so awful. She wouldn't even mind staying back here in the past if Drake came along as part of the package. But only if he loved her as much as she loved him . . . which didn't seem possible after all the things she had done to him.

So, staying here was out. She'd just have to stick with her original plan and save the man's life, then catch the next time portal back to the twenty-first century.

She sighed. Now that that was settled, she needed something to do. Bored since the bathhouse and the offices were still closed to clean up after the fire, she decided to find Drake. Though a funny feeling shot through her every time she saw him—part love, part desire, part pain—she couldn't help but seek him out, wanting to spend as much time with him as possible.

Scruffy whined when she went to the door, so she took him along. The poor dog had been cooped up too much and she was beginning to feel guilty. As she passed through the hotel, she couldn't appreciate how festive it looked decorated for Christmas in its greenery and bright ribbons. All it did was remind her how little time she had left.

She found Drake in his room as usual and expected him to be studying his notes, but this time, the police chief was with him.

Scruffy fawned over Drake, and when he bent to scratch the dog's ears, Gina spoke to the police chief. "So, have you learned anything about Shorty?"

Garrett nodded toward Drake. "I was just about to tell Mr. Manton what I learned."

"Good," she declared as Drake rose. "Then you won't have to repeat it. What did you find out?"

He frowned, glancing around at Drake's room. "Perhaps we should find somewhere else . . . ?"

Oh, good idea. It might look odd if people found her in Drake's bedroom with two good-looking single men. And she couldn't afford to be banned from The Chesterfield now that she was so close to the winter solstice.

They found an unused sitting room and Garrett told them what he had learned, concluding, "We have been unable to place Mr. Callahan at The Chesterfield the night of the fire."

"He wasn't here?" Gina exclaimed. "But he had to be."

"I didn't say he wasn't here," Garrett corrected her. "I said we haven't been able to *prove* he was here."

"Have you been able to prove he was anywhere else?" Drake asked.

"I'm afraid not. He claims he was asleep in his room at Mrs. Zimmerman's boardinghouse at the time of the fire, but since no one saw him there either, I'm unable to verify his whereabouts."

"Well, it had to be Shorty," Gina exclaimed. Jeez, wasn't it obvious? "Who else could it have been?"

Garrett shrugged. "The fact is, ma'am, it might have been anyone. Without proof, I can't arrest Mr. Callahan."

"Did you even search his room?" Gina demanded. "To see if he had matches or rags?"

"Yes, ma'am, I did. But every gentleman carries matches, and it's no crime to possess rags, or every housewife in Hope Springs would be under suspicion.''

Her shoulders slumped. That made sense, but . . . "How about a pistol? Did you find a dueling pistol in his room?''

Garrett gave her an odd look and drawled, "Now why would you ask about that? Were there shots fired . . . or did someone hold a gun on you during the course of the fire? Is there something you're not telling me?''

"No, not at all, Chief," Drake interposed. "Miss Charles just has an overactive imagination.''

He shot her a warning look but she just shrugged, unrepentant. She had to find that pistol sooner or later. "Isn't there anything you can do? He's made threats against us several times.''

"I'm quite aware of that, which is why I'm keeping an eye on him. And the staff here at The Chesterfield has been alerted as well.''

"I'm sure you've done everything you can," Drake said firmly, casting Gina a quelling look. He rose and the police chief rose with him. "Please let us know if you learn anything else.''

"I will," Garrett said, then politely took his leave.

"Well," Gina said with a belligerent glance at Drake, "I don't believe for a minute that Shorty was sleeping at the time of the fire.''

"I don't either.''

"You don't? But you said—''

"I said the police chief had done all he could, which is true. He can't arrest anyone without proof.''

Gina snorted. "Ha. From what I hear, it was done all the time back in the old days—these days.''

Drake's eyebrows rose. "Perhaps in a more lawless area such as the West, but a man of Jess Garrett's caliber wouldn't stoop to manufacturing evidence or running a man out of town on a rail unless he had incontrovertible proof."

Shoot, he was right. Garrett did seem an honorable, upright, Dudley Do-Right kind of guy. A lot like Drake, in fact. Well, since Drake hadn't been able to convince Mrs. Rutledge to leave her husband yet and get them both out of harm's way, they had no choice but to find another way to get Shorty out of the picture. "We'll just have to take matters into our own hands, then."

Drake gave her a wary glance. "What do you have in mind?"

"Maybe we can scare him away."

"How? With the ghost trick? Oh yes, it worked so well before," he murmured.

"Very funny." Besides, it wouldn't work unless she could gain access to the room above Shorty's at the boardinghouse. "Do *you* have any ideas?"

"Yes, how about we just stay as far away from Shorty as possible?"

"I plan to, but if he's the one responsible for the fire on December 22, wouldn't it be better to get him to leave town?"

"Of course. But if he's the owner of the pistol you've been worrying about, I don't want to give him any more reason to use it on us."

"That's right—the pistol. Since you don't have it, and the Rutledges don't have it, Shorty *must* have it. We can't let him leave town until we get it."

"Wait a minute," Drake said, frowning. "There's

something I don't understand. I thought you said I would be killed in a fire."

"That's what the article said—you read it."

"Then why would the *pistol* be so important? Why would it be so significant to your task that it would send you back in time?"

She'd wondered about that, too. "Maybe a bullet ignites the fuse, or sets something on fire somehow. How would I know?" she asked, perturbed by questions she couldn't answer. "I'm not an arsonist. But I bet Shorty knows at least a hundred ways to start a fire with a gun."

"No doubt," Drake murmured.

"So, you'll help me?"

Drake looked startled. "Help you what?"

"Help me get the pistol from Shorty."

His answer was a brief and uncompromising, "No."

"Why not?"

"Because it's dangerous."

"And the threat of your death isn't?" she asked incredulously.

"We're not talking about my death here," he reminded her. "We're talking about your desire for a pistol which may or may not exist."

"Oh, it exists all right. Esme said so."

"Did she also say it belonged to Callahan?"

"No, but who else *could* it belong to? He's the arsonist. He's the one who wants you dead."

"I see your point, but it's still dangerous."

"Then I'll do it by myself," she declared.

"You'll do nothing of the kind," he said, sounding alarmed.

She raised her chin a notch. "All right, then I'll get Rupert to help me."

"You would involve that poor young man in yet another of your wild schemes?"

"It's not wild, and yes, if you won't help me search Shorty's room, I'll have to find someone else. I know I can trust Rupert."

Drake regarded her thoughtfully. "Is it that important to you to regain this pistol?"

"Of course it is." Jeez, didn't he remember anything she'd said? "I can't go home without it."

"And it's important that you return home?"

Again, she said, "Of course. What would keep me here?"

It was a very broad hint, almost a plea, for him to ask her to stay. But either he didn't pick up on it . . . or he didn't want to.

"I see," he said carefully. "Then, if it is that important to you, I'll help you find the gun."

Gina barely restrained herself from throwing her arms around his neck. "Great! It'll be just great. You'll see."

Before Drake could change his mind, Gina gathered up Scruffy and cornered the mesmerist early the next day to remind him of his promise. Reluctantly, he agreed to go down to Hope Springs with her.

Gina decided she would be too conspicuous in her uniform, so she put on the pretty green dress and covered it with a warm cloak. The chill December wind cut right through her, and she was glad of the shelter when they took the train spur down the few miles to the town. She didn't want to discuss their plans with passengers all around them, so she kept silent until they got off in Hope Springs and she was able to pull Drake aside.

"What do you have planned?" he asked warily.

"I'm not sure yet." Her only "plan" was to make it up as she went along. "First, we need to find his room. You heard Chief Garrett—Shorty is staying at Mrs. Zimmerman's boardinghouse. It shouldn't be hard to find."

"And once we're there, how do you propose to find Callahan's room?"

"I'll just ask Mrs. Zimmerman."

"You think she'll tell you?"

"Sure, why not? I'll tell her I'm Shorty's sister."

"And I?"

"You'll be my brother."

His eyebrow rose. "That would also make me Callahan's brother. You think she'll believe that?"

She glanced up at Drake, almost a foot taller than Shorty. "Well, maybe not," she conceded.

"Let's make it simple," Drake said. "We'll just tell her I'm your husband . . . if she asks."

"All right," Gina said with an odd look at him. She wasn't quite sure how to take that, but decided it didn't mean anything. He was just trying to be logical and efficient.

It was odd seeing the town from the perspective of the past after seeing it as it had changed in the future. Things were a little skewed, not quite the same, but not all that different either. It was disconcerting.

And she didn't remember seeing the boardinghouse in the future, so they obtained directions from the stationmaster. It was on one of the main streets, so they strolled casually in that direction, but the effect was spoiled when they had to huddle against the wind. Fearing poor Scruffy might be blown away, she carried him under her cloak.

As they neared the boardinghouse, Drake pulled her into a doorway, his shoulders hunched against the cold. "It's early yet. He might still be inside."

Darn, he was right. She hadn't thought about that. "I guess we'll just have to wait for him to come out, then. If we don't freeze to death first."

Drake glanced around at their meager shelter. "This won't do. Come, let's wait in the mercantile."

The mercantile lay across the street from the boardinghouse and had a display window in front that they could peer through, so it was a good idea. And, as they entered the store, blessed warmth surrounded them, courtesy of the prominent potbellied stove.

The storekeeper nodded politely and didn't even blink at the presence of a dog in his store. Gratefully, Gina loosened her cloak and put Scruffy down to heel. They spent a few minutes warming themselves at the stove and surreptitiously keeping an eye on the boardinghouse through the window, but she knew they had to move soon or the storekeeper would get suspicious.

"Let's pretend we're shopping and take turns keeping an eye on the window," she murmured.

Drake nodded and they both moved to different parts of the store to browse through the merchandise. After fifteen minutes or so, Gina felt guilty for not buying anything, so she picked up a few odds and ends—some stationery for Esme, some sweet-smelling soap and hair ribbons for Bridget, and a pocketknife for Rupert.

Though the guy worked hard to send money home to his family, he rarely bought anything for himself. Besides, it was nearing Christmas and though she didn't plan to be here for the holiday, she wanted to do a little something for the people who had been so kind to her in this time. What else could she do with her earnings, anyway?

Another fifteen minutes passed and she glanced up to see Drake at the counter. Apparently, he had picked up a few guilt items as well, for he was paying for them now. He caught her eye and gave her a significant glance.

Finally—he must have seen Shorty leave. She approached the counter. "Is it time to go now?"

"Yes, I think I've found everything I need. How about you?"

"Me, too," Gina said and paid for her merchandise, barely able to restrain her eagerness. Finally, she was going to find the pistol that would take her back to her own time.

As they left the store with her quaint paper-wrapped parcel, she whispered, "I take it you saw him leave."

"Yes," Drake whispered back. "He headed up the street at a brisk pace. I don't think he'll be back soon."

When Drake lingered in the doorway, she asked, "What's wrong?"

"Perhaps it would be better to wait a few minutes. It might seem suspicious if we arrive too soon after Callahan's departure."

He had a point. Sighing, she said, "Okay," and gave a longing look back at the warm store as she wrapped her cloak more securely around her. "Do we just stand here, then?"

"Well, since we have a few minutes . . ." Drake dug around in his own parcel and pulled out a small box. He handed it to her, saying, "This is for you."

"You bought something for me?" Touched, Gina

could do nothing but stare down at the box. What did this mean?

He shrugged. "I know you don't plan on being here much longer, so I thought I'd give you a little something to remember me by. Go ahead, open it," he urged.

She opened the box to see an exquisite etched silver heart suspended from a silver bow. "It's beautiful," she breathed as she touched it with trembling fingers.

"It's a brooch," he said. "And a locket."

"A locket?" She opened it to find it empty. "What do people of this time keep in their lockets?"

He shrugged, seeming embarrassed. "Small photographs, miniature paintings, small mementos, a lock of hair. . . ."

She smiled up at him, immeasurably touched by his sweet gesture. "Then may I have a lock of your hair?" There was no time to arrange for a photo, and it would be something tangible she could take with her—something of his.

He seemed both pleased and embarrassed. Clearing his throat, he said, "Of course. I'll, er, give you one when we get back to the hotel."

All of a sudden, she didn't feel the wind anymore. Instead, she was intensely aware of Drake's closeness. His gaze locked with hers, and she swayed toward him, hoping for a kiss. Hmm, a hot tub wouldn't go amiss right now, either.

Scruffy whined at her feet, breaking the spell. Sighing, Gina handed her parcel to Drake and picked up the shivering little dog. "What's the matter with you?" she asked, rubbing him briskly. "You're the one with a fur coat—you should be warm."

Drake merely smiled and said, "Perhaps we can try Mrs. Zimmerman's now."

Gina nodded and they crossed the street and knocked on the door. A large, sturdy-looking woman came to the door. "Yes? May I help you?" There was only the faint trace of a German accent lingering in her speech.

"Yes," Gina said eagerly. "I'm looking for my brother, Shorty Callahan. Is he here, please?"

"No, he left," the woman replied brusquely.

"Do you know when he'll be back?"

"He didn't say."

The woman's tone was uncompromising and not at all encouraging, but Gina produced her best smile. "May I wait for him, then?"

"It's very cold out here," Drake interjected, "and we've come a long way to visit er, Shorty."

Gina grinned to herself as she realized they didn't even know his real first name. Hopefully, the landlady wouldn't know him by anything else either.

"All right," the woman said grudgingly and frowned down at Scruffy. "But the dog must behave."

"Oh, don't worry," Gina assured her. "He's a perfect gentleman."

Mrs. Zimmerman looked dubious but opened the door wider to let them in. "All right. You wait in the parlor."

The parlor? That wouldn't do at all. Gina's mind raced as she tried to find a plausible reason for them to wait in Shorty's room. As they entered the immaculately clean house and neared the parlor, she heard voices coming from it. Good—just the excuse she needed.

"Oh dear," she exclaimed. When Mrs. Zimmerman turned to her with a questioning look, Gina shrank away from the other guests. Placing her hand on her brow, she swayed and said, "The noise. I don't think I can bear it."

Luckily, Drake caught her cue and moved forward to support her supposed faintness, patting her hand with an anxious expression. It would have been rather nice if she didn't know it was all an act.

"We've come a long way," he explained. "And it was a very trying trip for my wife. Perhaps you have somewhere quiet where we can wait?"

The woman scowled, and looked around as if hunting for a suitable place, but Drake added, "Her brother's room, perhaps? If she could just lie down for a half hour or so, I'm sure she'd feel much better."

"Oh yes, please," Gina said in a weak voice as she tried to look suitably limp and faint.

"All right," Mrs. Zimmerman said. "You wait upstairs. I take you."

She led the way up the stairs as Drake solicitously helped Gina up after her. Once the woman left them alone, Gina dropped the die-away airs and Drake released her, unfortunately removing his warmth as well.

"Are you quite certain you've never been on the stage?" he asked with a twinkle in his eye.

"Look who's talking—I've never seen someone pick up on a cue so fast in my life."

He grinned and gestured at the room. "Shall we?"

"Yes, let's."

She opened the door just wide enough for Scruffy to see out and put him on guard. Then she and Drake methodically searched the whole room, trying not to unduly disturb anything. Mrs. Zimmerman must have whisked in here right after Shorty left, for the bed was freshly made and the room was spotless—she doubted Shorty would have kept it that way.

They looked everywhere they could think of, even a few places she doubted anyone else would have thought of, but no pistol.

Finally, Gina collapsed on the bed in frustration. "It's not here."

Drake nodded. "I'm afraid you're right."

"But where could it be?" Gina wailed. "He must have hidden it somewhere else—or he has it on him."

"There is another possibility," Drake suggested.

"What?"

"Perhaps he hasn't acquired it yet."

Gina's shoulders slumped. "I didn't even think about that. That must be it. Now what do we do?"

"There's nothing we can do," Drake said in a matter-of-fact tone. "Except . . ."

"What?"

"May I have a piece of that paper you just purchased?"

"Sure." She rummaged through the package and handed him one. "What are you going to do with it?"

Drake sat at the small desk and used the pen Mrs. Zimmerman had so thoughtfully provided. "I'll leave him a note."

"You're not going to tell him we were here, are you?"

"No, but I'm sure he'll figure it out once Mrs. Zimmerman describes us."

"Oh, I hadn't thought of that." With that white streak in his hair, Drake was very distinctive, and how many women walked around with a small black dog? Yes, Shorty would know they'd been there.

"I just want to give him something else to think

about,'' Drake said and blew on the ink just as Scruffy let out a sharp bark.

"Someone's coming," Gina hissed.

Quickly, she cast herself down on the bed and held her hand dramatically to her brow as Drake sat next to her and patted her hand solicitously. She peered around him and was glad to see it was only Mrs. Zimmerman at the door.

"You stay here all day?" she asked, scowling.

"No, I think not," Drake answered. "My wife is feeling much better now, so we'll just find a hotel room and come back later."

The landlady nodded. "Good."

He folded the paper and left it on the desk. "I've just left a note for her brother to let him know where we'll be staying." Helping Gina to her feet, he said, "We won't impose upon you any longer, but we do thank you for your hospitality."

"Yes," Gina said with a weak smile. "I feel much better now. Thank you so much."

The woman nodded grudgingly, and they made their way out the door, Scruffy following as they heard her lock the door behind them.

Then, once they were outside and she was able to drop the act, Gina asked, "What did you put in that note, anyway?"

Drake grinned. "Nothing much. From what I've heard, the man seems to equate mesmerism with spiritualism, and he's afraid I have occult powers. So, I just told him that I had a warning from his mother not to start any more fires or he would be doomed forever."

Gina's eyes widened in admiration. "Good idea— he seemed afraid of his mother."

"I also suggested it might be best if he left town for good. That way he won't be able to set any fires."

"Another great idea," Gina said in admiration, then frowned.

"What's wrong?"

"Nothing, really," she said. "But if he leaves, how am I ever going to find the pistol that will take me home?"

Chapter Eighteen

Drake looked up from his desk to see Gina at the door.

"We have a few minutes before Annabelle's session," she said. "Can we talk?"

"Of course."

She entered with that stubborn look he knew so well. "Well, another week has slipped away from us."

"Yes, I know." Another week closer to his predicted death. Had she imagined he could forget?

"How can you be so complacent?"

"I'm not," he answered calmly. On the contrary, he found it necessary to continuously fight off any stirrings of fear and despair. But his overriding determination to save Annabelle Rutledge gave him the strength to do just that.

"Don't you realize you're going to die in two weeks?"

Yes, he believed that implicitly now. "If I must, I

must. But I can't call myself a man if I leave without
taking Charlotte with me."

"Annabelle."

"What?"

"You mean Annabelle," Gina said gently.

He felt himself flush. "Of course."

Her face softened. "I understand this situation
seems like it's your sister all over again, but Charlotte
is dead. You can't bring her back."

"No, but I can save Mrs. Rutledge from meeting
the same fate."

"Not if both of you are killed in two weeks."

"I know that," he said as patiently as he could,
despite the fact that they'd had endless variations on
this conversation since they'd met. "I shall just have
to convince her to leave soon. I've been working up
to it, and I think she may finally be ready." Lord
knew he had worked hard enough to get her to this
point. And this morning, finally, he had received the
means to convince her.

Gina looked relieved. "Then you'll speak to her
today?"

"Yes." He rose, smiling. "That is, if you'll ask her
to come in?"

"Sure."

Gina called her in then sat in the corner as Drake
made sure Mrs. Rutledge was comfortable.

The woman seemed more frightened than ever.
Disturbed by this evidence that she might be sliding
back into her earlier state of abjection, he asked,
"How have things gone these past few days with your
husband?"

The blonde just shook her head and lifted her
handkerchief-filled hand to her mouth. She was
trembling badly, unable to speak.

Drake felt so inadequate. There was so much he didn't know, so much he didn't understand. He hadn't even known *how* much he was lacking until he'd listened to Gina talk about what was "commonly known" about mesmerism in her time—only she called it psychiatry. In the face of her knowledge, he felt like a caveman groping in the dark.

But that wouldn't stop him from using the knowledge he did have to help his patients. "It didn't go well?" he ventured.

Gina silently handed Mrs. Rutledge a glass of water, which seemed to help calm her. She took a sip, then gestured helplessly and set the glass down. "I—I don't know what to do. Everything I do anymore makes him angry, especially if I stand up to him. I can't seem to please him." She looked up at Drake with a pleading expression, as if begging him to make it all better.

Well, he only knew one way of doing that, but he needed to lead up to it gradually. "Did he hurt you again?" he asked gently.

"No." She sniffled. "But . . ."

Since she seemed unable to finish the sentence, he completed it for her. "But you fear he will."

Tears welled up in her eyes again and she brought her handkerchief to her mouth. "Yes," she whispered. "I'm so frightened."

He glanced helplessly at Gina. He wanted to comfort the woman, but feared it was inappropriate in his professional capacity as a mesmerist. Thank heavens Gina understood his silent plea and dragged her chair over next to Mrs. Rutledge's. She hugged her and patted the woman's hand reassuringly, saying, "It'll be all right. Just listen to Mr. Manton."

Mrs. Rutledge nodded silently and looked up at

Drake as if he were the answer to her prayers. Well, he planned to be . . . if she would only listen.

Taking a deep breath, he said, "I want to tell you a story."

She looked puzzled, but Drake continued anyway. "I had a sister, Charlotte. She was a lovely child, and so loving and giving that everyone adored her. So, when my parents received a very flattering offer for her hand that would help consolidate my father's position in the banking world, they asked her to consider it, assuming the man would adore her as we did."

He paused, assessing her reaction. So far, nothing but polite interest, and perhaps a bit of confusion as to why he was telling this story. "She did consider it, and seeing the advantages to our family of marrying this man, who seemed handsome and kind, she did so."

He paused. The next part was far more painful. "But he wasn't nearly as kind as he appeared. In private, he berated Charlotte, telling her she was worthless, denigrating everything she did, and destroying any sense of value she had."

Now Gina regarded him with concern, but he was determined to get this out. Staring earnestly at the trembling Mrs. Rutledge, he said, "Since no one else understood what was happening, she had no choice but to believe him. Finally, it was too much for Charlotte. . . ."

He paused, unable to go on for a moment.

"What happened?" the woman asked breathlessly.

Drake took a deep breath and forced himself to finish. "She took her own life."

Mrs. Rutledge gasped and covered her mouth, her eyes wide with horror.

Then, to make sure the point went home, Drake added, "I fear the same may happen to you if you don't leave your husband."

She shook her head violently. "No, no, I can't."

"Yes, you can. I hope you'll forgive me, but I took the liberty of contacting your family and informing them of your situation."

If possible, Mrs. Rutledge's eyes widened even further. "You *told* them? Oh, no. How could you tell them of my shame?"

Had she learned nothing? "It's not *your* shame," he said firmly. "It's your husband's." He pulled a telegram from the desk and handed it to her. "Here's their answer. Your parents want you to leave him and return home where they'll take care of you. They're prepared to help you sue for divorce or anything else it takes to get you away from this man."

Mrs. Rutledge buried her head in her hands and sobbed. Drake looked helplessly at Gina, uncertain if he'd done the right thing. Gina, whose arms were occupied with holding Mrs. Rutledge and offering her much-needed comfort, nodded reassuringly at him above the weeping woman's head.

Finally, Mrs. Rutledge's sobs subsided and she wiped her eyes to read the telegram. When she finished, her lips trembled even more and she pressed the letter to her bosom, obviously too overcome with emotion to speak.

"You see?" Drake said gently. "Your parents love you. The disgrace of a divorce means nothing to them, only your safety."

She nodded and it appeared her tears would brim over once more.

"So you'll do it?" he asked. "You'll leave him?"

She straightened in her chair and he could almost

see her spine stiffen as she resolutely wiped away her tears. "Yes, I'll leave him," she said with determination. Good—her family's promised support had given her the courage she needed to leave her abusive husband. "But . . . how?" she asked, looking uncertain again.

"I'll help," Drake said reassuringly.

"We'll both help," Gina added.

For the first time, Drake saw a glimmer of hope in Mrs. Rutledge's eyes and he knew without a shadow of a doubt that he couldn't disappoint her now.

Though she seemed to draw strength from their assurances, Mrs. Rutledge glanced toward the door. "He's just outside."

"We weren't suggesting you leave now," Drake reassured her. "Do you think you could get away from him at some point in the next few days?"

"I don't know. He watches me so closely. I'd never be able to pack anything without him noticing and becoming suspicious."

"Then you mustn't pack," Drake said firmly. "Take only those things that are most important to you— give them to Gina to hold for you ahead of time if you must, but don't pack a bag."

When she looked doubtful, he added, "What's more important? A few items of clothing . . . or your life?"

She nodded. "Yes, I see." And her shoulders firmed and she even seemed to gain more confidence from somewhere deep within her. "Of course, you're right."

"And don't worry," Gina added, patting her hand consolingly. "Drake will buy you whatever you need on your journey."

When that only served to make Mrs. Rutledge look

more dubious, Drake added, "With a full accounting to your father, if you wish."

Mrs. Rutledge relaxed then, and with dawning hope, said, "But how shall we do this?"

"Is there any time of the day or week when your husband regularly leaves you alone?"

She paused to think. "Yes—he plays billiards every afternoon at four with his cronies. Since women aren't allowed in the billiard room, I don't go with him."

"Excellent. Shall we say day after tomorrow, then?" He wanted another day with his other patients so he didn't leave them hanging, though none of them needed him as much as she did. He wouldn't be able to tell them it was their last session for fear word would get back to Rutledge and make him suspicious, but he had to do what he could to tie up any loose ends.

"Yes. Where?"

"As soon as your husband leaves for his billiard game, meet me in the tower." It wouldn't be open for guests until the New Year. He paused, wondering if she would change her mind as soon as she left. "Don't leave any notes and don't tell anyone else where you're going or he might find out. You won't fail me?"

"No," she said in a firm voice, and glanced down at the telegram. "I won't fail you." With trembling fingers, she held the piece of paper out to him. "Will you hold this for me? I—I don't want Clyde to find it."

He took it from her. "Yes, of course. I'll hold it for you until we meet at the tower."

Much more composed now, and seeming happier

than he had ever seen her before, Mrs. Rutledge left the office.

Drake, too, was finally content. Once he spirited her away to her family in Boston, he would have fulfilled his promise to Charlotte, and could regain some peace himself.

The door closed behind the woman and Gina turned to him with a sigh. "That's it, then. You're really going to leave."

"Yes, I really am."

"It's hard to believe. After so many months of hassling you, you're finally going to do it."

He smiled. "You won't know what to do with yourself once I'm not around to harass anymore."

She smiled back, an oddly wistful expression on her face. "Maybe. So, what are you going to do? Are you going to come back here once the danger is over?"

He shook his head. The resort would always remind him of Gina, but it wouldn't be the same without her. "No, I have been offered a position in Richmond. A progressive doctor there thinks I'll make a good addition to his practice. I think I'll take it."

Her eyes widened. "Richmond? Why, that's ideal."

"Yes, since it lacks the transient nature of the resort, I'll be able to help a lot more people there."

She smiled at him. "Good, I'm glad. You'll do wonderfully."

Will I? How could he, without Gina beside him, to bully him, laugh with him, love him?

He desperately wanted to ask her to come with him, but kept silent. She had made it very clear there was nothing for her here.

Though he had hoped *he* would be enough. . . .

* * *

Two days later, Gina waited for Drake at the tower with mixed emotions. She was glad he would finally be safe, but it also meant this was the last time she would see him.

She touched the place over her heart where the locket lay. Since employees weren't allowed to wear jewelry while on duty, she had kept it pinned to her undergarments ever since he had given it to her. This was all she would have left of him after today. This, and the small lock of hair inside.

Drake arrived then, alone and with not even a bag in his hands. "Where's your luggage?" she asked, alarmed. "Aren't you going?"

"Of course," he soothed. "But I didn't want to advertise that I was leaving, so I left my things in my room. I've paid up through the end of the week, so no one should bother them until then. Here." He handed her a slip of paper. "After I see Mrs. Rutledge safely to her family, I'll go on to Richmond to take up my new practice. Will you see that my trunk and bags are sent to this address?"

"Of course." It was the least she could do. She folded it carefully and put it in her pocket. "So, what's the plan?"

"Sean Quinn has a buggy standing by, waiting to whisk us away to the Hope Springs station so we can avoid the curious eyes at The Chesterfield's spur. We'll catch the first train heading north, then make our way to Boston."

She nodded. Now, all that was left was figuring out how to say good-bye. And it was best to do it now, in the tower and away from prying eyes. "Drake, I—"

She broke off, not knowing how to let him go gracefully, without tears.

Well, it wasn't going to happen. She felt the telltale pricking behind her eyelids and knew her eyes were filling with moisture. Grasping his lapel, she smiled tremulously up at him and blinked away the tears. "I—I'm going to miss you."

How inadequate. It didn't begin to describe the feeling of loss and desolation she experienced at the thought of never seeing him again. Nor did it convey the love she knew would never fade.

He smiled sadly down at her and wiped away one of her tears. "Don't cry," he murmured. "I thought this is what you wanted."

"It is," she managed to choke out. No, that was a lie. She wanted to scream for him to stay, or to take her with him, but kept silent. He had to go, and if he had wanted her with him, he would have asked her by now. Begging him to take her would only make her look foolish . . . and embarrass him.

But she couldn't let him go without one last kiss. Stretching to her full height, she twined her arms around his neck and brought his face down to hers. Their lips met and fused in a moment of sheer longing and stark need. She put her entire being into that kiss, to create a memory that would have to last for the rest of her life.

Drake matched her intensity, as if he, too, felt the same. But as much as she wanted to pretend he loved her, she knew it wasn't true. It was lust he felt, not love.

And if she wasn't careful, this kiss would escalate out of control very soon, and Annabelle was likely to show up to find them tearing each other's clothes off.

Where was Annabelle, anyway? Gina pulled away reluctantly and asked, "What time is it?"

Drake checked his pocket watch. "It's after four-thirty."

She frowned. "Shouldn't she be here by now?"

"Yes, but she might have had a little trouble getting away, or needed time to pack the few things she plans to take with her."

Gina fumed. After all they'd done for the woman, after all the risks Drake was taking to save her life, she could at least be on time. Unless there was another reason. . . . "Or she got cold feet, and decided to stay with that idiot husband of hers."

Drake frowned. "I hope not."

"I'll just go check on her, then."

"No." Drake stayed her with a hand on her arm. "That's not a good idea. What if Rutledge or someone else sees you? He might suspect something."

"What do you want to do then? Just wait? If she hasn't shown up by now, she isn't going to. She probably chickened out."

"No, I—" Drake broke off as Rupert stuck his head around the corner.

"Mr. Manton? Mrs. Rutledge gave me this for you."

Rupert handed him a folded note, then went off with a jaunty salute after Drake tipped him.

"What does it say?" Gina asked impatiently as Drake read the note.

He sighed. "She isn't coming."

"Hell, I figured that out. Why not?"

"She says she must have done something to make Rutledge suspect her. He didn't go to his billiard game today and seems reluctant to leave her alone."

"Yeah, he suspects something all right. And we'll probably never pry her loose now." Gina nodded decisively. "That settles it—you'll just have to leave without her."

"What?" Drake stared at her incredulously. "You know I can't do that."

"Sure you can. Look, you've done every possible thing you could to help her, so it's time to cut your losses."

"I haven't done everything," he reminded her. "I still haven't helped her with the one thing she needs most—escape from her husband."

"But you have everything arranged—the buggy, the train, your luggage. It would be a shame not to take advantage of it." Seeing he was about to protest again, she added, "Besides, I'll follow up with Annabelle."

"What do you mean, follow up?"

"I'll follow up to make sure she gets out of here."

"I don't think—"

"You don't think I will, do you?" And it really ticked her off. "Look, I don't want to see her hurt any more than you do. And it doesn't take a mesmerist to get her to a train. Anyone could do that."

"I didn't doubt your veracity," Drake protested. "But I don't think that would work."

"Why not?"

"Because she is the sort of woman who needs a man to lean on—"

"And why does it have to be you?" Gina spit out, jealousy running rampant through her. Was the article turning out to be true after all? Was Drake coming to care for the clinging vine?

"Because I'm the only one who knows her predicament and is willing to help her," Drake explained patiently. "She needs someone to bolster her courage the entire trip, or she's liable to give up and go running back to Clyde at the first sign of a problem. You can't help her with that—you have to stay here.''

He sighed, adding, ''She's not strong like you, Gina. She needs constant reassurance that she's doing the right thing.''

Well, strength was overrated if it felt like this. For a brief moment, Gina wondered if playing the clinging vine would make Drake want her to stay around, but discarded the idea immediately. He would never buy it, and she would never be able to sustain the act for long. She stared up at him with a belligerent expression, wondering what she could do to convince him to leave now. Besides, she didn't think she could say good-bye again.

''It isn't going to work,'' Drake said softly.

''What isn't?''

''Whatever you're planning in that busy little brain of yours—it isn't going to work. For Charlotte's sake, and Mrs. Rutledge's, I'm going to see her out of here if it's the last thing I do.''

''And it just might be, if you're not careful,'' Gina snapped.

And she didn't care what he said. She was going to make sure he got out of here—no matter what she had to do to make it happen.

Chapter Nineteen

Gina fretted as another ten days passed with agonizing slowness. Clyde had become very suspicious and the only time he left Annabelle alone now was in her sessions with Drake. So, rather than set a specific time to steal away, they had agreed to have Annabelle escape whenever possible and send word to Drake to meet her at the tower.

It was now December 21, and Gina was beginning to panic. Would he ever get away? She glanced at the office door behind her in exasperation. How could he sit there calmly and see patient after patient when he knew he was destined to die in this hotel tomorrow?

Rupert provided a welcome distraction as he arrived with a folded piece of paper in his hand. "I have a note for Mr. Manton, from Chief Garrett."

Gina knew better than to expect Rupert to turn

the note over to her—Drake tipped too well. "He'll be done in a minute," she said.

In less than that, the door opened and Drake's latest patient left. Gina followed Rupert in. She wanted to know what it said, too.

Rupert handed over the note and received his tip. "I'll wait outside to see if there's a reply."

"What does it say?" Gina asked when Rupert had closed the door behind him. "Is it about Shorty?"

"Yes," Drake said with a smile. "Chief Garrett informs me that Mr. Callahan has left town. For good, it appears. He took all his things and paid his shot at Mrs. Zimmerman's. The chief doesn't think he'll be back."

Hope surged through her, and Gina pulled the article from her pocket. Lately, she didn't keep it far from her. But as she glanced at it, her hopes faltered. "It didn't change anything."

"That doesn't make sense. If Shorty is gone, how can he set the fire that causes my demise?"

"I don't know—maybe he's convinced one of his friends to do it, or maybe he just wants us to *think* he went out of town, and he's gonna sneak back to do you in. I wouldn't put it past him."

Drake frowned and perused the note once more. "I don't think so—the chief seems fairly certain he's gone for good."

"But the article didn't change—you still die."

He shrugged. "Maybe it won't change until the date has come and gone."

He was putting entirely too much stock in this little note from the chief. "No, that wasn't true with Madame Rulanka—her article changed immediately after she decided to change her itinerary."

"Regardless, you know I can't leave unless Mrs.

Rutledge goes with me." He folded the note carefully and placed it in his desk. "Could you send the next patient in, please?"

Sighing, Gina left, knowing argument was futile. Ordinarily she wouldn't give in so easily, but after six months' experience in trying to beat some sense into Drake, she knew argument wouldn't sway him. The only way to deal with him was to take matters into her own hands.

There was no hope for it—she would just have to put her plan into action.

Rupert was waiting for her, bouncing impatiently on his toes. "Is there an answer?"

"No, but wait a moment. There's something else I need to talk to you about."

She sent in the next patient, then pulled Rupert into the hallway where they could converse without being overheard. "Okay, it's time."

"Time for what?"

"Time to put Plan B into action." Luckily, word had gotten around the resort that a spirit summoned by Madame Rulanka had predicted Drake's death if he stayed at The Chesterfield. Since many of the staff believed firmly in the spiritualist and her claims, Gina hadn't found it difficult to convince a few of her friends that what she was about to do was for Drake's own good.

"He won't leave?" Rupert said with anxiety.

"No, he thinks he'll be safe."

"Are you certain this is the right thing to do?"

"I'm sure," Gina said firmly and decided to fib, just a little. "Madame Rulanka told me she even knew the date of his death. He'll die in a fire on December 22—tomorrow—unless we do something to prevent it. Can't you see this is the lesser of two evils?"

When Rupert didn't answer, she pressed further. "You want Mr. Manton to live, don't you?"

"Yes, but—"

"Then we have to do this. Trust me, he'll thank you later." Then, without giving him a chance to have second thoughts, she said, "Do you still have that special note I gave you?"

He patted his chest. "Yes, right here."

"Then let me have it. I'll make sure Drake gets it, and you go tell Sean Quinn it's time." The stablemaster would take it from there.

Rupert headed off with obvious reluctance, but she knew he wouldn't let her down.

Well, it was time for her performance, and she'd better make it convincing. Gina burst into Drake's office, ignoring the startled look on his patient's face. "Excuse me," she said breathlessly, "but this note just came for you."

Drake scowled at first, but as she knew he would, he must have figured the note was from Annabelle or she wouldn't have disturbed him otherwise.

"Excuse me," he said to the patient, "but this is a very important missive." He skimmed it quickly, then added, "I'm sorry, but an emergency has come up. I'm afraid I'll have to cut our session short."

Though the woman appeared a little disgruntled, she left with good grace.

"It's from Annabelle, isn't it?" Gina asked, though she knew very well what the note said since she'd written it herself.

"Yes—she's gotten free and wants me to meet her at the stables." He frowned. "I wonder why we aren't meeting at the tower as we arranged? And why now?"

Why was he asking questions? "Who cares? Come on, I'll go with you."

"That's not necessary—"

"Oh, yes it is," Gina said forcefully. She wanted to make sure nothing went wrong.

Shrugging, Drake grabbed his hat and hurried out the door. Gina followed him, sending up a silent prayer that they wouldn't encounter the Rutledges on the way.

Her luck held and they made it to the stables without encountering anyone. The stablemaster was waiting outside and gave Gina a questioning look.

She nodded significantly and a look of determination came over the middle-aged man's face.

"Where's Mrs. Rutledge?" Drake asked.

"Just inside," Sean assured him.

Then when Drake passed him, the small man brought up a cloth and pressed it with surprising force against Drake's nose, using all his wiry strength to hold it there as Drake struggled briefly.

Gina stifled a shriek as Drake crumpled to the ground, unconscious. She'd known it was necessary, but she hated to see him like this. "What did you use?"

"Chloroform," Sean said. "We keep it around for the animals, but it works just as well on humans."

Well, at least Drake wasn't hurt.

Sean signaled to a couple of his stablehands and they lifted Drake's inert body and placed it in a wagon. Then, for good measure, Sean tied his hands together in front of him, then his feet, and covered him with a blanket.

"All right, Jem," Sean said, addressing one of the stablehands. "Take him as far away as you can."

"Yes," Gina added. "He mustn't be able to make it back here until day after tomorrow."

The stablehand nodded. Then, since Sean had

already hitched the horses to the wagon, he rode away with Drake covered up in the back.

Gina stared longingly after him. She would have liked another chance to say good-bye, but they had already said their farewells and it would have only made him suspicious. A tear tracked down her cheek, and Sean patted her on the shoulder.

"It's all right, young Gina. You did the right thing. He'll be safe now."

Gina brushed away a tear. Yes, she'd done the right thing. She'd accomplished the task she was sent here to do, so now all she had to do was find the pistol that would send her home tomorrow.

Drake woke, woozy and disoriented. When he tried to move, he found his hands and feet had been tied, and he couldn't see anything because a rough blanket lay over him. At first, he had thought he was lying on some kind of wooden floor, but since the floor was moving, he realized he must be in a wagon.

A few minutes more of trying to focus his scattered thoughts, and he remembered Gina leading him to the stable. Was she responsible for this, or had both of them been kidnapped?

He managed to get some of the blanket off his face and squinted up into the sun to see who was driving the wagon. It was a young man he recalled working in the stables. Since there was no one else sharing the wagon bed with him, he put the pieces of the puzzle together . . . Gina strangely not arguing, her leading him to meet Annabelle at a different place from the one they had agreed upon, and the strange expression on Quinn's face.

No doubt about it—Gina was responsible for this.

The realization stunned him for a moment, until he realized it was exactly what he should have expected of her. And though he should feel betrayed and angry, he felt nothing but disgust—at himself. It was his own fault. He should have been more careful.

And he should have taken her into his confidence. He had received a note from Mrs. Rutledge the day before saying her husband had planned an all-male hunting trip for tomorrow. Since Rutledge planned to be gone most of the day, it was the ideal time to slip away.

Drake had planned to spirit Mrs. Rutledge away and be long gone before Shorty could find them and set any fires, but knew Gina would panic at the thought of waiting until the last minute, so he hadn't told her.

He grimaced ruefully. If he had told her, she might not have gone to such lengths to protect him. Now, he needed to figure out how to get back to The Chesterfield in time to meet Mrs. Rutledge and get her to Boston.

But how? He recognized the lingering, distinctive sweet odor of chloroform as the agent they'd used to make him unconscious. He couldn't have been out for more than a couple of hours, so it must be late afternoon . . . and the position of the sun confirmed it. Now, if he could just find a way out of this, he might be able to get back in time.

Tilting his head back to peer at the driver, he called out to get the lad's attention, glad that they'd spared him a gag at least.

Startled, the driver jerked and stared down at Drake with wide eyes.

"What's your name?" Drake asked.

"Jem."

"Well, Jem, could you see your way clear to getting me a drink of water?"

"I'm not supposed to let you loose until late tomorrow," Jem said dubiously.

"I'm not asking you to let me loose," Drake said in a reasonable manner, though his heart sank at this confirmation of his fears. "I just want some water. That drug your stablemaster used on me gave me a powerful thirst."

"All right," Jem said, pulling the wagon over and bringing it to a stop. "But don't try to pull nothin'. If'n you do, I'm supposed to bash you on the head." With a stubborn look, he brandished a stout cudgel.

"I won't," Drake promised. At least, not until he was certain he could overpower the stablehand and get away on his own.

He got a better look at the lad and found they had made a good choice. Jem was big and hefty, though he couldn't be more than seventeen. He would be difficult to overpower, especially since Drake was bound and had no weapons at his disposal.

Drake wriggled until he was able to achieve a sitting position and as Jem dipped water from the barrel someone had so thoughtfully provided, Drake looked around. His heart sank. They weren't on a main road, and he didn't recognize any landmarks. All he could see was a small stream alongside the small road, flowing back the way they had come.

Jem raised the dipper to his lips, and Drake drank thirstily as the young man watched him with wary eyes. Maybe if he could engage Jem in conversation, he might find out a few things.

"So," he said conversationally, "why are you doing this?"

Jem shrugged as he hooked the dipper back on

the barrel. "Mr. Quinn tol' me to." He paused, then added as if it were justification, "Fer yer own good, he said."

"I see." He did, too. It explained how Gina had been able to convince them to go along with this harebrained scheme.

Drake glanced casually around. "Where are you taking me?"

"Nowhere—jus' makin' sure ya can't get back tomorrow."

"Where are we now? A few hours north of Hope Springs, would you say?"

"Mebbe."

Drake frowned. Jem was more close-mouthed than he'd hoped. "Well—"

" 'Nuff talkin'," the stablehand said, and abruptly returned to his seat, setting the horses in motion again.

After that, Jem wouldn't respond to any of his questions, so Drake was left to brood and make plans. But how could he get loose when he didn't have any weapons? He wracked his brain until he finally realized he did have one weapon at his disposal—his mind—though he was going to have to wait to employ it.

A few hours after it turned dark, Jem finally decided to stop again. After he took care of the horses and set up camp by the stream, he came to check on Drake. By then, Drake was getting rather cold and grateful for the meager shelter of the blanket.

Brandishing his cudgel at Drake once more, Jem warned him to be still, then set about doing something with the rope at his ankles. When he was through, Drake's feet were still bound, but now hobbled so he could at least walk.

Grateful to get out of the wagon, Drake shook off the pins-and-needles sensations and walked over to the fire at Jem's gesture.

"Siddown," the boy said.

Drake sat. He would have to wait for a chance to put his plan into action, but it wouldn't hurt to have a good meal first. He huddled close to the warmth of the fire and watched as Jem cooked the food he had brought.

When Jem finished and brought him a plate, Drake held up his bound hands. "Aren't you going to release me?"

"Nope."

"Why not?"

"You kin eat like that," he said uncompromisingly.

And so he could. Drake ate the generous meal someone had provided, and brooded over how long this was taking. He had to get back to the resort by tomorrow morning or he wouldn't be able to get Mrs. Rutledge to safety. Nor would he be able to say his final good-byes to Gina before she went back to the future.

Strange, but he wasn't angry at her or any of the employees she had talked into kidnapping him. By now, he knew this was just Gina's way of showing she cared enough about him to make certain he didn't die.

He shook his head. He never thought he'd actually come to understand and sympathize with her crazy schemes. He must be in love or something.

Yes. . . .

The realization blossomed within him, slow but sure. He loved her. Not just as a dear friend, and not just because they had been intimate. He loved her as a man loves a woman, a woman who was kind, funny, enchanting, strong, and never ever boring. She had brought him back to life with her engaging and unexpected ways, breathing life into the humdrum, bleak existence he had been living since Charlotte died.

Now he understood why he had made all those marriage proposals. It wasn't to satisfy propriety or to atone for compromising her, it was because he very simply wanted—no, he *needed*—Gina in his life. His own mind had known it before he had. And she must love him, too. She had to, to go to so many lengths to save his life.

All of a sudden, he realized he couldn't let her leave without making some attempt to ask her to stay, to ask her to be his wife. If he didn't at least try, he would never forgive himself and always wonder what would have happened if he had broached the subject.

Sudden urgency filled him. If he was to get back tomorrow early enough to catch her before she left for the future, he must find a way to escape. Soon.

Jem came back from washing the dishes and stowed them in the wagon, then sat across from him at the fire. Good—this was a perfect time to put his plan into effect.

As Jem stared into the fire, Drake said, "Intriguing, aren't they? The flames . . . each one is different and ever changing."

Jem grunted acknowledgment and Drake watched him carefully as he continued to stare into the flames. Softly, he said, "Legend says that if you continue to watch, to let the images in the flames fill your mind, you will see everything that ever existed, everything that ever will be." He paused. "Do you see them, Jem?"

Jem nodded slowly, and Drake continued in a

monotone, telling him what he saw in the fire, letting
the leaping flames slowly mesmerize the stablehand.

Once it was clear Jem was under, Drake felt a leap
of excitement as he realized this was really going to
work. "Look around you," he said. "Can you see the
signs? We're in for a devil of a storm tonight." They
weren't, of course, but Drake had to find some way
to convince him to return to the resort.

Jem's expression turned concerned and he nodded.

"We have to return to The Chesterfield or we'll be
in danger. You see that, don't you?"

Jem nodded again, slowly. To reinforce his suggestion, Drake said, "We need to leave now, so we can
get back to The Chesterfield by tomorrow morning."

"But I'm not s'posed to let you back until day after
tomorrow."

"The storm overrides everything," Drake said.
"You said yourself they don't want me killed, and we
will both surely die if we have to stay out in this
weather. Look, a few snowflakes are beginning to
fall."

Seeing that Jem believed firmly in his imaginary
snowflakes, Drake added, "There's no shelter further
up the road, so we have to return to the resort or
we'll both die. You know this is what Mr. Quinn would
want you to do."

"We'd best be goin', then."

Drake sighed in relief. "Yes, we must hurry. And
it will go much faster if you untie my hands and feet."

Jem paused and Drake added, "We're going where
I want to go, so I won't be any trouble."

Then, after Jem untied him, Drake reinforced his
suggestions so Jem would continue to believe in the
storm and brought him out of the trance.

Drake spared a moment of apology for the horses,

though at least they had had a couple of hours of rest. And they weren't in any danger. Now that night had fallen, it would take longer to get home than it had to get here, but the track was visible enough in the bright moonlight. He just hoped it was enough to get back in time.

He had to. Not only did Drake have to keep his promise to meet Mrs. Rutledge, but he had to find Gina and convince her to be his wife before she found the pistol and went out of his life forever.

Chapter Twenty

Gina woke the morning of December 22 with very mixed feelings. She wanted to go home so badly to all the conveniences of the twenty-first century, but she had come to appreciate some of the amenities of this time, too ... like the slower, more relaxed lifestyle of this century, and men who acted like gentlemen. Men like Drake who still believed in things like honor and keeping promises, and who knew how to treat a woman with gentleness and consideration.

Those types were rare in her time. Or at least, *she'd* never run into one.

She sighed. Well, she couldn't have everything, and since it appeared Drake didn't love her as much as she loved him, going back to the future was the thing to do. But first, she had to find that blasted pistol or she wasn't going anywhere.

Gina dressed hastily and glanced around the room. She had been careful not to acquire too many possessions here since she knew she wouldn't be staying, so there was nothing she really wanted to take except for the locket Drake had given her, and she was already wearing that.

Then of course there was Scruffy. She needed to make sure he stayed close to her side all day today just in case she ran across the pistol. Leaving him behind was unthinkable—he was the only one in the world who truly loved her.

She rubbed his ears, saying, "We're going home today, Scruffy. Would you like that?"

He barked joyously, though Gina doubted he really understood. He had taken to these times faster than she had, due to the generosity of Sasha's table scraps, which were of far better quality than the dog food she fed him at home. And of course, there were two humans here that he adored—her and Drake. Leaving both the food and Drake would be hard on him.

And leaving her friends would be hard on her. She was glad she had gone back to the mercantile a few days ago and picked up things for Jack, Sasha and Sean as well. They had all been so good to her and though the gifts were small tokens indeed for the genuine friendship they had offered, Gina hoped they would serve to remind them of her long after she was gone.

She labeled the packages and left them on her bed where Esme would find them after she left, certain the housekeeper would get them to the right people.

Gina glanced sadly down at the items there, realizing there was nothing for Drake. She blinked back tears and reminded herself she had given Drake the most precious gift of all—his own life. He was probably in no condition to appreciate it now, but he would thank her some day.

Well, enough maudlin sentiment. It was time to get on with the rest of her life. Gina left her room to look for Esme, noticing that the resort was once again bustling with activity. They were preparing for another ball, this time to celebrate the winter solstice and Christmas. But, she reflected sadly, she would be gone before this one even started.

Gina found Esme in the linen room and pulled her aside. "Do you know what day this is?"

"Of course." But the housekeeper's calm words were belied by her worried expression.

"Will I be able to go home today?"

Esme frowned. "That's entirely up to you."

"What do you mean?"

"Whether you go or stay is entirely your decision— no one can make that for you."

"Then I will be given the opportunity? I will find the pistol?" Gina pressed.

"Oh, yes," Esme said, though she sounded a bit disapproving. "I would say it's inevitable."

"Where? When?"

"That will be revealed in due course."

Esme's cryptic pronouncements were beginning to irritate Gina. "Why won't you tell me more?"

Esme's disapproval faded, to be replaced by resignation. "I really cannot tell you more without compromising the desired outcome. And I don't really know that much more for certain myself."

Desired outcome? "You mean, there's more than one way this could go?"

"Of course. You have free will, you always have had. What choice you make once the alternatives are presented to you is yours alone to make."

"And which way would you like it to go?"

"I would like you to stay, of course."

Gina frowned. It sounded like there was a great deal more to this than just Esme's desire for her company. "But what——"

"I can say no more," Esme said firmly. "But if you decide to stay, you know you will always have a friend in me."

"Sure," Gina said, baffled by the housekeeper's attitude.

With that, Esme nodded crisply and walked away.

Gina stared down at Scruffy. "Now what was that all about?" she wondered aloud.

Scruffy had no answer, so Gina shrugged and stood indecisively, wondering what to do next. Would the pistol just appear somewhere? Did she need to go looking for it? What the heck was she supposed to do?

Esme made it sound like her portal would show up no matter what she did, so she supposed it didn't matter.

Gina sighed. All right, since Drake had canceled all his sessions for the rest of the holiday week, she would just visit her friends one last time and find a way to let them know how much they meant to her without saying good-bye. The resourceful Esme could come up with some explanation to tell them once Gina was gone for good.

And here was one of those people now——Rupert, striding fast up the hallway. "There you are," he exclaimed. "I've been looking everywhere for you."

"Why?" she asked, bewildered. If the Major had some sort of menial task for her, forget it. After today, she didn't need to stay on his good side anymore. She'd be long gone.

He leaned down to whisper with intensity, "It's Mr. Manton. He's back."

"Back?" Gina repeated in rising panic. "You mean, he's here, at the hotel?"

"Yes, he's here. I just saw him, heading toward his room and looking mighty stone-faced."

"But how could that be? Jem was supposed to take him far, far away."

"I don't know," Rupert said. "I only know he's back here in the hotel. If I were you, I'd keep well out of his reach for awhile." With that dire warning, he strode off without a backward look.

Drake, here? What the hell had happened? Before she confronted him, she had to know. So, trying not to trip over Scruffy who insisted on playing his little game of walking beneath her skirt, Gina headed off to the stables and Sean Quinn.

Sean was standing outside, and when he saw her, he just frowned and shook his head.

"Is it true?" Gina demanded. "Is Mr. Manton back already?"

Sean nodded. "Yes, he arrived back about an hour ago."

"But how? What happened?"

"I don't rightly know," Sean admitted. "And neither does Jem, really. I think it had something to do with Mr. Manton's mesmerizing ways."

Of course. It hadn't been enough to bind his hands and feet—she should have covered his mouth and eyes as well. Well, hindsight was twenty-twenty, but it didn't help her at all now. What could she do? He was bound and determined to get himself killed no matter what she did.

"What are you going to do now?" Sean asked.

Her first instinct was to flee, to get as far away from this situation as possible. She had done all she could to save the man's life. If he chose to throw it away for the sake of a woman who reminded him of his dead sister, that was his business. She didn't have to stay around and watch him do it to himself.

Yes, that was the ticket. Esme said it was inevitable that Gina would find the pistol today. Well, she could find it in Hope Springs just as easily as she could at The Chesterfield.

In answer to Sean's question, she said, "I'm catching the next train down to Hope Springs."

"What good will that do?" Sean asked. Then, after a disbelieving pause, he said, "Surely you're not going to abandon him to his fate?"

"I tried to save his life, but he's done everything he could to make sure he dies today. How can I fight that?" she asked in exasperation. "I don't want to watch him die."

"So you're going to just run away?"

Unfortunately, Sean had chosen the only words that would make her stop and think. Run away? That's what Drake had said. *You run away every time things don't go your way.*

Okay, so he was right. So what?

So, running away doesn't solve anything, a little voice inside her said.

She decided to ignore it—she didn't trust little voices anyway. What did they know? Running away had stood her in good stead her whole life. It was much easier than staying around to face the consequences. And if she wasn't around to see the bad things happen, she could pretend they didn't exist.

But they still happen, the voice said, *whether you pretend they do or not.*

But—

And Drake will still die, whether you pretend he does or

not. Can you live with yourself if you do nothing to prevent it?

Do nothing? Nonsense—she'd done nothing but try to save the man's life for the past six months. But he obviously didn't want her help and was determined to get himself killed.

But now is when he needs you the most, the voice insisted. *And you can't do that if you run away.*

"Well?" Sean asked. "What are you going to do?"

Gina pulled the article out of her pocket once more and read the headline. It was unchanged, implacable. If she did nothing, Drake would die. If she tried to save him, he might still die, but at least she would have done what she could to save him.

Sean was right—this time, she couldn't run away.

Sighing, Gina put the article back in her pocket. "I'm staying," she said with determination. And though it scared the hell out of her, it kind of felt good for a change.

"Good," Sean declared. "What can I do?"

The article already accounted for two dead bodies, and she didn't want to put Sean in danger and possibly add a third. But maybe she could do some damage control. "Send someone down to Jess Garrett's office and ask him to come right away. Tell him . . . tell him Shorty Callahan must be back in town and a crime is about to be committed at The Chesterfield. Uh, and maybe you'd better notify the fire chief as well." She needed every possible advantage to keep Drake alive.

"And what are you going to do?"

"Me? I'm going to do my best to save Drake's life." She only hoped her best would be good enough.

She hurried off to find him, but he wasn't in his

room, nor was he in his office. Now what? Where could he be?

Annabelle—she was the key. She was slated to die in the fire along with Drake, so wherever Annabelle was, Drake would be, too. Could they have decided to meet at the tower? Yes, Annabelle must have finally gotten away. They had to be at the tower.

Gina ran the long distance in record time, Scruffy's little legs twinkling like mad to keep up with her. Sure enough, Drake was there, and he whirled around when she arrived with a rustle of skirts and an explosion of breath. "Good, I found you," she exclaimed as Scruffy greeted him joyously.

Drake's expression was tense and strained. That was good, too. At least he didn't underestimate his danger.

"Do you have a death wish?" she demanded. "What are you doing here?"

"I'm waiting for Mrs. Rutledge," he said. "She should be here at any minute." He checked his watch and put it back in his pocket. "We had this arranged days ago when we learned her husband planned to leave on a hunting trip this morning."

"Why didn't you tell me?" she demanded.

"Because I knew you would object since this is the day . . ."

"The day of your death, I know. You have to get out of here."

"And I will, just as soon as Mrs. Rutledge arrives."

"No, you have to leave now."

"What are you going to do? Have Sean Quinn kidnap me again?"

Gina felt herself flush, but he didn't seem too upset about it. "I'm sorry about that, but you know why I did it."

His expression softened. "Yes, I know. Which leads me to something I should have asked long ago. Gina—"

But she didn't know what he would have asked, for Annabelle arrived then, breathless and extremely agitated. And Drake turned away from Gina toward the distraught woman as if Gina didn't even exist.

Damn, she hadn't realized how much this would hurt. As Drake tried to soothe Annabelle, Gina spit out, "You'd better leave now, before it's too late." Drake and Annabelle together on the winter solstice was a combustible combination.

"Yes," he said, his concentration all on Annabelle. "I think it's—"

"It's too late already," a deep voice declared.

Annabelle screeched and as Scruffy dived beneath Gina's skirt, they all turned in surprise to see Clyde Rutledge at the door, holding a pistol on them—a very familiar-looking pistol.

The dueling pistol! It had finally turned up, but in entirely the wrong hands. No, it couldn't be—they hadn't been able to find the pistol in his room.

He closed the door carefully and set a small bag down beside his foot, not taking his eyes off Drake and Annabelle. "I knew something was up," he said with a sneer. "You couldn't keep a secret if your life depended on it. I knew you had a lover—I just didn't figure it would be him." Clyde gestured toward Drake with contempt.

Drake shoved Annabelle behind him and faced Clyde bravely. Annabelle backed away, trembling badly, until she hit the wall.

Gina wanted to shout, *No, forget Annabelle and run,* but knew Drake would never do it. As for herself, she seemed frozen in place, not knowing what to do, afraid any move would only place Drake in more danger than he already faced.

"We're not lovers," Drake said in a placating tone. "I'm just helping her take a little vacation, that's all."

"Well, she ain't going nowhere," Clyde declared. "I knew she was a no-good, unfaithful slut when I married her, and I ain't letting no woman make a fool outta me. You're going to die. Both of you."

He cocked the pistol and trained it on Drake. With a small shriek, Annabelle slid down the wall to the floor and covered her eyes, shaking like mad. Gina couldn't blame her and wished she could emulate her, but Drake's life was still in danger.

Drake slowly moved to his right, his hands outstretched in a calming gesture. "Someone will hear the shots—you'll never get away with it."

"Not likely, with all this noise going on in preparation for the ball. They'll just think it's the hunting party having a little fun."

He moved a little more. "But killing us won't do you any good. You'll be caught and hanged."

Gina wondered what Drake was doing, then realized he was trying to draw fire away from Annabelle, and was speaking in the monotone he used to mesmerize his patients. *It won't work,* she wanted to scream. Clyde was too intent and focused to be diverted by mesmerism.

"No, I won't," Rutledge insisted, tracking Drake's slow progress with his pistol. "I have this all figured out—I stole the pistols from a shop in town last week, so no one can connect me with them."

So that's why they hadn't been able to find them. Clyde chuckled—an evil sound that made her shiver as hard as Annabelle. "And that idiot Callahan gave me an idea. I saw him set the fire at your office, though he botched it." Clyde nudged the bag with his toe and several rags spilled out, drenching the air with the smell of kerosene. "But I won't. After I kill you both, I'm gonna light your funeral pyre with this." He grinned wolfishly. "It'll hide the bullets and everyone will blame Callahan, not me."

Dear God, he was right. He *would* get away with this. And now she knew where the rumor had come from about Drake and Annabelle being lovers.

No! Gina screamed silently. She couldn't let it happen. But how could she stop it? She had no weapon, no skill in martial arts—the only thing she knew how to do was train dogs.

That's it! Scruffy would be her weapon. Mentally crossing her fingers and praying, Gina took a deep breath as Clyde grinned and slowly drew a bead on Drake's heart.

Now! "Scruffy, attack," Gina yelled, pointing frantically at Clyde.

With an incredible, super-canine effort, Scruffy burst out from beneath her skirt and took a running jump, soaring into the air to sink his jaws into Clyde's gun hand. The pistol flew off, and landed next to Annabelle's outstretched foot as Clyde cursed and shook Scruffy off with a snap of his thick wrist.

Scruffy landed in a heap with a yelp, and Gina ran to him, thanking God when she found him he was still moving and didn't seem to be hurt. Now she could do nothing but watch helplessly as Drake, who had moved swiftly into the breach, grappled with Clyde. Where the hell was Sean with Jess Garrett?

There was nothing she could do here—she had to get help. "Don't let Clyde have the pistol," she yelled at Annabelle who was peeking through her fingers at the fight.

Thankfully, Annabelle seemed to have snapped out of her stupor. As she scrambled for the gun, Gina headed for the door but was halted by the sound of a meaty smack and a thud. The big man had overpowered Drake and was now standing over him, wiping his mouth.

With a grin, Clyde reached behind him and she watched in horror as he pulled another pistol from the back of his belt, aiming it at Drake who was scrambling to his feet.

Aw, shit. She should have remembered that dueling pistols always came in pairs.

She made an abortive attempt toward him, but Clyde waved the gun at her. "Stay back," he warned. "Or I'll get you next, and your little dog, too."

Gina obediently froze as he turned his attention back to Drake. Now what? Should she tackle him anyway? Hell, why not? She had nothing to lose.

She was just prepared to launch herself into the fray and damn the danger when she heard a shot. Her hands flew to her mouth, but to her surprise, Drake remained standing.

Instead, it was a very surprised Clyde who jerked, arching backward as he slid to the floor, shot neatly in the back by his loving wife.

Annabelle dropped the gun with a moan and buried her face in her hands, sobbing her heart out as Clyde lay unmoving.

Gina and Drake exchanged puzzled glances. Could it really be over now? But before they could make a move, the police chief burst in the door, followed by several men he had evidently deputized . . . and Miss Sparrow.

As Garrett took in the tableau with a well-trained glance, Drake blurted out, "It was self-defense. He was about to murder us all."

Garrett nodded slowly. "I can see that."

Anyone could. The gun still clasped in Rutledge's lifeless hand bore mute testimony to his intentions, not to mention the kerosene now seeping into his clothing.

Esme ran to the weeping Annabelle and pulled her into her comforting arms. And as Garrett went to examine the body, Drake, bless him, headed straight for Gina.

She entered his arms with a sob. "I was so scared."

"Me, too," he admitted, stroking her hair. "I didn't expect Rutledge—that report about the fire threw me off."

"Yes, Clyde was more clever than we gave him credit for."

He smiled down at her. "Well, it looks like you saved my life after all, sending Scruffy into the fray like that."

"Well, I tried, but that didn't do it," she admitted. "Annabelle did."

"Yes, but your move put the gun into her hands."

"And you put the stiffening in her backbone," Gina shot back. "She would have never been able to find the courage to shoot her husband before you worked with her."

He smiled down at her. "Well, I think we can both take credit for that. I just hope she can survive this."

Suddenly remembering the article, Gina moved reluctantly out of his arms to pull the piece of paper out of her pocket. She scanned it quickly, then exclaimed, "Look, it's changed." Where the paper had once spelled doom for Drake, it now announced

Clyde's death. "It says that the police will exonerate Annabelle of all guilt—and that her family is coming to the resort to take her home."

"Good," Drake murmured with evident relief. "With her family coming, she won't need me so much anymore."

Well, that was a switch. "Don't you want to help her through the trauma of killing her own husband?"

"If she wants to follow me to Richmond for treatment, I'd be happy to help her. But I've done what I set out to do, what I promised Charlotte. Mrs. Rutledge won't have any reason to commit suicide now, and she'll have the strength of her family to help her through this."

"I thought she was all you cared about," Gina murmured, not meeting his eyes.

Drake tipped her chin up so their gazes met. "All? No, toward the end there, all I could think about was the danger you were in. I was afraid you were going to try for the pistol yourself . . . and disappear."

Oh, yes, the pistol. In all the excitement, she had forgotten that her means back to the future lay in this very room. Not only that, but she had not just one, but two pistols to choose from. "I forgot," she admitted.

He drew her back into his arms and hugged her tight. "Could I persuade you to forget about it forever?" he murmured into her hair.

Her heart jumped with excitement. Could he mean . . . ? She drew back, needing to see his face, needing to know every nuance of his expression. All he revealed was a plea and a hope.

She swallowed hard. "What are you saying?" she asked and held her breath.

He searched her face as worry etched lines in his

face. "I'm saying that I don't want you to go. I want you to stay here—with me."

Her heart did that leapfrog again but she forcibly calmed it, not wanting to hope too much. "Why?" she asked. "Why do you want me to stay?"

He tenderly pushed a stray strand of hair away from her face. "Because I love you, and I want to make you my wife, forever."

That was the answer she'd been waiting for. She dropped all constraints and let her heart soar. Wrapping her arms around his neck, she said, "Oh, Drake, I love you, too. I think I always have."

Relief dawned on his face and he grinned. "Then you'll marry me?"

"Of course. I'd like nothing better than to stay here with you for the rest of my life." He was right. There was nothing in the future for her. This is where she belonged—with Drake.

"Then how would you like a Christmas wedding?" he asked.

"Perfect."

They kissed hungrily to seal their engagement and only came up for air when they heard a polite clearing of the throat next to them.

As Gina looked around in surprise, she realized that she and Drake were alone in the room except for Scruffy and Esme. Scruffy was leaning against both their legs and Esme stood regarding them with amusement, cradling both dueling pistols in her hands. Garrett must have gotten rid of the body and spirited Annabelle away while they weren't paying attention.

Gina looked down at the pistols with distaste. "What are you doing with those?"

Esme glanced down at them. "I asked the chief if I could have them and he agreed." She paused, then added, "I take it one of these was the pistol that drew you back in time?"

"Yes, definitely." Even though they were unmarred by fire, there was no doubt that one of them was the instrument that had taken her back in time. The one on the left, no doubt the one that had killed Drake in the original timeline, pulsed with energy that both attracted and repelled her.

Esme cocked her head and smiled. "I also take it you don't need it anymore?"

"That's right. Take them away," Gina said, unable to contain her happiness. "I'm staying here. Drake and I are getting married Christmas Day."

"Excellent choice," Esme said approvingly, and Gina had never seen the housekeeper smile so wide. "You don't mind if I keep one, then?"

It seemed an odd sort of souvenir, but Gina didn't really care what happened to them—they would have no more impact on her life. "Sure."

Esme unerringly chose the pistol that had created the time portal, then placed the other one in Drake's hand. "Here," she said. "Keep this as a reminder of your wife's love and what she gave up for you."

Drake took it with a smile and placed it at the small of his back. "Thank you. I'll do that."

With that, Esme said, "I'll just leave you two alone then." Picking up her odd souvenir, she left Drake, Gina, and Scruffy alone to plan their lives together.

EPILOGUE

Christmas Day, 1885

Esmerelda Sparrow retired to her room with a sigh. This had been the best Christmas of her life. Drake and Gina had been married in a lovely ceremony with the entire resort in attendance. Gina had made a beautifully radiant bride and Esme had never seen the solemn mesmerist smile so much in all the time he'd been here. They were truly soul mates, and she had done the right thing in bringing them together.

In return, Esme had the only Christmas present she needed. She polished the pistol to a mirror bright shine and laid it carefully in her hope chest, staring down at it with a smile and dawning hope of her own.

One down, four to go. . . .

Author's Letter

Dear Reader,

This series came about when Deb Stover suggested our critique group (the Wyrd Sisters) write a series for Kensington's new Ballad line. Though Deb and Yvonne Jocks couldn't participate due to other commitments, they helped the rest of us brainstorm the "Hope Chest" series. And, to be consistent with the Wyrd tradition, we naturally couldn't write straight historicals, so we made each book a time travel.

If you enjoyed this book, I hope you'll return to Hope Springs, The Chesterfield, and the mysterious Miss Sparrow to read the others in the series: *Fire with Fire* by Paula Gill, *Grand Design* by Karen Fox, *Stolen Hearts* by Laura Hayden, and *At Midnight* by Maura McKenzie.

I love to hear from my readers—you can find

me on the Web at http://www.pammc.com or write to me at P.O. Box 648, Divide, CO 80814. Until then, I hope you all find a little enchantment in your lives. . . .

Pam McCutcheon

We hope you've enjoyed ENCHANTMENT, by Pam McCutcheon, the first of the Ballad time-travel series Hope Chest, by five talented authors. Now look for the next installment of this captivating series, FIRE WITH FIRE, by Paula Gill, available July 2001 in stores everywhere!

With two weeks off at Christmas and no one to go home to, Corrinne Webb accepts the loan of a cabin in a small town. An unexpected snowstorm forces her to seek shelter in the ruins of the historic Chesterfield resort. After finding a hope chest—and the rusty sheriff's badge in it—she is thrown back in time to 1886. Now she is desperate to help Sheriff Jesse Garrett so that she can return to her own time. Things soon begin to heat up all around them—catastrophic fires, heated gun battles . . . and fiery passion. Jesse has vowed never to kill again. So when he was forced to don the role of sheriff, he and his family, a clan of lawmen, drifted apart. He can't seem to dismiss the willful yet vulnerable vixen named Corrie, who seems intent on reconciling Jess with his family . . . and with her heart.

COMING IN JULY FROM
ZEBRA BALLAD ROMANCES